Constant, Elizabeth Gilbert Martin

Memoirs of Constant

First valet de chambre of the emperor, on the private life of Napoleon, his family

and his court. Vol. 4

Constant, Elizabeth Gilbert Martin

Memoirs of Constant
First valet de chambre of the emperor, on the private life of Napoleon, his family and his court. Vol. 4

ISBN/EAN: 9783337350277

Printed in Europe, USA, Canada, Australia, Japan

Cover: Foto ©Raphael Reischuk / pixelio.de

More available books at **www.hansebooks.com**

Memoirs of Constant

First Valet de Chambre of the Emperor

on the

Private Life of Napoleon

His Family and His Court

TRANSLATED BY

Elizabeth Gilbert Martin

WITH A PREFACE TO THE ENGLISH EDITION

BY

Imbert de Saint-Amand

Vol. IV

NEW YORK

CHARLES SCRIBNER'S SONS

1895

MEMOIRS OF CONSTANT

CHAPTER I

Passage of the Beresina — The deliberation — The eagles burned — The Russians have their ashes only — The Emperor lends his horses to be harnessed to the pieces of artillery — The officers simple cannoneers — Generals Grouchy and Sébastiani — Great shouting near Borizoff — Marshal Victor — The two army corps — The confusion — Voracity of the soldiers of the retreating army — An officer despoiling himself of his uniform to give it to a poor soldier — General disquietude — The bridge — Credulity of the army — Sinister conjectures — The enemy abandons his positions — The Emperor transported with joy — The rafts — M. Jacqueminot — Count Predziceski — The chests of the horses cut by ice — The Emperor himself lays hold of the teams — General Partonneaux — The bridge breaks — The cannons pass over thousands of crushed bodies — The officers harness themselves to sledges — Arrival at Malodeczno — Confidential interviews between the Emperor and M. de Caulaincourt — Twenty-ninth bulletin — The Emperor and Marshal Davoust — The project of the Emperor's departure known to the army — His agitation on leaving the council — The Emperor speaks to me of his project — He will not have me depart on the seat of his carriage — Impression made on the army by the news of His Majesty's departure — Birds frozen by the cold — The slumber that death gives — Cartridge powder used to salt the pieces of roasted horseflesh — Young Lapouriel — Arrival at Wilna — Prince d'Aremberg half dead with cold — The burned carriages — The alarm — The treasure carriage pillaged.

THE day that preceded the passage of the Beresina was one of dreadful solemnity. The Emperor seemed to have come to his decision with the cold

resolve of a man who attempts a despairing deed;
nevertheless, a council was held. It was determined
that the army should despoil itself of all useless bur-
dens which might impede its march; never was there
more unity in the opinions; never was deliberation
more calm; it was the calm of men who commit
themselves for the last time to the will of God and
their own courage. The Emperor had the eagles of
all the corps brought together; they were burned;
he thought there was nothing else for fugitives to
do. It was a sad spectacle, these men stepping from
the ranks one by one, and throwing down there what
they loved more than their life; I have never witnessed dejection more profound, shame more bitterly
felt; for this strongly resembled a general degrada-
tion of all the veterans of the Moskowa. The
Emperor had attached a talisman to these eagles;
then he made it too well understood that he no
longer had faith in it. He must be very unfortunate to have come to that; at least it was a consola-
tion for the soldiers to think that the Russians would
have nothing but their cinders. What a picture was
that of the burning of the eagles, especially for those
who, like me, had been present at the magnificent
ceremony of their distribution to the army at the
camp of Boulogne, before the campaign of Austerlitz!

Horses were lacking for the artillery, and at this
critical moment the artillery was the safeguard of
the army. The Emperor gave orders that his horses
should be taken; he estimated that the loss of even

one cannon or artillery wagon would be incalculable;
the artillery was confided to a corps composed
entirely of officers; it amounted to about five hundred men. It affected His Majesty to see these
brave officers become soldiers once more, putting
their hands to the pieces like simple cannoneers,
and going back through devotion to the lessons of
the school. The Emperor called this his *sacred
squadron!* For the same reason which made the
officers become soldiers, the other superior commanders descended from their rank without disturb-
ing themselves about the designation of their grade.
Generals of division Grouchy and Sébastiani resumed
the rank of simple captains.

Near Borozino we were arrested by loud shouting;
we thought ourselves cut off by the Russian army;
I saw the Emperor turn pale; this was a thunder-
bolt; several lancers were despatched as quickly as
possible; we saw them return waving their flags;
His Majesty comprehended the signals, and long
before we could have been reassured by the cuirassiers, he said: "*I bet that it is Victor*"; so accurately
present to his mind were even the possible positions
of each corps of the army. Marshal Victor was, in
fact, awaiting our passage with keen impatience.
It seemed that his army had received some vague
tidings of our misfortunes, and was, therefore, prepared to give the Emperor an enthusiastic welcome.
His soldiers, still fresh and vigorous, at least in
comparison with the rest of the army, could not

believe their eyes when they saw us in such a miserable condition; the shouts of *Long live the Emperor!* resounded none the less on that account.

But when the rear portion of the army began to defile before them, another impression was produced. A great confusion ensued. All those in the Marshal's army who recognized any of their companions left their ranks and ran toward them, offering bread and clothes; they were frightened by the voracity with which these wretches ate; many embraced each other weeping. One of the brave and kindly officers of the Marshal took off his own uniform to give it to a poor soldier whose ragged garments exposed him naked to the cold, putting on his own back a tattered old infantry coat, because he was more capable of resisting the rigors of the weather. If excessive misery withers the soul, on the other hand it sometimes expands it to the highest point, as one may see. Many of the most wretched blew their brains out in despair. In that act, the last which nature indicates to put an end to wretchedness, there was a resignation and coolness that made one shudder. Those who thus assailed their own lives were not seeking death so much as a term to insupportable sufferings, and in this disastrous campaign I saw what vanities are physical force and human courage where that moral force which is born of a determined will is non-existent.

The Emperor marched between the army of Marshal Victor and that of Marshal Oudinot. It was frightful to see these moving masses sometimes halting progressively, the advance corps first, then those that followed, then the last; when Marshal Oudinot, who was ahead, suspended his march for some unknown reason, there would be a movement of general uneasiness, then alarming speeches would begin, and, as men who have seen everything are inclined to believe everything, both true and false tidings easily found credit; the fright would last until the front of the army began to move on, when a degree of confidence was restored.

By five o'clock in the evening of the 25th some trestles had been fixed above the stream, constructed of wooden beams taken from Polish cabins. It was rumored in the army that the bridge would be finished during the night. The Emperor was much annoyed when the army deceived itself in this way, because he knew that people grow much more quickly discouraged when they have indulged in vain hopes; for this reason he took great care to have the rear of the army made acquainted with the slightest incidents, so as never to leave the soldiers under so cruel an illusion. The trestles gave way at a little past five o'clock. They were not strong enough. It was necessary to wait until the next day, and the army relapsed into its dismal conjectures. It was plain that next day it would have to sustain the enemy's fire; but there was no room for choice. At the end of that night of anguish and sufferings of every sort, the first trestles were driven down into the river. People do not comprehend that the soldiers had stood up to their lips in water full of floating ice, summoning every force with which nature had endowed them, and all the remaining courage born of energy and devotion in order to drive the piles several feet deep into a miry river bed; struggling against the most horrible fatigues; pushing away with their hands enormous masses of ice which would have knocked them down and submerged them by their weight; fighting, in a word, and fighting unto death with cold, the greatest enemy of life. Well, that is what our French pontonniers did. Several of them were either dragged down by the currents or suffocated by the cold. That is a glory, it seems to me, which outweighs many another.

The Emperor awaited day in a wretched hovel. In the morning he said to Prince Berthier: "Well! Berthier, how are we to get out of this?" He was sitting in his chamber. great tears were rolling down his cheeks, which were paler than usual. The Prince was near him.

But they exchanged very few words. The Emperor seemed overwhelmed with sadness. What was passing in his mind I leave to the imagination. It was then that the King of Naples spoke frankly to his brother-in-law, entreating him, in the name of the army, to think of his own safety, the peril being so imminent. Some brave Poles offered to form the escort of the Emperor. They could go further up the Beresina and reach Wilna in five days. The

Emperor shook his head in sign of refusal, but said nothing. The King understood, and there was no further mention of it.

In great misfortunes, the least relief is doubly appreciated. A thousand times I have observed this in the case of His Majesty and his unhappy army. On the banks of the Beresina, when the first supports of the bridge had scarcely been thrown out, Marshal Ney and the King of Naples rode up at full speed toward the Emperor, shouting that the enemy had abandoned his positions. I saw the Emperor, quite beside himself and unable to believe his ears, run at full speed to look in the direction which Admiral Tschitzakoff was said to have taken. The news was true. The Emperor, transported with joy and out of breath with running, exclaimed: " I have tricked the Admiral!" This retrograde movement of the enemy, when he had so good a chance to crush us, was not easy to comprehend; and I do not know whether the Emperor, in spite of his apparent satisfaction, was very sure about the happy results which were to accrue to us from this retreat.

Before the bridge was finished, some four hundred men were partially transported from the other side of the river on two miserable rafts which they could with difficulty steer against the current. From the shore, we saw them greatly shaken by the great pieces of ice which clogged the river. These masses would come to the very edge of the raft; meeting an obstacle, they would stop for a while and then be drawn underneath those feeble planks and produce horrible shocks. Our soldiers would stop the largest ones with their bayonets and make them deviate insensibly beyond the rafts.

The impatience of the army was at its highest pitch. The first to arrive on the other bank were the brave M. Jacqueminot, aide-de-camp of Marshal Oudinot, and Count Predziecski. This was a brave Lithuanian whom the Emperor greatly liked, especially when he shared our sufferings through fidelity and devotion. Both of them crossed the river on horseback. The army uttered shouts of admiration on seeing that its leaders were the first to give the example of intrepidity. There was, in fact, enough to disturb the strongest minds. The current forced the poor horses to swim obliquely across, which doubled the length of the passage. Then came the masses of ice, which, striking against their chests and sides, inflicted piteous gashes.

At one o'clock, General Legrand and his division blocked up the bridge constructed for the infantry. The Emperor was on the opposite side. Several cannons got entangled in each other and stopped the march for an instant. The Emperor sprang on to the bridge, put his own hands to the teams, and aided in freeing the pieces. The enthusiasm of the soldiers was extreme. It was to shouts of *Long live the Emperor!* that the infantry landed on the other shore.

Not long after the Emperor learned that General Partonneaux had laid down his arms. He was

keenly affected by the news, and broke into somewhat unjust reproaches against the General. Later
on, when better informed, he did full justice to the
claims of necessity and despair. It is fair to say
that this brave general did not take such an extreme
step without having done all that a courageous man
could do in such circumstances. It is permissible
for a man to reflect when he can do nothing but
allow himself to be killed to no purpose.

When the artillery and the baggage were crossing,
the bridge was so thronged that it broke. Then
ensued that retrograde movement which crowded
back in horrible confusion the whole multitude of
stragglers who were advancing, like driven cattle,
behind the artillery. Another bridge had been hastily constructed, as if in sad prevision of the breaking
of the first one; but the second one was narrow and
unprotected at the sides. However, it was a make-
shift which at first glance seemed very precious in
such an appalling calamity; but what miseries
ensued! The laggards flocked thither in droves.
As the artillery, the baggage,— in a word, the entire
material of the army,— had been in advance on the
first bridge, when it broke, and by the sudden recoil
which took place the catastrophe became known,
then those who had been behind were the first to
gain the other bridge. But it was necessary that
the artillery should cross first. It pressed forward
then with impetuosity toward the only way of salva-
tion which was left. Here the pen refuses to

describe the scene of horrors that took place. It was literally over a road of crushed bodies that the wagons of every sort reached the bridge. On this occasion one saw what hardness, what systematic ferocity even, can be imparted to the soul by the instinct of self-preservation. There were some of the stragglers, the craziest of any, who wounded and even killed with bayonet thrusts the unfortunate horses who did not obey the whip of their drivers. Several wagons had to be abandoned in consequence of this odious proceeding.

I have said that the bridge had no ledges at the sides. Crowds of poor wretches who were trying to cross it were seen to fall into the stream and be sucked under the masses of ice. Others tried to cling to the miserable planks of the bridge, and would remain hanging over the abyss until their hands, crushed by the wheels of the wagons, would let go their hold; then they went to rejoin their comrades and were engulfed by the waters. Whole artillery wagons, horses and drivers alike, were plunged into the stream.

Poor women were seen holding their children out of the water, as if to retard their death by a few moments, and the most frightful of deaths. A truly admirable maternal scene, which the genius of painting has believed itself to divine in delineating the deluge, and of which we have seen the touching and terrible reality! The Emperor wished to retrace his steps, hoping that his presence might restore order; he was dissuaded from this, and in a manner so significant that he struggled against the impulse of his heart and stayed where he was, and assuredly, it was not his grandeur that riveted him to the shore. You could see what sufferings he endured when, at every instant, he would ask how the passage was getting on, if the cannons could still be heard rolling over the bridge, if there were fewer cries from that side. "Imprudent people!" he would say; "why could they not have waited a little longer?"

There were fine examples of devotion on this unfortunate occasion. A young artilleryman sprang into the water to save a poor woman who, encumbered by her two children, was trying to reach the other shore in a small boat. The load was too heavy. An enormous piece of ice struck the boat and it foundered. The cannoneer seized one of the children and swam to shore with it. The mother and the other infant perished. This good young man brought up the little orphan as his son. I do not know whether he had the happiness of returning to France.

Some officers harnessed themselves to sledges so as to fetch along a number of their companions who had been made helpless by their wounds. They wrapped the poor fellows up as warmly as possible, comforted them occasionally with a glass of brandy when any could be procured, and lavished on them the most touching attentions.

There were many who acted thus; and yet how

many whose names are unknown! how few returned to enjoy in their own country the most beautiful memories of their life!

The bridge was burned at eight o'clock in the morning. The 29th, the Emperor left the banks of the Beresina, and we went to pass the night at Kamen. There His Majesty occupied a wretched wooden house. A freezing wind entered it on every side through windows nearly every pane of which was broken. We closed the apertures with trusses of hay. Not far away from us, on a vast, open space, the unfortunate Russian prisoners, whom the army was driving before it, were penned up like cattle. Truly, I found difficulty in comprehending that air of being victorious which our soldiers still assumed by dragging along a wretched superfluity of prisoners, who could only hamper them by requiring superintendence. When the victors are dying of hunger, what becomes of the vanquished? Hence these miserable Russians, worn out by want and marching, nearly all perished that night. In the morning we saw them huddled close together. They had hoped to find a little warmth in this way. The feeblest of them had succumbed, and all night long their dead bodies had been embraced by the survivors without the latter having noticed it. There were some who, in their voracity, devoured their dead companions. The firmness with which the Russians endure pain has often been spoken of; I can give an instance of it which almost surpasses belief. One of these poor fellows, having wandered away from the corps to which he belonged, was struck by a cannon ball which cut off both his legs and killed his horse. A French officer, making a reconnoissance on the bank of the river where the Russian had fallen, perceived, at a distance, a mass which he recognized as a dead horse, and yet he saw that this mass was not without movement. He approached it and saw the head and shoulders of a man whose extremities were hidden in the body of the horse. The unfortunate man had been there four days, shutting himself up inside his horse as a shelter from the cold, and feeding on infected scraps from this frightful lodging.

December 3, we arrived at Malodeczno. All day long the Emperor seemed thoughtful and unquiet. He had frequent confidential interviews with his grand equerry, M. de Caulaincourt. I suspected some extraordinary measure. Nor was I deceived in my conjectures. At two leagues from Smorghoni, the Duc de Vicenza had me summoned, and told me to go forward and give orders for the six best horses of the teams to be harnessed to my calash, which was the lightest of the carriages, and kept constantly in the traces. I was at Smorghoni before the Emperor, who only arrived at nightfall. The weather was excessively cold. The Emperor alighted at a poor house in the place, where he established his headquarters. He ate a light repast, wrote the twenty-ninth bulletin of his army with his own hand, and sent for all his marshals.

Nothing had as yet transpired concerning the Emperor's project; but in great and final measures there is always something unwonted which does not escape those who are clear-sighted. The Emperor had never been so amiable, so communicative. He felt that it was necessary to prepare his most devoted friends for this overwhelming news. He talked for a long time of vague matters; then he spoke of the great things that had been done during the campaign, returning with pleasure to the retreat of Marshal Ney, whom *they had at last found again.*

Marshal Davoust seemed thoughtful; the Emperor said to him: "But talk a little, Marshal." For some days there had been a slight coolness between him and the Emperor. His Majesty reproached him with the infrequency of his visits; but he could not dispel the cloud which lowered on all brows, for the secret had not been kept so well as he had hoped. After the repast, the Emperor requested Prince Eugène to read the twenty-ninth bulletin; then he frankly unbosomed himself about his plan, adding that his departure was *essential in order to send assistance to the army.* He gave his orders to the marshals; all were gloomy and discouraged. It was ten o'clock in the evening when the Emperor said it was time to go to rest; he embraced all the marshals affectionately, and withdrew. He felt the need of this separation, for he had suffered greatly from the constraint of this interview; one might conclude so, at least, from the extreme agitation of his countenance after the council. About half an hour later, the Emperor summoned me to his chamber and said: "Constant, I am starting, I thought I could take you with me; but I have reflected that several carriages would attract attention; it is essential that I should experience no delay; I have given orders that you shall start at once after the return of my horses, so you will not be far behind me." I was suffering greatly from my malady; that is why the Emperor was unwilling to have me go on the seat as I requested, in order to be able to render him all the attentions to which he was accustomed; he said to me: "No, Constant; you will follow me in a carriage, and I hope you will arrive not more than a day at most after I do." He set off with the Duc de Vicenza and Roustan on the seat; the horses were taken from my carriage, and I remained behind, to my great regret. The Emperor started in the night.

By daybreak next morning, the army knew all. The impression produced by the news is indescribable. Discouragement was at its height. Many soldiers blasphemed and reproached the Emperor for having abandoned them. There was a universal cry of malediction. Prince de Neufchâtel was in great anxiety, and asking every one if they had heard the news, although he must have been the first to receive it; he feared lest Napoleon might be taken by the Cossacks, for he had an insufficient escort, and if his departure were known, no doubt great efforts would be made to capture him.

On that night of the 6th the cold increased; it must have been very great when we found birds lying frozen on the ground. Some soldiers who were sitting down, their heads in their hands and leaning forward, so as to feel the emptiness of their stomachs somewhat less, fell asleep and were found dead in that position. When we breathed, the vapor of our breath congealed on our eyebrows; tiny white icicles formed in the beards and moustaches of the soldiers; to get rid of them they would warm their chins at the bivouac fires, and as one may fancy, a good many did not do so with impunity; the artillerymen held their hands to the nostrils of their horses, seeking a little warmth from the powerful breath of these animals. Their flesh was the ordinary nutriment of the soldiers; you could see them throwing large cuts of this meat on the coals, and as the cold froze it, it could be carried along without spoiling, like salted pork, the powder of the cartridge boxes taking the place of salt.

That very night we had with us a young Parisian belonging to a very wealthy family, who had desired employment in the Emperor's household. He was very young, and had been received as one of the apartment waiters; the poor child was making his first journey. He had been attacked with fever as we were leaving Moscow, and he was so ill that night that he could not be taken from the wardrobe wagon in which he had been put until he should be better. He died there during the night, greatly regretted by all who knew him. Poor Lapouriel was a charming character, very well taught, and the hope of his family; he was an only son. The ground was so hard that we could not dig a grave, and we experienced the grief of abandoning his remains without sepulture.

I set off the next day, provided with an order from Prince de Neufchâtel that I should be furnished with horses all along the route in preference to any other person. At the first post beyond Smorghoni, which the Emperor had left with the Duc de Vicenza, this order was of the greatest utility, for there were only horses enough for one carriage; I found myself competing for them with Count Daru, who arrived when I did. I need not say that but for the Emperor's order to rejoin him as soon as possible, I could not have availed myself of my right to take precedence of the intendant-general of the army; but commanded by my duty, I showed Prince de Neufchâtel's order to Count Daru, who, after examining it, said to me: " That is right, M. Constant; take the horses; but, I entreat you, send them back to me as soon as possible."

How disastrous was that retreat! After many pains and privations we arrived at Wilna. It was necessary to cross a long and narrow bridge to enter the city; the artillery and baggage wagons so obstructed the space as to prevent all other vehicles from passing; it was all very well to say: " Service of the Emperor;" we were received with maledic-

tions. Seeing that it was impossible to advance,
I alighted from my calash, and saw Prince d'Aremberg, an orderly officer of the Emperor, in a pitiable
condition; his face was distorted, his nose, ears, and
feet were frozen. He was sitting down behind my
carriage. I was heart-broken. I said to the Prince
that if he had acquainted me with his distress, I
would have given him my place. He could scarcely
answer me. I supported him for some time; but
seeing how urgent it was for both of us to go forward, I concluded to carry him. He was slight,
supple, and of medium height. I took him in my
arms, and with this burden, elbowing, pushing, hurt
and hurting, I at last arrived and deposited the
Prince at the headquarters of the King of Naples,
advising that he should be given the care demanded
by his condition; after which I looked out for my
carriage.

We lacked everything. Long before reaching
Wilna, the horses being dead, we had received orders
to burn our carriages with all they contained. I
lost considerable in this journey. I had made several
costly purchases. All were burned with my effects,
of which I had always a great quantity on my journeys. A large part of the Emperor's effects were
burned in the same way.

A very fine carriage belonging to Prince Berthier,
which had just arrived and not yet been used, was
also burned. Four grenadiers were stationed at each
fire, who with presented bayonets were to prevent

any' one from taking what must be sacrificed. The next day, the carriages which had been spared were examined to see that no luggage of any sort was left in them. All I was able to keep were two shirts. We slept at Wilna. But the alarm was given early next morning. The Russians were at the gates of the city. Frightened men arrived shouting: "*We are lost!*" The King of Naples, rudely awakened, sprang from his bed, and in an instant orders were given that the service of the Emperor should set off at once. I leave to the reader's imagination the confusion that all this occasioned. There was no time to make any provision. We were obliged to start without delay. Prince d'Aremberg was put into one of the King's carriages with whatever could be procured for the most pressing needs. Hardly had we left the city when we heard loud cries behind us, and discharges of cannon, accompanied by quick volleys of musketry. We had to ascend a mountain of ice. The horses were fatigued. We made no progress. The treasure wagon was abandoned, and part of the money was stolen by men who, a hundred paces further on, were obliged to throw away what they had taken in order to save their lives.

CHAPTER II

The Emperor badly lodged throughout the whole campaign —
Hovels infested with vermin — Manner in which the Emperor's
apartment was arranged — The council hall — Proclamations
of the Emperor — Inhabitants of Russian hovels — How the
Emperor was lodged when houses were lacking — The tent —
Marshal Berthier — A momentary coolness between the Emperor and him — M. Colin, kitchen superintendent — Roustan
— The Emperor's sleepless nights — His care of his hands — He
is much affected by cold — Demolition of a chapel at Witepsk —
Dissatisfaction of the inhabitants — Singular spectacle — Soldiers
of the guard mingling with the bathers — Review of the grenadiers — Installation of General Friant — The Emperor gives him
the accolade — Refutation of those who think that the Emperor's
suite fared better than the rest of the army — The generals gnaw-
ing munition bread — Community of sufferings between generals
and soldiers — The marauders — Straw beds — M. de Bausset
— Anecdote — A night of those in the Emperor's suite — I undress only once during the entire campaign — Canvas bags as
beds — The Emperor's solicitude for the members of his suite —
Vermin — We sacrifice our mattresses to the needs of wounded
officers.

DURING the whole Russian campaign the Emperor was usually very badly lodged. We had
to comply with necessity. The thing was a trifle
hard, to be sure, for people who had nearly always
lived in palaces. The Emperor resigned himself to
it courageously, and all the rest followed suit in consequence. Thanks to the system of burning adopted

by the Russian policy, those who were in easy circumstances throughout the country, when retiring further into the interior, would abandon their houses in ruins to the enemy. To tell the truth, all along the road conducting to Moscow, some rather important towns alone excepted, the habitations were wretched enough. After long and fatiguing marches we thought ourselves very lucky if we found a hovel on the place indicated by the Emperor for head-quarters. In quitting these miserable holes, their proprietors would sometimes leave there two or three poor seats and wooden bedsteads swarming with the vermin which no invasion frightens. The least dirty room was taken when it fortunately proved to be the best ventilated. When the cold weather came, draughts never failed us. When the place was selected and it was decided to remain there, a carpet was laid on the ground. The Emperor's bed was set up. On a wretched table was placed the open dressing-case containing whatever might be agreeable or useful in a sleeping-chamber. The dressing-case included a breakfast service for several persons. All this luxury was displayed whenever the Emperor invited his marshals. There was no choice about coming down to the ways of small provincial burghers. If the house had two rooms, one served both as sleeping-room and dining-room; the other was taken for His Majesty's cabinet. The chest of books, the geographical charts, the portfolio, and a table covered with a green cloth were all the furniture. This was the council hall. It was from these beggars' hovels that were issued those prompt and trenchant decisions which changed an order of battle and often the fortune of a day; those vivid and energetic proclamations which so quickly reanimated the discouraged army. When our apartment comprised three rooms, a case which was extremely rare, then the third room or cabinet was given to Prince de Neufchâtel, who always slept as near by as was possible. We often found old worm-eaten furniture of odd shapes in these wretched habitations, and little images of saints in wood or plaster which the proprietors had left behind. But usually we found poor people in these dwellings. Having nothing to save from conquest, they stayed where they were. These good people appeared much ashamed of receiving the Emperor of the French so badly. They gave what they had, and we thought none the worse of them. More poor people than rich ones in Russia have received the Emperor in their houses.

The Kremlin was the last palace of foreign kings in which His Majesty slept during the Russian campaign.

When we found no houses on the route, we put up the Emperor's tent. It was divided into three rooms by curtains, so as to contrive several apartments. In one the Emperor slept, in the second was his cabinet, in the third his aides-de-camp and chief attendants were accommodated. In this room the Emperor usually ate his meals, which were prepared outside. I alone slept in the chamber. Roustan, who followed His Majesty on horseback when he went out, slept in the couloirs of the tent, so as not to be interrupted in a repose very necessary for him. The secretaries slept either in the cabinet or the couloirs. The great officers and chief attendants ate where and as they could. Like common soldiers, they had no scruples against taking a snack when they could get it.

Prince Berthier had his tent close to that of His Majesty. He always breakfasted and dined with the Emperor. They were inseparable friends. This intercourse was very touching. It was seldom interrupted. Still, I think there was a slight falling out between the Emperor and the Marshal when His Majesty quitted the army of Moscow. The old Marshal wished to go with him. The Emperor refused him. A somewhat lively discussion ensued which entailed no consequences.

On campaign the meals were served by M. Collin, superintendent of the kitchen, and Roustan as a valet de chambre.

In this campaign, more than in any other, the Emperor frequently rose during the night, put on his dressing-gown, and worked in his cabinet. Very often he had fits of insomnia which he could not overcome. Then, as he found the bed unendurable, he would suddenly spring up, take a book, and read as he walked up and down the room. When he found his head somewhat refreshed, he would go back to bed. He rarely enjoyed uninterrupted sleep for two nights together. He would often remain at work in the cabinet until it was the hour for the toilet. Then he would return to his chamber and I would dress him. The Emperor took great care of his hands. Yet in this campaign he often relaxed this petty vanity. During the great heats he no longer wore gloves, finding them too uncomfortable. Hence, through being exposed to the sun, his hands became very much tanned. When the cold weather set in, what had been a coquettish device became a sanitary precaution. The Emperor resumed his gloves. He endured the cold with great courage. Still, it was plain that physically he was much affected by it.

It was at Witepsk that the Emperor had several wretched houses pulled down to enlarge the place in front of the house he inhabited, because it was too small to hold reviews there. There was a dilapidated old chapel which it was likewise necessary to eliminate to attain his end completely. The demolition had already begun when the inhabitants assembled in large numbers, expressing loudly their dissatisfaction with this proceeding. But they were appeased when the Emperor gave them permission to take away all the sacred objects contained in the chapel. In consequence of this authorization, several persons entered the holy place, and we saw them come out again bearing, with great pomp, some wooden images of saints of large dimensions, which they deposited in other churches.

One morning I was present at a grand review of the foot grenadiers of the guard. All the regiments seemed very joyful. It was because General Friant was about to be installed as commander of the corps. The Emperor gave him the accolade. It was the only time I ever saw His Majesty do this on campaign. As the General was much beloved by the army, this favor of the Emperor was received with universal acclamations. All the promotions were usually welcomed with great enthusiasm by the soldiers, for the Emperor insisted on their being made with formality and display.

Many persons fancy that to be near the Emperor was enough to ensure one's being perfectly well off, even on campaign. This is a great error, which could be contradicted by the kings and princes who followed His Majesty to his wars. If such grand personages as these lacked necessary conveniences, one should reflect that the employees of the different services were very uncomfortable. The Emperor himself often dispensed with those ordinary commodities which would have been very agreeable to him after his fatiguing days. One might say that at the hour for the bivouacs there was a general *loge-qui-peut* (lodge who can). Never did the poor soldier find his own destitution made more grievous by the sight of abundance and scandalous luxury in the quarters of his superiors. The chief generals of the army ate their munition bread with as much pleasure as the common soldiers. Never was want more general than during the retreat. This idea of a misfortune shared by all came most opportunely to rekindle hope and energy in the most discouraged. It may also be said that sympathy was never more reciprocal between chiefs and soldiers. Thousands of examples might be cited in support of what I advance.

When evening came, the fires were lighted; the most fortunate of the marauders would invite some of their companions to share their feast. On days of dearth, cuts of roasted horse were a very poor repast to offer, and yet a very good one. Many soldiers would deprive themselves of a good prize to offer it to their leaders. Selfishness was not so general as to prevent this noble French courtesy from reappearing occasionally to recall the happy days of France. We all lay on straw; and those of the marshals who slept in excellent feather-beds in Paris did not find this couch too hard in Russia.

M. de Bausset gave me a very droll account of one of these nights when, lying pell-mell in very narrow quarters on a little straw, the aides-de-camp summoned to the Emperor would pass mercilessly over the legs of their sleeping companions. Luckily enough, the rest had not the pains of gout from which M. de Bausset was suffering, and which were not diminished by such rough and repeated pressures. He cried out in a doleful voice: "It is a butchery then;" and drew his legs up under him, skulking in his corner until the comings and goings should cease for a time.

Imagine large, dirty, unfurnished rooms, open to the wind through every window, the panes of which were for the most part broken, dilapidated walls, a fetid atmosphere which we warmed as well as we could by our breathing, a vast litter of straw shaken down as if for horses, and on this litter men shivering with cold, tossing about, pressing against each other, murmuring, swearing; some unable to close an eye, others, more lucky, snoring in fine style; and, from the midst of this pile of feet and legs the alarm cries in the night when an order from the Emperor would come; and you will have an idea of the hostelry and the guests.

For my part, so long as the campaign lasted, I never once undressed myself to go to bed, for we found none anywhere. Something else had to be substituted in their place. Now, one knows that necessity is never at a loss for inventions. This is how we supplied for this defect in our furnishings: We had great bags of coarse canvas made, in which we enveloped ourselves completely, and then threw ourselves down upon a little straw, when we were so lucky as to find any. It was in this manner that I took a little repose during the night for several months together; and even at that, I have several times passed five or six nights without being able to avail myself of it, my service being continual.

If you reflect that all these petty sufferings were renewed daily, that when night came we had not even the repose of the bed to refresh our weary limbs, you will get a notion of the burdensome character of our service. Never did the least murmur of impatience escape the Emperor when assailed by so many inconveniences. His example endowed us with great courage; and in the end we so accustomed ourselves to this nomadic and fatiguing life, that in spite of the cold and the privations of every kind to which we were subjected, we often jested over the poor appearance of our apartments. The Emperor was never affected during the campaign but with the sufferings of others. Not infrequently his health was affected to such a degree as to inspire anxiety, especially when he refused himself all unusual repose. Yet I always saw him taking pains to find out how everything was going, and if there were resting places for all. He was never tranquil until he had been perfectly informed concerning all these details.

Although the Emperor nearly always had his bed, yet the wretched shelters in which it was set up were frequently so dirty that in spite of all the pains taken to cleanse them, I more than once found in his clothes a sort of vermin extremely uncomfortable and very common in Russia. We suffered still more than the Emperor from this filthiness, deprived as we were of clean linen and other changes of clothing; for the larger part of our effects had been burned with the carriages that contained them. This extreme measure had been taken, as is known, for a good reason. All the horses were dead of cold and hunger.

We were not much better off for beds in the palace
of the Czars, than at the bivouac. We had mattresses
for several days; but a large number of wounded
officers were without any, and the Emperor made
us give them ours. We made the sacrifice with very
willing hearts, and the thought that we were solacing
those who were still more unfortunate than ourselves
would have made us find the hardest couches good.
Besides, throughout this war we had more than one
occasion of learning to put aside all egotistic sentiment and narrow selfishness. We might have been
guilty of such forgetfulness if the Emperor had not
been always there to recall us to this simple and easy
duty.

CHAPTER III

THE too famous twenty-ninth bulletin of the grand army was not published in Paris, where it was well known what a consternation it produced in all classes, until December 16; and the Emperor,

coming close on the heels of this solemn manifesto of
our disasters, arrived in his capital forty-eight hours
later, as if to paralyze by his presence the bad effect
which this communication must produce. At half-
past eleven in the evening, December 28, His Majesty
alighted at the palace of the Tuileries. It was the
first time since his advent to the Consulate that Paris
beheld him return from a campaign without bringing
with him a peace conquered by the glory of our arms.
On this occasion the numerous persons who, through
attachment for the Empress Josephine, had always
seen or thought they saw in her a sort of talismanic
protector of the Emperor's successes, did not fail to
remark that the Russian campaign was the first that
had been undertaken since his marriage with Marie-
Louise. Without being superstitious, it cannot be
denied that if the Emperor was always great, even
when fortune was against him, there was a very
marked difference between the reigns of the two
empresses. The one saw nothing but victories followed by peace, the other only wars, not without
glory but without results, up to the great and final
result of the abdication of Fontainebleau.

But it would be anticipating events too far to con-
cern ourselves about misfortunes which very few men
dared yet forebode, even after the disasters of Moscow. Everybody knew that cold and a biting temperature had contributed more toward our reverses
than the enemy whom we had sought even in the
midst of his burning capital. France still afforded

immense resources, and the Emperor was there to accelerate their employment and multiply their value. Besides, no defection had yet been manifested, and with the exception of Spain, Sweden, and Russia, the Emperor had none but allies in all the powers of the European continent. It is true that the moment was approaching when General Yorck would give the signal; for, as well as I can recollect, the first news of it reached the Emperor about the 10th of the following January, and it was easy to see that His Majesty was profoundly affected by it, for he plainly foresaw that Prussia would not fail to find imitators in the other corps of the allied army.

At Smorghoni, where the Emperor had left me, setting off himself, as I have said, with the Duc de Vicenza in the calash intended for me, little was thought of but how to get out of the frightful plight that we were in. Still, I remember that after some moments of regret because the Emperor was no longer in the midst of his lieutenants, the idea of knowing that he was out of all danger became the prevailing sentiment, such confidence had we in his genius! Moreover, in departing he had left the command to the King of Naples, whose valor was admired by the army, although I have been told that some of the marshals were secretly jealous of his royal crown. I learned afterwards that the Emperor reached Warsaw on the 10th, after having avoided passing through the city of Wilna, which he had gone around by way of the faubourgs, and that at last, after crossing

Silesia, he arrived at Dresden, where the good and faithful King of Saxony, sick as he was, had had himself carried to the Emperor. From there, His Majesty followed the route of Nassau and Mayence.

I also took that route, but not with the same rapidity, although I lost no time. Everywhere, and especially in Poland, in all the places where I halted, I was amazed to find such security as I saw displayed. I constantly heard people saying that the Emperor was about to return at the head of an army of three hundred thousand men. Such surprising things had been seen from the Emperor that nothing seemed impossible, and I learned that he had himself spread these rumors as he passed by in order to rouse the courage of the populations. In several places I found difficulty in procuring horses: hence, in spite of my eagerness, I did not reach Paris until six or eight days after the Emperor.

Hardly had I left the carriage when the Emperor, having been informed of my arrival, summoned me. As I made the person whom he had sent observe that I was not in a state which permitted my presenting myself before His Majesty: "That is no matter," was replied; "the Emperor wishes you to come at once, just as you are." I obeyed to the minute, and went, or rather ran to the cabinet of the Emperor where he was with the Empress, Queen Hortense, and another person whom I do not remember positively enough to be able to name. The Emperor deigned to give me the most benevolent reception; and as the Empress seemed to pay no attention to me, he said with an accent of kindness which I shall never forget: "Louise, don't you recognize Constant?" "I perceived him." Such was the sole response of Her Majesty the Empress. But it was different with Queen Hortense, who welcomed me as her adorable mother had always done.

The Emperor was very cheerful and seemed to have forgotten all his fatigues. I was about respectfully to withdraw when His Majesty said to me: "No, Constant, stay a moment longer. Tell me what you saw along the road." Even had I had the intention of disguising a part of the truth from the Emperor, I was taken unawares and had no time to invent a courteous lie; therefore I told him that everywhere, as far as Silesia, my eyes had been smitten with a frightful spectacle, that in every place I had seen the dead and the dying, and unhappy wretches hopelessly contending against cold and famine. "It is well," said he; "go and rest yourself, my child; you must need it. To-morrow you will resume your service."

The next day I did, in fact, resume my duties about the Emperor, and found him absolutely the same as he had been before entering on campaign: one might have thought the past no longer existed for him, and that, living already in the future, he beheld victory ranging herself once more beneath his banners, and his enemies humiliated and overthrown. It is true that the language of the numerous addresses he received, and of the speeches delivered in his presence by the presidents of the Senate and the Council of State, were not less laudatory than in the past; but it was easy to discern in his replies that if he had been able to feign forgetfulness of the disasters experienced in Russia, he was much more keenly preoccupied with the ill-concerted scheme of General Mallet than with anything else.[1] For my part, I shall not disguise the painful sentiment I experienced the first time I went out in Paris, and when I frequented the public promenades in my hours of leisure, I was struck with the extraordinary number of people in mourning whom I met. They were the wives and sisters of our heroes, mown down in the plains of Russia; but I kept this painful observation to myself.

---

[1] In the Emperor's response to the Council of State, the following passage was remarked, which it is perhaps not inappropriate to recall here as a thing very singular at present.

"It is to ideology, to that gloomy metaphysics which, in subtly searching for first causes, wishes to establish the legislation of peoples on its fundamental principles, instead of adapting laws to the knowledge of the human heart and the lessons of history, that the misfortunes which our fair France has experienced must be attributed. These errors ought to, and actually have, brought on the régime of the men of blood. In fact, who has proclaimed the principle of insurrection as a duty? Who has flattered the people by ascribing to it a sovereignty it is incapable of exercising? Who has destroyed the sanctity and the respect due to laws, by making them depend not on the sacred principles of justice, the nature of things, and civil justice, but merely on the will of an assembly of men who know nothing about civil, criminal, political, or military law? When one is called to regenerate a state, it is the principles constantly opposed which one must follow." — *Note by the editor.*

Some days after my return to Paris, Their Majesties were present at a representation at the Opéra, where the *Jerusalem Delivered* was rendered. I too went into a box lent me for that evening by Count de Rémusat, first chamberlain of the Emperor, and in charge of the theatres. I witnessed the reception given to the Emperor and Empress. Never had I seen more enthusiasm, and I must avow that I found the transition rather brusque between the recent crossing of the Beresina and this truly magical spectacle. It was a Sunday; I left the theatre a little before the end of the play, so as to be at the palace when the Emperor returned. I was in time to undress him, and I remember His Majesty spoke to me that evening of the quarrel which Talma had had a few days before his arrival with Geoffroy. The Emperor, although he was very fond of Talma, considered him altogether in the wrong. He repeated several times: "An old man! . . . An old man! . . . That was inexcusable! . . . Parbleu!" he added, smiling, "has nobody spoken ill of me? . . . Have I not also my critics, who seldom spare me? He ought not to be more susceptible than I am."

The affair passed off, however, without disagreeable consequences for Talma; for, I repeat, the Emperor liked him very much, and overwhelmed him with pensions and presents.

In this respect, Talma was one of the small number of privileged persons; for the chapter of presents was not His Majesty's strong point. We were then nearing the 1st of January, but we had no castles in Spain to build upon that epoch, because the Emperor never gave New Year's presents. We knew that we need count on nothing but our emoluments, and for me, in especial, it was most impossible to make any savings, since the Emperor wished my toilet to be extremely elaborate. Truly, it was a most extraordinary thing to see the master of the half of Europe not disdaining to occupy himself with the toilet of his valet de chambre: but he did so, and to such an extent that when he saw me in a new coat which pleased him, he never failed to compliment me on it, and to add: "You are very fine, M. Constant."

Even at the time of the marriage of the Emperor and Marie-Louise, and at that of the birth of the King of Rome, the persons in His Majesty's private service received no presents; the Emperor found that the expenses of these two ceremonies reached too high a figure. Once, however, but not because of any special circumstance, the Emperor said to me as I was finishing his toilet: "Constant, go and find M. Menneval, I have ordered him to buy you national bonds bearing eighteen hundred francs interest."[1] Now it happened that the bonds having risen during the interval between the order and the purchase, instead of eighteen hundred francs income I had only seventeen hundred, which I sold not long afterwards; and it was with the proceeds of this sale that

---

[1] Roustan obtained the same favor the same day.

I bought a modest property in the forest of Fontaine-bleau.

Sometimes the Emperor made presents to the princes and princesses of his family. I was nearly always charged with delivering them, and I can affirm that, with some two or three exceptions, the functions of porter were perfectly gratuitous ones —a circumstance which I recall here as a simple souvenir. Queen Hortense and Prince Eugène were never included, at least not to my knowledge, in the distribution of the imperial largesses; the Princess Pauline was the person most favored.

In spite of the numerous occupations of the Emperor, who, since his return from the army, spent a considerable portion of the days and a part of the nights in working in his cabinet, he showed himself more frequently in public than ever before. He would go out almost unattended. January 2, 1812, for example, I remember that he went, accompanied by Marshal Duroc only, to visit the basilica of Notre-Dame, the works of the archbishop's palace, and those of the central depot of wines; then, crossing the bridge of Austerlitz, the public granaries, the Elephant fountain, and finally the palace of the Bourse, which His Majesty frequently spoke of as the most beautiful monument which would exist in Europe. However, the passion for monuments, next to that for war, was the keenest that the Emperor had. The cold was severe enough during these almost solitary excursions of His Majesty; but, in truth, the cold of Paris was a very mild temperature for those who returned from Russia.

I noticed at this epoch, that is to say, at the close of 1812 and the commencement of 1813, that the Emperor had never hunted so frequently. Two or three times a week I would help him to put on his livery coat, which, like all the members of his suite, he wore in conformity with the renewed customs of the former monarchy. Several times the Empress accompanied him in an open carriage, although the cold was severe ; but when he had said anything, there was no observation to be made. Knowing how irksome His Majesty usually found the pleasure of hunting, I was surprised at his new liking for it; but I soon learned that there was a political motive at the bottom of it. One day when Marshal Duroc was in his chamber as I was putting on his green coat with gilt lace, I heard the Emperor say to the Marshal : "I must move about and the papers must talk about it, since those imbeciles of English journals are daily repeating that I am ill, that I cannot stir, that I am no longer good for anything. Patience! . . . I'll soon make them see that I am as sound in body as in mind." Moreover, I think that the exercise of hunting, taken in moderation, was very favorable to the Emperor's health; for I never saw him in better condition than when the English papers were amusing themselves by making him out a sick man, and possibly their lying announcements helped to make him better still.

CHAPTER IV

JANUARY 19 the Emperor sent word to the Empress that he was going to hunt in the woods of Grosbois, that he would breakfast at the house of the Princesse de Neufchâtel, and that Her Majesty would accompany him. The Emperor told me also to go to Grosbois to assist him in changing his linen after the chase. This party took place as the Emperor had announced. But what was the surprise of all his suite when, at the moment of re-entering the carriages, His Majesty ordered them to be driven towards Fontainebleau! The Empress and the ladies who accompanied her had absolutely nothing but their hunting costumes with them, and the Emperor diverted himself somewhat with the tribulations of coquetry experienced by the ladies on finding themselves engaged in a campaign unprovided with toilet ammunition. Before leaving Paris, the Emperor had given orders to have everything that the Empress might require despatched in all haste to Fontainebleau; but her ladies were taken unawares, and it was a curious thing to see them sending messenger on messenger as soon as they arrived, in order to have the objects of prime necessity which they required despatched to them without delay.

However, it was known very soon that the hunting party and the breakfast at Grosbois were mere pretexts, and that the Emperor's object was to terminate in person with the Pope the differences which still existed between His Holiness and His Majesty. Everything having been prepared and agreed, the Emperor and the Pope signed, on the 25th, an arrangement, under the name of Concordat, of which the following is the text:

"His Majesty the Emperor and King and His Holiness, desiring to put an end to the differences which have arisen between them, and to provide for the difficulties that have supervened in several affairs of the Church, have agreed upon the following articles as a suitable basis for a definitive arrangement.

"ART. 1. His Holiness will exercise the pontificate in France and in the kingdom of Italy in the same manner and the same forms as his predecessors.

"2. The ambassadors, ministers, chargés d'affaires of the powers near the Holy Father, and the ambassadors, ministers, or chargés d'affaires whom the Pope may have near foreign powers, shall enjoy the immunities and privileges enjoyed by the members of the diplomatic corps.

"3. The dominions which the Holy Father possessed, and which are not alienated, shall be exempt from every sort of tax; they shall be administered by his agents or chargés d'affaires. Those which will be alienated shall be replaced to the extent of two million francs of revenue.

"4. Within the six months that follow the customary notification of nominations by the Emperor to the archbishoprics of the empire and kingdom of Italy, the Pope will give canonical institution, conformably with the concordats and in virtue of the present indult. The preliminary information will be given by the metropolitan. The six months expiring without the Pope having granted the institution, the metropolitan, or, in default of him when there is question of the metropolitan, the oldest bishop of the province shall proceed to the institution of the bishop nominated, so that a see shall never be vacant for more than a year.

"5. The Pope will nominate, either in France or in the kingdom of Italy, to ten bishoprics which will be subsequently designated in concert.

"6. The six suburbicarian bishoprics shall be re-established. They will be appointed to by the Pope. The actually existing properties will be restored, and measures taken for those that have been sold. On the death of the bishops of Anagni and Rieti, their dioceses will be reunited to the said six bishoprics, conformably to the concert which will exist between His Majesty and the Holy Father.

"7. With regard to the bishops of the Roman states, absent from their dioceses through force of circumstances, the Holy Father may exert in their favor his right of giving bishoprics *in partibus.* A pension, equal to the income they enjoyed, will be given them, and they may be replaced in vacant sees, whether of the empire or the kingdom of Italy.

"8. His Majesty and His Holiness will concert together at an opportune time on the reduction to make, if there is occasion for it, in the bishoprics of Tuscany and the territory of Genoa, and also on the bishoprics to be established in Holland and the Hanseatic departments.

"9. The propaganda, the penitentiary, the archives shall be established in the Holy Father's place of residence.

"10. His Majesty will restore to favor the cardinals, bishops, priests, and laics who have incurred his disfavor in consequence of actual events.

"11. The Holy Father resorts to the above arrangements through consideration for the existing state of the Church, and in the confidence inspired in him by His Majesty that the latter will grant his powerful protection to the very numerous needs of religion in our times.

"NAPOLEON.   PIUS VII.

"FONTAINEBLEAU, January 25, 1813."

Every possible means has been sought of casting odium on the conduct of the Emperor on this occasion. He has been accused of insulting the Pope, and even of threatening him; all that is signally untrue. Things occurred in the most becoming manner. M. Devoisin, Bishop of Nantes, an ecclesiastic highly esteemed by the Emperor, and his favorite intermediary in the frequent discussions that arose between the Pope and His Majesty, came to the Tuileries January 19. After remaining in private conference with His Majesty for two hours, he went to Fontainebleau. It was immediately after this interview that His Majesty entered a carriage with the Empress, in hunting costume, followed by all his attendants, likewise in hunting costume.

Having been notified by the Bishop of Nantes,

the Pope was expecting His Majesty. As the important points had been agreed upon and regulated beforehand, there was nothing now in question but certain clauses accessory to the principal end of the Concordat; hence it is impossible that the interview should not have been amicable. This verity will become increasingly evident to those who will reflect on the excellent dispositions of the Holy Father toward the Emperor, their mutual friendship, and the admiration inspired in the Pope by the great genius of Napoleon. I affirm then, because I think I can do so, that everything passed off in an honorable way, and that the Concordat was signed freely and without constraint by His Holiness in the presence of the cardinals assembled at Fontainebleau. It is an atrocious calumny to have dared assert that, on the reiterated refusals of the Pope, the Emperor put a pen dipped in ink into his hand, and seizing him by the arm and the hair, forced him to sign by saying that *he ordered him to do so*, and that his disobedience would be punished by perpetual imprisonment. One must have had little knowledge of the Emperor's character to lend credence to this absurd story.

A person who was present at this interview, the circumstances of which have been so maliciously distorted, related them all to me; it is in conformity with his account that I am speaking. As soon as he arrived at Fontainebleau, the Emperor paid a visit to the Holy Father, who returned it the following day. This visit lasted for at least two hours; during which time His Majesty's countenance was, in truth, invariably calm and firm, yet full of kindliness and respect for the venerable person of the Pope. Some stipulations of the treaty alarmed the conscience of the Holy Father. The Emperor perceived it, and, without waiting for complaints, declared that he abandoned them. This proceeding conquered what remaining scruples there may have been in the mind of His Holiness; a secretary was called, and drew up the articles of the treaty, which the Pope approved, one after another, with a truly paternal bounty.

January 25, the Concordat having been definitively agreed upon, the Holy Father entered the apartments of Her Majesty the Empress. The two contracting parties seemed equally satisfied; an additional proof that there had been neither trickery nor violence. The Concordat was signed by the august personages in the midst of a magnificent circle of cardinals, bishops, military men, etc. Cardinal Doria acted as grand master of ceremonies, and it was he who received the signatures.

I could not describe the ensuing multitude of felicitations offered and received, the favors asked and granted, the relics, decorations, rosaries, snuff-boxes distributed on either side. Cardinal Doria received the gold eagle of the Legion of Honor from His Majesty's own hand. The grand eagle was also given to Cardinal Fabricio-Ruffo. Cardinal Maury, the Bishop of Nantes, and the Archbishop of Tours received the grand cross of the order of the Reunion; finally, the Cardinal of Bayonne and the Bishop of Evreux were made senators by His Majesty. Doctor Porta, the Pope's physician, was given a pension of twelve thousand francs, and the ecclesiastical secretary, who had come into the cabinet to transcribe the articles of the Concordat, was presented with a magnificent ring in brilliants.

His Holiness had scarcely signed the Concordat when he repented of it. It was in this fashion that the Emperor described the matter to Marshal Kellermann when he was with him at Mayence toward the end of April:

"The Pope was to dine in public with me on the day after the signing the famous Concordat of Fontainebleau; but during the night he was ill, or pretended to be so. He was really a lamb, a thoroughly good man, a truly virtuous man whom I esteem, whom I greatly love, and who returns my feeling somewhat, I am sure.

"Would you believe," continued His Majesty, "that he wrote me eight days afterwards that he was very sorry that he signed, that his conscience reproached him for it, and that he urgently requested me to consider the Concordat as null and void? That is because, as soon as I left him, he fell back into the hands of his habitual counsellors, who made a frightful bugbear out of what he had just agreed upon. If we had been alone, I could have done

what I pleased about it. I answered him that what
he asked was contrary to the interests of France,
that, moreover, being infallible, he could not have
made a mistake, and that his conscience was too
ready to take the alarm.

"As a matter of fact, what was ancient Rome, and
what was it now? Injured by the imperative consequences of the Revolution, could it retrieve and
maintain itself? A government vicious in the
political order had succeeded to the ancient Roman
legislation which, without being perfect, was yet
capable of forming great men of every kind. Modern
Rome has applied to the political order principles
which may be worthy of respect in the religious
order, and has given them an extension fatal to the
welfare of peoples. . . .

"Thus *charity* is the most perfect of Christian virtues. . . . Hence charity must be given to those who
ask it. That is the reasoning which has made Rome
the receptacle of the scum of all nations. There
you see assembled (so I am told, for I have never
been there) all the drones of the earth, who come
thither for refuge, certain to find abundant nourish-
ment and considerable gifts. So it is that the papal
territory, destined by nature to produce immense
riches by its position under a fortunate sky, by the
multitude of the streams that water it, and yet more
by the fertility of the soil, is languishing for want
of cultivation. Berthier has often told me that
you may traverse considerable regions without per-

ceiving the imprint of man's hand. Even the women, who are regarded as the most beautiful in Italy, are indolent, and their minds are incapable of any activity for the ordinary cares of life: it is the softness of Asiatic manners.

"Modern Rome has confined itself to maintaining a certain pre-eminence by the marvels of art which it contained. But we have somewhat lessened that pre-eminence; the museum is enriched with all those masterpieces of which it was so vain; and before long the beautiful monument of the Bourse, which is being erected in Paris, will surpass all those of Europe, ancient or modern.

" France before all.

"To return to the political order, what could the papal government amount to in its actual condition, in presence of the great sovereignties of Europe? Old and petty sovereigns ascend the pontifical throne at an age when one no longer aspires to anything but repose. At that period of life all is routine, all is habit; all they think of is to enjoy their grandeur and make it reflect upon their family. A pope does not arrive at sovereign power but with a mind contracted by long recourse to intrigue, and with the fear of making powerful enemies who, in the end, may avenge themselves upon his family; for his successor is always unknown. In fine, all he desires is to live and die tranquilly. For one Sixtus Fifth, how many popes have there not been who occupied themselves with trifles only, as uninteresting from the truly religious point of view as they are calculated to inspire contempt for such a government? But this would carry us too far."[1]

Since his return from Moscow, His Majesty had been devoting himself with unparalleled activity to the means to be taken for preventing the invasion of the Russians, who, having joined the Prussians since the defection of General Yorck, were forming a most formidable mass. New levies had been decreed; and, during two months, there had been received and utilized innumerable offers of horses and riders, made by all the cities of the Empire, administrations, rich individuals nearly connected with the court, etc. The imperial guard was reorganized by the brave Duc de Frioul, who was, alas! to be taken away from his numerous friends a few months later.

Amidst these serious occupations His Majesty did not lose sight of his favorite plan,— that of making Paris the most beautiful city in the world. Not a week passed without architects and engineers being admitted to present him with their designs, make their reports, etc.

"It is a shame," the Emperor said one day to M. Fontaine, while looking at the barracks of the guard,

---

[1] This remarkable speech of His Majesty to Marshal Kellermann has been already recorded in another work ; but I thought it permissible to reproduce it here, because it is so well adapted to corroborate the information I have been able to collect concerning the interview with the Pope at Fontainebleau, which has just been read.

a sort of black and smoky outhouse, "it is a shame
to construct buildings as frightful as those of
Moscow. I ought never to have allowed such work
to be done; are not you my first architect?" Thereupon M. Fontaine excused himself by calling His
Majesty's attention to the fact that he had nothing
to do with the constructions of Paris, that he had,
indeed, the honor of being the Emperor's first architect, but merely for the Tuileries and the Louvre.
"That is true," replied His Majesty; "but could
there not be constructed in place of that wooden
dockyard, which makes a frightful effect here,"
pointing to the quay, "a hotel for the Italian
minister?" M. Fontaine replied that the thing was
very feasible, but would cost between three and four
millions. Whereupon the Emperor seemed to abandon that idea, and thinking of the Tuileries garden,
possibly on account of General Mallet's conspiracy,
he told him to arrange all the fastenings of the
palace in such a way that one key would answer for
all the locks. "This key," added His Majesty,
"must be remitted to the grand marshal every
evening after the doors are closed."

Some days after this conversation with M. Fontaine, the Emperor sent to him, for himself and M.
Costaz, the subjoined note, a copy of which has
fallen into my hands. His Majesty had gone that
morning to examine the buildings of Chaillot.

"There will be time to discuss the construction of
the palace of the King of Rome.

"I am unwilling to be dragged into foolish expenses; I want a palace smaller than that of Saint-Cloud and larger than that of the Luxembourg.

"I want to be able to live in it by the time the sixteenth million shall have been expended; that would be a medium which I could enjoy; if, instead of this, pretentious things are made for me, it will be as it is with the Louvre, which has never been completed.

"You will have to begin with the plantations, determine the space to be enclosed, and enclose it.

"I want this palace to be a little finer than that of the Elysée; now the Elysée did not cost eight millions to build; and yet it is one of the finest palaces in Paris.

"That of the King of Rome will be the second palace after the Louvre, which is a large palace. It will be, so to say, merely a country seat for Paris; for people will always prefer to spend the winter at the Louvre or the Tuileries.

"I find difficulty in believing that it cost sixteen millions to build Saint-Cloud.

"Before seeing the plan, I wish to have it well discussed and settled by the building committee, so that I shall have the assurance that this sum of sixteen millions will not be surpassed; I do not want a chimera but a real thing for me, and not for the amusement of the architect. The completion of the Louvre will be enough for his fame. When the plan is once adopted, I will carry it forward very fast.

"The Elysée does not please me, and the Tuileries are uninhabitable. Nothing can please me unless it is extremely simple, and built in accordance with my tastes and manner of life. Then this palace will be useful to me. I would like to have it a more substantial *Sans-souci*. I especially desire to have it an agreeable palace rather than a fine garden, two conditions which are incompatible; that it should be between court and garden, like the Tuileries; that from my apartment I can go and promenade in the garden and park, as at Saint-Cloud; but at Saint-Cloud there is the inconvenience of having no park for the house.

"The exposure must be studied also, in order that my apartment shall lie to north and south, so that I can change my room according to the temperature.

"My dwelling room must be that of a rich private individual, like that of my small apartment at Fontainebleau.

"My apartment must be very near that of the Empress and on the same floor.

"In fine, I must have *a convalescent's palace or habitation for a man in the decline of life*. I want a small theatre, a small chapel, etc.; and, above all, take care that there is no stagnant water around the palace."

The taste for building was, at this time, pushed to excess by the Emperor; he was like a more active architect, one more in haste to execute his plans, more jealous of his ideas than all the architects in the world.

And still, the notion of putting the palace of the King of Rome on the heights of Chaillot was not altogether his; M. Fontaine might claim the better part of it. On the first occasion mention had been made of the palace of Lyons, which, to have a fine appearance, said M. Fontaine, needed to be situated on an eminence that might dominate the city, as, for example, the heights of Chaillot dominate Paris. The Emperor did not seem to notice what M. Fontaine had just said; two or three days before he had given orders to have the château of Meudon put into condition to receive his son. But one morning he summoned the architect, and told him to prepare a plan for the embellishment of the Bois de Boulogne, adding to it a pleasure house built on the top of Mount Chaillot. "What do you think of it?" he added, smiling; "do you think the site well chosen?"

One morning in March the Emperor had his son taken to a grand review held in the Champ-de-Mars. There was an indescribable enthusiasm, the sincerity of which could not be doubted, for it was easy to see that the shouts proceeded from the heart; hence the Emperor was much affected by it. He re-entered the Tuileries in the most charming mood; he caressed the King of Rome, covered him with kisses, calling M. Fontaine's attention and mine to the precocious intelligence displayed by this dear child. "He was not afraid of anything," said His Majesty; "he seemed to know that all those brave fellows were acquaintances of mine." That day he chatted for a long time with M. Fontaine, playing, meanwhile, with his son, whom he held in his arms. The conversation happening to turn on Rome, M. Fontaine spoke of the Pantheon with the most profound admiration. The Emperor asked whether he had ever lived in Rome, and on M. Fontaine's replying that when he went there first he remained three years, "It is a city I have not seen," continued His Majesty; "I will surely go there some day. It is the city of the King's people." And as he said it his eyes were fixed upon the King of Rome with all the pride of paternal tenderness.

When M. Fontaine had departed, the Emperor made a sign for me to approach, and began by pulling my ears, as was his habit when in good humor. After some personal questions, he asked me what my salary was. "Sire, six thousand francs." — "And M. Colin, how much has he?" "Twelve thousand francs." — "Twelve thousand francs! That is not just; you ought not to have less than M. Colin; I will see about that." His Majesty did, in fact, have the kindness to make inquiries at once, but he was told that the accounts of the year were made. Whereupon the Emperor told me that until the end of the year it would be Baron Fain who would give me five hundred francs monthly, out of his privy purse, wishing, so he said, that my salary should equal that of M. Colin.

CHAPTER V

Murat quitting the army to return to Naples — Eugène commanding
in the Emperor's name — Still more disquieting news — Resolution to depart — Rumors spread beforehand — The Empress regent
— Oath of the Empress — Our departure for the army — Rapid
march on Erfurt — Visit to the Duchess of Weimar — Satisfaction of the Emperor with his reception — The Emperor's house
for the campaign of 1813 — The little town of Eckartsberga
transformed into headquarters — The Emperor in the midst of
an unusual disturbance — Arrival at Lutzen and battle gained
next day — Death of the Duc d'Istrie — The Emperor's letter
to the Duchesse d'Istrie — Monument erected to the Duke by
the King of Saxony — Fine behavior of the young conscripts —
Ney's opinion concerning them — The Prussians commanded
by the King in person — The Emperor amidst the balls — His
Majesty enters Dresden the day that the Emperor Alexander
leaves it — Deputation, and response of the Emperor —
Explosion, and the Emperor slightly wounded — General
Flahaut's mission to the King of Saxony — Long conference
between the King of Saxony and the Emperor — The Emperor
complains of his father-in-law — Felicitations of the Austrian
Emperor after the victory — M. de Bubna at Dresden — The
Emperor taking no repose — His faculty of sleeping in all places
and at all hours — Battle of Bautzen.

SINCE the time when the Emperor quitted the
army, leaving, as the reader knows, the command to the King of Naples, His Sicilian Majesty
had likewise abandoned the authority conferred on
him, remitting it to Prince Eugène when he de-

parted to his own dominions. The Emperor was very eager for the news he received from Posen, where the grand headquarters were toward the end of February and the beginning of March; but the Prince Viceroy had little under his command but the débris of different corps, some of which were no longer represented save by a very small number of men.

Moreover, all that he could do whenever the Russians presented themselves in force was to retreat; and every day of March brought news which constantly grew more disquieting. Hence, toward the end of the month, the Emperor decided to depart for the army very soon.

Long preoccupied with the attempt Mallet had made during his last absence, the Emperor had already expressed himself on the danger of leaving his government without a head, and the journals had been filled with inquiries concerning the ceremonies in use when in former times the regency of the kingdom had been intrusted to the queens. As this was generally known to be the means frequently adopted by His Majesty in order to foster opinion in advance concerning what he intended to do, no one was surprised to find him conferring the regency on the Empress Marie-Louise before his departure, circumstances not yet permitting him to have her crowned as he had long desired. The Empress took the solemn oath at the Elysée palace, in presence of the princes, great dignitaries, and ministers. The

Duc de Cadore was appointed secretary of the regency, to advise Her Majesty in concert with the archchancellor; the command of the guard was intrusted to General Cafarelli.

The Emperor started from Saint-Cloud April 15, at four o'clock in the morning. He entered Mayence at midnight the next day. On arriving, His Majesty learned that Erfurt and all Westphalia were a prey to the most vivid alarms; nothing could express the rapidity which this tidings imparted to his march; in eight hours he was at Erfurt. His Majesty did not stop long in that city; the information he received there tranquilized him completely concerning the results of the campaign. On leaving Erfurt, the Emperor wished to pass through Weimar to salute the Grand Duchess; he paid his visit the same day and hour that the Emperor Alexander went from Dresden to Töplitz to see the other Duchess of Weimar (the hereditary princess, his sister).

The Grand Duchess received the Emperor with a grace that enchanted him. Their interview lasted for nearly half an hour. On quitting her, His Majesty said to Prince de Neufchâtel: "That woman is always astonishing; really she has the head of a great man." The Duke accompanied the Emperor to the market town of Eckartsberga, where His Majesty kept him to dinner with him.[1]

---

[1] The household of the Emperor, partly renewed for this campaign of 1813, comprised the following persons: grand marshal of the palace, the Duc de Frioul; grand equerry, the Duc de Vicenza,

The Emperor was quartered on the Place of Eckartsberga; he had only two rooms; his suite camped on the landing and the staircase. Nothing could be more extraordinary than the aspect of this little town thus transformed for some hours into head-quarters. Across a square surrounded by camps, bivouacs, and parks of artillery, amidst more than a thousand vehicles which crossed, got mixed up with, and entangled in each other in every way, you saw regiments slowly defiling, convoys, trains of artillery, baggage wagons, etc. Behind these came herds of cattle, preceded or cut into by the little carts of sutlers and canteen-women, equipages so light and frail that the least shock damaged them; and then marauders with their plunder; peasants forced into driving the vehicles, and cursing and swearing to

---

aides-de-camp, Generals Mouton, Comte de Lobau, Lebrun, Duc de Plaisance, Generals Drouot, Flahaut, Dejean, Corbineau, Bernard, Durosnel, and Hogendorp; first orderly officer, Colonel Gourgaud; orderly officers, Baron de Mortemart, Baron Athalin, M. Béranger, M. de Lauriston, Barons Desaix, Laplace, and de Caraman, MM. de Saint-Marsan, de Lamezan, Pretet, and Pailhou; he had M. d'Aremberg also, but at this period he was shut up in the city of Dantzic; first chamberlain, master of the wardrobe, Comte de Turenne; prefect of the palace, Baron de Beausset; quartermaster of the palace, Baron de Canouville; equerries, Barons Van Lenneps, Montaran, and de Mesgrigny; secretaries of the cabinet, Barons Mounier and Fain; clerks of the cabinet, MM. Jouanne and Prevost; interpreting secretaries, MM. Lelorge, Dideville, and Vonzowitch: director of the topographical bureau, Baron Bacler d'Albe; geographical engineers, MM. Lameau and Duvivier; pages, MM. Montarieu, Devienne, Sainte-Perme, and Ferreri.

the accompaniment of the laughter of our soldiers; and couriers, orderlies, aides-de-camp darting at a gallop through this curiously diversified and motley multitude of men and beasts. And if to this you add the whinnying of the horses, the lowing of the cattle, the noise of wheels upon the pavement, the cries of soldiers, the trumpets, the drums, the bands, the complaints of the inhabitants, four hundred persons all asking the same thing at the same time, talking German to Italians, French to Germans, how will you ever comprehend that it was possible for His Majesty to be as tranquil, as entirely at his ease in the midst of this infernal racket as if he were in his cabinet at the Tuileries or Saint-Cloud? Yet so it was; the Emperor, seated before a wretched table covered with a sort of cloth, a map under his eyes, compass and pen in hand, wrapt in his meditations, showed not the least impatience; one might have thought that not a sound of the exterior din had reached his ears . . .; but let a cry of pain arise from any quarter, and on the instant the Emperor would raise his head and order some one to go and find out what had happened. The power of isolating one's self so completely from all that is going on around us is very difficult to acquire; no one in the world has possessed it like His Majesty.

May 1, the Emperor was at Lutzen. The battle was not fought until the next day. On that day, about six o'clock in the evening, the brave Marshal

Bessières, Duc d'Istrie, was carried off by a cannon-ball at the moment when, mounted on a height, wrapped in a long cloak which he had put on to escape notice, he had just ordered the burial of the brigadier of his escort, whom a first ball had killed but a few paces away from him.

The Duc d'Istrie had seldom quitted the Emperor since the first Italian campaigns; he had followed him everywhere, been present at all his battles, and always distinguished himself by a courage equal to every trial, and an uprightness and candor too rare among the great personages by whom His Majesty was surrounded. He had passed through nearly every grade of the command of the imperial guard; and his wide experience, his excellent qualities, his good heart, and his unalterable attachment had greatly endeared him to His Majesty.

The Emperor was deeply affected on learning the Marshal's death. For several moments he remained silent, his head bent and his eyes fixed upon the ground. "At last," said he, "he has died the death of Turenne; his fate is to be envied;" then he passed his hand across his eyes and precipitately left the place.

The body of the Marshal was embalmed and taken to Paris; the Emperor wrote the following letter to Madame the Duchesse d'Istrie:

"My cousin, your husband is dead on the field of honor! The loss that you and your children have sustained is doubtless great; but mine is yet more so. The Duc d'Istrie died the most beautiful of deaths and without suffering. He leaves a reputation without a spot; it is the finest heritage he could have bequeathed to his children. My protection is assured to them. They will inherit, also, the affection that I bore their father. Find in all these considerations some consoling motives to alleviate your sorrows, and never doubt my sentiments toward you.

"This letter having no other purpose, I pray God, my cousin, that He may have you in His safe and holy keeping.

"NAPOLEON."

The King of Saxony erected a monument to the Duc d'Istrie on the spot where he fell.

The victory, long disputed in this battle of Lutzen, was all the more glorious for the Emperor on that account. It was principally the young conscripts who gained it. They fought like lions. Marshal Ney expected this, moreover; for before the battle he said to His Majesty: "Sire, give me plenty of those little young fellows yonder. . . . I will lead them wherever I please. The old moustaches know as much as we do; they reflect; they have too much *sang-froid;* but those intrepid children do not know the difficulties; they always look straight ahead, never to right or left."

In the middle of the fight the Prussians, commanded by the King in person, did, in fact, make so furious an assault on the Marshal's corps that it recoiled; but the conscripts did not take to flight; they awaited the blows, rallied by platoons, and thus turned round the enemy while shouting *Long live the Emperor!* with all their might. The Emperor made his appearance; then, recovering from the terrible shock they had sustained, and electrified by the presence of the hero, they attacked in their turn with incomparable violence. His Majesty was surprised by it. "I have been commanding French armies for twenty years," said he, "and I never before saw such bravery and devotion."

You should have seen those young soldiers, wounded, one deprived of an arm, another of a leg, and with but a breath of life remaining, trying to rise up from the ground as the Emperor approached, and shouting *Long live the Emperor!* with all the voice they had left. Tears come to my eyes when I think of those lads so brilliant, so strong, and so courageous.

There was the same bravery, the same enthusiasm on the part of our enemies; the chasseurs of the Prussian guard were nearly all young men who were under fire for the first time; they sprang to meet death and fell by hundreds before they gave way a foot.

In no battle, I think, did the Emperor seem more visibly protected by his destiny. Balls whistled past his ears; as they went by they carried off scraps from the harness of his horse; balls and grenades rolled to his feet; nothing touched him. The men saw all this, and their enthusiasm was redoubled.

At the commencement of the battle, the Emperor saw a battalion advancing whose chief had been suspended from his functions two or three days before for a rather trifling fault of discipline. The poor officer was marching in the second rank of his soldiers, by whom he was adored. Perceiving him, the Emperor halted the battalion, took the officer by the hand, and put him back at the head of his troop. The effect produced by this scene cannot be described.

May 8, at seven o'clock in the evening, the Emperor made his entry into Dresden and took possession of the palace which the Emperor of Russia and the King of Prussia had quitted that very morning. At some distance from the barriers, the Emperor was saluted by a deputation from the municipality of this city. "You deserve," said he to these ambassadors, "that I should treat you as a conquered country. I know all that you have been doing while the allies occupied your city; I have the list of the volunteers whom you have clothed, equipped, and armed against me with a liberality that astonished even the enemy; I know what insults you have heaped on France, and how many infamous libels you have had to hide or burn to-day. I am not ignorant of your noisy transports of joy when the Emperor of Russia and the King of Prussia entered within your walls. Your houses are still decked with garlands, and we yet see on your pavements the flowers which your young girls scattered along their path. Yet I will pardon all. Thank your king, for it is he who has saved you, and I pardon only through love of him. Let a deputation from among you go and beg him to restore you his presence. My aide-de-camp, General Durosnel, will be your governor. Your good king himself would not choose a better."

At the moment of entering the city, the Emperor learned that a part of the Russian rear-guard was trying to keep a foothold in the new city, separated by the Elbe from the old one, which had fallen into our hands. His Majesty at once ordered that everything should be done to drive out these remaining troops, and during an entire day there was constant cannonading and firing in the city from one bank to the other. Balls and grenades fell like hail on the ground occupied by the Emperor. Close beside him a grenade broke the partition wall of a powder magazine and hurled the fragments at his head. Happily the fire did not reach the powder. A few minutes afterwards, another grenade fell between His Majesty and several Italians; they stooped down to avoid the effects of the explosion. The Emperor saw this movement and, beginning to laugh, he said to them: "Nonsense, that doesn't do any harm."

May 11, in the morning, the Russians were flying and pursued, and the French army entered into all parts of the city. The Emperor stayed all day long on the bridge, watching the troops file by. At ten o'clock next day, the imperial guard took arms and put itself in battle array on the road from Pirna to Grow Garten; the Emperor reviewed them and sent General Flahaut forward; the King of Saxony arrived about noon. On meeting, the two sovereigns dismounted from their horses and embraced each other; they afterwards entered Dresden amidst universal acclamations.

General Flahaut, who had gone to meet the King of Saxony with a portion of the imperial guard, received the most flattering tokens of satisfaction and gratitude from this good king. No one could display more good nature, more gentleness than the King of Saxony. The Emperor said of him and his family that it was a patriarchal family, and that all the members of it united to great virtues an expansive goodness that should make them adored by their subjects. His Majesty always paid the most affectionate attentions to this royal personage. So long as the war lasted, he sent couriers daily to acquaint the King with the slightest circumstances; he came himself as often as he could; in fine, with him he was always full of that amiability he knew so well how to assume and to render irresistible when he chose.

Several days after his arrival in Dresden, His Majesty had a long conversation with the King of Saxony, which turned chiefly upon the Emperor Alexander. The qualities and defects of that prince were amply analyzed, and the result arrived at was, that the Emperor Alexander had been sincere at Erfurt, and that very complicated intrigues had been required to bring about this rupture of all bonds of amity. "Sovereigns are so unfortunate!" said His Majesty; "always circumvented, always surrounded by flatterers or faithless counsellors, whose first necessity is to prevent the truth from reaching the ears of their master, whom it so greatly concerns to know it."

Afterwards, the two sovereigns began to talk about the Emperor of Austria. His Majesty seemed profoundly afflicted that his union with the Archduchess Marie-Louise, whom he had done everything in the world to render happy, should not have had the result he hoped for, that of gaining him the confidence and friendship of his father-in-law. "But I was not born a sovereign," said the Emperor; "perhaps that accounts for it. And yet, I should have thought this circumstance would have been an additional title to the friendship of Francis. Never, I am sure, could I have persuaded myself that such ties would not be strong enough to retain the Emperor of Austria in my alliance. For, after all, I am his son-in-law; my son is his grandson; he loves his daughter; she is happy. . . . How then can he be my enemy?"

On hearing of the victory of Lutzen and the entry into Dresden, the Emperor of Austria made haste to despatch M. de Bubna to his son-in-law. He arrived the evening of the 16th, and the interview he at once obtained from His Majesty lasted until two hours after midnight. That giving us hopes that peace would soon be made, we formed a thousand conjectures, one more reassuring than the other; but two or three days elapsed, during which we saw nothing but preparations for war, which cruelly undeceived us. It was then that I heard these words issue from the mouth of the unfortunate Marshal Duroc: "This is lasting too long! We shall all die at it." He had the presentiment of his death.

Throughout the entire campaign the Emperor had not an instant of repose. The days slipped by in combats or excursions, always on horseback; the night in cabinet work. I have never comprehended how his body could resist such fatigues, and yet he enjoyed almost uninterrupted good health. The eve of the battle of Bautzen he went to bed very late, after having visited all the military posts. As the orders were given, he slept profoundly. May 20, the day of the battle, the evolutions began at daybreak, and, at headquarters, we awaited the result with keen impatience. But the battle was not to end that day. After a succession of combats, all to our advantage, though bitterly disputed, the Emperor returned to headquarters at nine o'clock in the evening, took a slight repast, and remained with Prince Berthier until midnight. The rest of the night was spent in work, and at five o'clock in the morning the Emperor was up and ready for the fray.

Two or three hours after his arrival on the battle-field, the Emperor could not resist the slumber that overcame him. Foreseeing the issue of the day, he fell asleep on the slope of a ravine, amidst the batteries of the Duc de Raguse. They awoke him to say that the battle was won.

This fact, which he related to me in the evening, did not amaze me; for I had already remarked that when he was obliged to yield to slumber, that imperious necessity of nature, the Emperor took the repose essential to him how and where he could, like a true soldier.

Although the battle was decided, yet the fighting went on until five o'clock in the evening; at six o'clock the Emperor had his tent set up near an isolated tavern which had served as the headquarters of the Emperor Alexander the two preceding days. I received orders to go thither and I hastened to do so; but His Majesty passed that night also in receiving and congratulating the principal chiefs, as well as in working with his secretaries.

All the wounded who were able to walk were already marching on the road to Dresden, where ample assistance awaited them; but on the field of battle lay more than ten thousand men, French, Russians, Prussians, etc., scarcely breathing, mutilated, and in a piteous condition. The efforts of the good and indefatigable Baron Larrey, and a multitude of surgeons, encouraged by his heroic example, did not suffice even for the first dressings.

And what means of transportation for these poor wretches could be found on this desolate plain, all of whose villages had been sacked and burned, where there no longer remained either carriages or horses? Must all these men be left to perish in the most atrocious anguish for lack of means to carry them to Dresden?

Then it was that this population of Saxon villagers, who must have been embittered by the disasters of the war, who beheld their dwellings burned, their fields ravaged, willingly afforded to the whole army the spectacle of what pity can inspire, of what is most sublime in the heart of man. They perceived the cruel anxieties of M. Larrey and his companions concerning the fate of so many unfortunate wounded. In an instant, men, women, children, old people, ran up with wheelbarrows; the wounded were raised, placed upon these frail vehicles; two or three persons took hold of each wheelbarrow and conducted them to Dresden in this way, stopping whenever by cry or sign the wounded soldier asked to rest, stopping to replace the bandages disarranged by the movement, stopping near a spring to give him a drink and allay thus the fever that devoured him. I have never seen anything so touching.

Baron Larrey had a very lively dispute with the Emperor. Among the wounded a great number of young soldiers had been found with two fingers of the right hand shattered. His Majesty believed that these poor young fellows had done it expressly to dispense themselves from service. He said so to M. Larrey, who hotly denied it, saying that it was impossible, and that such cowardliness was not in the character of these brave conscripts. As the Emperor insisted, M. Larrey went so far as to tax him with injustice. Things had arrived at this point when certain proof was supplied that these uniform wounds were all caused by the precipitation with which the young soldiers charged and discharged their guns, to the handling of which they were not accustomed. Then His Majesty saw that M. Larrey had been in the right, and was grateful to him for his firmness in maintaining what he knew to be true. "You are a thoroughly good man, M. Larrey," said the Emperor; "I wish I were surrounded with none but men like you, but men like you are very rare."

CHAPTER VI

WE were on the eve of the day when the Emperor, still deeply affected by the loss he had sustained in the person of the Duc d'Istrie, was to receive the blow that he probably felt more than all others inflicted by the sight of his old companions in arms falling at his side. The very next day after the sort of dispute I have recorded in the previous chapter between the Emperor and Baron Larrey, was signalized by the irreparable loss of the excellent Marshal Duroc. The Emperor's heart was broken by it, and there was not one of us who did not shed honest tears for him; so just and good was he, although grave and severe with all who were brought into contact with him by the nature of their duties. This was a loss not merely to the Emperor, who possessed in him a real friend, but I venture to say that it was one to all France, which he passionately adored, and for which he never ceased to lavish his counsels, although they were not always listened to. The death of Marshal Duroc was one of those events which are so painful and so unexpected that one hesitates to credit them, even when a too evident reality no longer permits one to cherish the least illusion.

These are the circumstances in which this baleful event came to spread consternation throughout the army. The Emperor was pursuing the Russian guard, which constantly escaped him. It had just done so for, perhaps, the tenth time since morning, after having killed and made prisoners of a good number of our men, when two or three cannon-balls, which ploughed up the ground at his feet, attracted the Emperor's attention and made him say: " What, no result after such a butchery! no prisoners! These fellows will not leave me a pin." Hardly had he spoken when a ball passed and upset a mounted chasseur of the escort almost between the legs of His Majesty's horse. "Ah! Duroc," said he, turning to the grand marshal, "fortune has a heavy grudge against us to-day." "Sire," said an aide-decamp, who came up at a gallop, "General Bruyères has just been killed." "My poor comrade of Italy! Is it possible? Ah! we must get through with this all the same." And, seeing on his left an eminence from whose summit he could observe better what was going on, the Emperor turned in that direction through a cloud of dust; the Duc de Vicenza, the Duc de Trevise, Marshal Duroc, and General of Engineers Kirgener followed His Majesty very closely; but the wind blew the smoke and dust so violently that one could hardly see. A tree near which the Emperor was passing was suddenly struck by a cannon-ball which half destroyed it. His Majesty, having reached level ground, turned to ask for his glass, and saw no one but the Duc de Vicenza. Duc Charles de Plaisance came up; a deadly pallor overspread his countenance; he bent toward the grand equerry and said a few words in his ear. "What is the matter?" quickly demanded the Emperor, "what has happened?" "Sire," said the Duc de Plaisance, weeping, "the grand marshal is dead." — "The grand marshal is dead? Duroc? But you are mistaken, he was beside me just now!"

Several aides-de-camp arrived with a page who brought His Majesty's spy-glass. The fatal news was in great part confirmed. The Duc de Frioul was not yet dead, but his entrails had been struck and all the assistance of art was unavailing. The ball, after hitting the tree, had ricochetted on General Kirgener, who fell dead on the spot, and then upon the Duc de Frioul. MM. Yvan and Larrey were with the wounded man, who had been transported to a house in Makersdorf; there was no hope of saving him.

To describe the consternation of the army, the grief of His Majesty at this frightful event, would be impossible. The Emperor mechanically gave some orders and came back to camp. Arriving in the square of the guard, he sat down on a stool in front of his tent, with head bent down and joined hands, and remained thus for nearly an hour without uttering a single word. Yet essential measures must be taken for the next day; General Drouot approached him and, in a voice broken by sobs, asked him what was to be done. "Time enough for all that to-morrow," replied the Emperor; he said not another word. "Poor man!" muttered the old grumblers of the guard as they looked at him; "he has lost one of his children."

At nightfall the enemy was in full retreat, and the army having taken its positions, the Emperor left the camp and went to the house where the grand marshal had been carried, accompanied by

Prince de Neufchâtel, M. Yvan, and the Duc de Vicenza. The scene was terrible. The disconsolate Emperor several times embraced this faithful friend and sought to impart some hopes; but the Duke, who knew his condition perfectly, only replied by entreating him to have them give him opium. At these words the Emperor went out; he could restrain himself no longer.

The Duc de Frioul died next morning. The Emperor ordered his body to be taken to Paris and deposited under the dome of the Invalides. He bought the house in which the grand marshal died, and charged the pastor of the village to have a stone placed on the spot where the bed had stood, on which the following inscription should be engraved:

"Here General Duroc, Duc de Frioul, grand marshal of the palace of the Emperor Napoleon, struck by a cannon-ball, died in the arms of the Emperor, his friend."

The preservation of this monument was made obligatory on the tenant of the house. This was the condition of the gift of it which was made him by His Majesty. The pastor, the village magistrate, and the donee were summoned, for this purpose, into His Majesty's presence. He made them acquainted with his intentions, which they solemnly pledged themselves to fulfil. Then His Majesty, taking the necessary funds from his cash-box, remitted them to these gentlemen.

It is well now that the reader should know how

this agreement, so religiously contracted, received its fulfilment. The following order from the Russian staff-office will apprise him:

"A protocol, bearing date March 16 (28), states that the Emperor Napoleon has remitted to minister of religion Hermann, at Makersdorf, the sum of two hundred gold napoleons, intended for the erection of a monument to the memory of Marshal Duroc, who died on the field of battle. His Excellency Prince Repnin, governor-general of Saxony, having ordered that a clerk from my office should repair to Makersdorf in order to take possession of the said sum so as to deposit it with me until the final disposition of it shall be decided on, Clerk Meyerheim is charged with this mission. In consequence, he will instantly present himself at Makersdorf, for the purpose of legitimating himself to Minister Hermann, by showing him the present order, and will seize from his hands the aforesaid sum of two hundred gold napoleons. Clerk Meyerheim will have no account to give of the execution of this order to any one but me.

"*Signed:* BARON DE ROSEN."
" At DRESDEN, this 20th day of March (April 11), 1814.

This document requires no comment.

After the battles of Bautzen and of Wurtchen, the Emperor entered Silesia. Everywhere he saw the combined army of the allies flying before his own, and this spectacle deeply flattered his self-love by nourishing the idea that he would soon behold himself master of a rich and fertile country, whose abundant resources would be favorable to his enterprises. Several times a day you would hear him saying: "Are we far from such a city?" His impatience did not, however, prevent his occupying himself with whatever attracted his attention, as a man might have done who was exempt from all cares; when he passed through any village he would examine the houses one after another; he noticed the direction of the rivers and mountains, and collected even the slightest information that any one could or would impart.

In the daytime of May 27, His Majesty being between two or three days' march from Breslau, he encountered, before a small village called Michelsdorf, several regiments of Russian cavalry which barred the way; they were already quite close to the Emperor and the staff, and yet His Majesty had not even thought of looking at them. Prince de Neufchâtel, seeing the enemy so near, hastened to the Emperor and said: "Sire, they keep on advancing." "Oh, well! we will advance also," returned His Majesty, smiling; "don't you see behind us?" And he pointed out to the Prince the French infantry which was approaching in serried columns. A few discharges soon routed the Russians from this position; but they turned up again half a league or a league further away; the thing was always to begin again. The Emperor knew this well; hence he manœuvred with the greatest precision. Directing in person the troops that were moving forward, he went from one acclivity to another, and made the round of all the cities and villages to reconnoitre the positions and see what resources he could extract from the soil. Through his cares, as a result of his indefatigable glance, the scene would change ten times a day. Had a column debouched through a sunken road, a wood, a village, it could, on the instant, take possession of a height, for the defence of which a battery was all ready. The Emperor indicated all the movements with admirable tact, so that it was impossible to take him unawares. He commanded only in the mass, transmitting his orders, either in person or by his orderly officers, to the commanders of corps and divisions, who transmitted them in turn or had them transmitted by their own officers to the chiefs of battalion. All the orders given by His Majesty were short, precise, and so clear that no explanation of them was ever required.

May 29, not knowing how far on the road to Breslau it would be prudent to advance, His Majesty established himself in a little farmhouse called Rosnig. It had been pillaged already and presented a wretched appearance. There was only one small room in the house with a cabinet for the use of the Emperor; Prince de Neufchâtel and the suite took up their quarters as best they could in thatched cabins, barns, and even in the gardens; for there was not shelter enough for all. Fire broke out the next day in a small grange close beside His Majesty's lodging. There were fourteen or fifteen baggage wagons in this grange, all of which were burned. One of them contained the cash-box of the paymaster of the journey; in another were some clothes and linen of the Emperor, as well as jewels, rings, snuff-boxes, and other costly objects. Very little was rescued from this fire, and if the reserve service had not promptly arrived, His Majesty would have been obliged to change his usual toilet customs for lack of stockings and shirts. The Saxon Major d'Ode-leben, who has written very interesting things concerning this campaign, says that everything belonging to His Majesty was burned, and that some breeches had to be hastily made for him in Breslau; it is an error. I do not think the wardrobe wagon was burned; but even if it had been, the Emperor would not have been minus clothing on that account, since he had always four or five ser-vices, either ahead or in the rear of headquarters. In Russia, where the order was given to burn all the vehicles for which there were no horses, the com-mand was rigorously executed with regard to all the members of his household, who had almost nothing left; but for His Majesty everything was kept which could be regarded as indispensable.

At last, June 1, at six o'clock in the morning, the French advance-guard entered Breslau, having at its head General Lauriston and General Hogendorp, whom His Majesty had previously invested with the government of this city, the capital of Silesia. Thus was partially fulfilled the promise made by the Emperor when returning from Russia by way of Warsaw: "I am going to find three hundred thousand men. Success will make the Russians audacious. I shall fight two battles with them between the Elbe and the Oder, and in six months I shall again be on the Niemen."

These two battles, fought and won by conscripts, and without cavalry, had re-established the reputation of the French armies. The King of Saxony had been brought back in triumph to his capital. The Emperor's headquarters were at Breslau; one corps of the grand army at the gates of Berlin, and the enemy driven from Hamburg; Russia was about to be thrown back within its own limits, when the Emperor of Austria, intervening in the affairs of the two sovereign allies, advised them to propose an armistice. They followed this advice, and the Emperor was weak enough to consent to what they asked. The armistice was granted and signed June 4; and His Majesty set out on his return to Dresden. An hour after his departure he said: "If the allies do not really desire peace, this armistice may become fatal to us."

June 8, His Majesty went to sleep at Görlitz. That night a fire broke out in a faubourg where the guard had established its quarters. One of the notables of the city came to the Emperor's quarters at one o'clock in the morning to give the alarm and say that all was lost. The troops extinguished the fire, and some one came afterwards to acquaint His Majesty with what had occurred. I dressed him at this time, because he wished to start at daybreak. "What does the loss amount to?" asked the Emperor. "Sire, to seven or eight thousand francs, at least for the most necessitous."—"Give them ten thousand, and let it be distributed at once." The population learned the generosity of the Emperor that very instant, and when he left the city, an hour or two later, he was saluted with unanimous acclamations.

On the morning of the 10th we were back in Dresden. The arrival of the Emperor dispelled some rather singular rumors which had been in circulation ever since the remains of Marshal Duroc passed through the city. People declared that the coffin that had been brought was that of the Emperor, that he had been killed in the last battle, and that his corpse was secretly locked up in a chamber of the château, through the windows of which candles could be seen burning all night long. When he arrived, these persons, persisting in their notions, went so far as to repeat what had already been said on another occasion, namely, that it was not the Emperor that was seen in his carriage, but a manikin with a wax face. However, when he appeared on horseback before everybody the next day, in a meadow outside the city gates, they were forced to believe that he was still alive.

The Emperor alighted at the Marcolini palace, a charming summer residence situated in the faubourg Friederichstadt. An immense garden, the beautiful meadows of Osterwise, on the banks of the Elbe, and the most agreeable exposure possible rendered this sojourn far more attractive than that of the winter palace; hence the Emperor was infinitely pleased with the King of Saxony for having prepared it for him. Here his life was like what it had been at Schönbrunn; reviews every morning, a great deal of work all day, and a trifle of diversion in the evening. In general there was more simplicity than display. The middle of the day was devoted to the cabinet work; then there reigned such a tranquillity in the palace that, but for the two mounted sentries and the two sentinels that announced the abode of a monarch, it would not have been easy to suppose that this beautiful dwelling was inhabited by even the simplest private person.

The Emperor had selected the right wing of the palace for his own quarters; the left wing was occupied by Prince de Neufchâtel. In the centre of the edifice were a grand salon and two smaller ones which answered for the receptions.

Two days after his return, His Majesty sent the necessary orders to Paris for the actors of the Comédie Française to spend the time of the armistice at Dresden. The Duc de Vicenza, acting *ad interim* as grand marshal of the palace, was commissioned to make due preparations for receiving them. He remitted the affair to MM. de Beausset and de Turenne, to whom the Emperor gave the superintendence of the theatre. For this purpose, a hall was constructed in the Orangery of the Marcolini palace. It communicated with the apartments and could accommodate some two hundred persons. It was built as if by enchantment, and was opened, while awaiting the début of the French troupe, by two or three representations given by the Italian comedians of the King of Saxony.

The tragedians who came from Paris were: MM. Saint-Prix, Talma; and Mademoiselle Georges.

The comedians: MM. Fleury, Saint-Fal, Baptiste junior, Armand, Thénard, Michot, Devigny, Michelot, Barbier; and Mesdames Mars, Bourgoin, Thénard, Emilie Contat, Mézeray. The direction had been intrusted to M. Després.

All these actors arrived June 19, and found everything arranged in the most suitable manner; tastefully furnished lodgings, domestics, all in fact that could aid them to endure with ease the tedium of a sojourn in a foreign country and prove to them meantime what consideration His Majesty had for their talents, — a consideration doubly merited by most of them on account of their excellent social qualities, and the nobility and good tone of their manners.

The French troupe made their début at the Orangery theatre June 22, with the *Gageure imprévue* and another piece very much in vogue in Paris at the time, and which has since been seen with pleasure, the *Suite d'un bal masqué.*

As the Orangery hall was not large enough for tragic representations, that sort of spectacle was reserved for the grand theatre of the city, to which no one was admitted on such days unless provided with tickets from Count de Turenne, for which no charge was made.

In the grand theatre, when the French actors played, as also in that of the Marcolini palace, the attendance of the boxes was performed by none but His Majesty's footmen, who offered refreshments during the entire performance.

After the arrival of the actors of the French theatre, the day's employment was regulated in this manner:

All was quiet until eight o'clock in the morning, unless some courier arrived, or some aide-de-camp were unexpectedly summoned. At eight o'clock I dressed the Emperor. At nine he held a levee at which all persons could be present who had the rank of colonel. The civil and military authorities of the country were also admitted; the Dukes of Weimar and Anhalt, and the brothers and nephews of the King of Saxony came sometimes. Then breakfast; after which the parade in the meadow of Osterwise, about a hundred paces distant from the palace. The Emperor always went there on horseback, dismounting after he arrived; the troops defiled before him and saluted him thrice with the usual enthusiasm.

The evolutions were sometimes commanded by the Emperor and sometimes by Comte de Lobau; as soon as the cavalry began defiling, the Emperor would re-enter the palace and set to work. Then commenced that tranquillity of which I have spoken. Dinner was not until very late, at seven or eight o'clock. The Emperor often dined alone with Prince de Neufchâtel, unless he had guests belonging to the royal family of Saxony. After dinner, people went to the play when there was one, and after the play the Emperor would return to his cabinet to work again, either alone or with his secretaries.

It was the same thing every day, unless, and this case was very rare, fatigued beyond measure by the tasks of the day, His Majesty took a whim to send for Mademoiselle G—— after the tragedy. Then she would spend two or three hours in his apartment, but never more.

Sometimes, also, the Emperor would invite Talma or Mademoiselle Mars to breakfast. One day, in conversation with this admirable actress, the Emperor spoke of her début. "Sire," said she, with that grace which everybody has recognized, "I commenced very humbly. I slipped in without being perceived." "Without being perceived!" replied His Majesty, briskly; "you are mistaken. Believe me, Mademoiselle, that, like all the rest of France, I have always applauded your rare talents."

The sojourn of the Emperor at Dresden diffused riches and plenty there. More than six millions of

foreigners passed through that city between May 8
and November 16, if one credits the lists published
by Saxon authority and the number of lodgings furnished. This passage was a rain of gold which was
carefully picked up by caterers, innkeepers, and mer-
chants. Those who took charge of the military lodgings, on account of the inhabitants, also made large
profits. At Dresden you found Parisian tailors and
bootmakers who were aiding the natives to work in
the French style; you even saw bootblacks crying
on the bridges of the Elbe as they had cried on those
of the Seine, "*Shine your boots!*"

Around the city several camps had been established
for the wounded, the convalescents, etc. Nothing
could be more pleasing to the eye than one of these
camps called the Westphalian. It was a succession
of charming little gardens. Yonder, was a fortress
of turf with its bastions crowned with hortensias.
Here, a building site had been converted into a ter-
race and alleys garnished with flowers like the most
carefully tended parterre. On a knoll you saw a
bust of Pallas. All the barracks were covered with
moss and hung with daily renewed foliage and
garlands.

As the armistice was to end August 15, the celebration of His Majesty's fête was anticipated by five
days. Magnificent preparations had been made by
the army, the city, and the court, so that the ceremonies might be worthy of him who was their object.
All that Dresden contained of wealth and power vied

with each other in balls, concerts, festivities, and rejoicings of every description. In the morning, before the hour for the review, the King of Saxony with all his family came to visit the Emperor; and the two sovereigns mutually displayed their friendship. They breakfasted, and then His Majesty, accompanied by the King of Saxony, his brothers and his nephews, went into the meadow behind the palace, where they were awaited by fifteen thousand soldiers of the guard, as carefully uniformed as for the finest parades on the Champ-de-Mars.

After the review, both the French and Saxon troops went to the churches to listen to the *Te Deum*. The religious ceremony ended, all these brave fellows sat down at banquets prepared for them, and the shouts of joy, the music, and dances were prolonged far into the night.

CHAPTER VII

THE entire duration of the armistice was employed
in negotiations for arriving at the conclusion
of peace. At that time the Emperor ardently desired
it, especially since he had seen the honor of his arms
repaired by the battles of Lutzen and of Bautzen.
Unhappily, he desired it on conditions to which the

enemies could not be persuaded to accede, and we were soon to see the opening of the second series of our disasters, which rendered peace increasingly impossible. Besides, from the beginning of the negotiations relative to the armistice now approaching its end, the Emperor Alexander, in spite of the three battles gained by the Emperor Napoleon, had declined to listen to direct propositions on the part of France and insisted on the intermediation of Austria. This distrust was ill calculated to promote a definitive reconciliation; being the victor, the Emperor must naturally have been irritated by it; nevertheless, in these grave circumstances, he had succeeded in mastering his legitimate susceptibility with regard to this adverse proceeding of the Russian Emperor. Time was lost at Dresden in consequence, as it had been when our stay in Moscow was prolonged, and on both occasions the time lost by us turned solely to the advantage of the enemy.

All hope of a peaceful adjustment of difficulties having vanished, the Emperor set off from Dresden in a carriage, August 15, and the war began anew. The French army was still magnificent and imposing: it comprised two hundred thousand foot soldiers, but only forty thousand cavalrymen, so impossible had it been to repair completely the great loss we had sustained in horses. As ill luck would have it, England was at this time the soul of the coalition of Russia, Prussia, and Sweden against France; its subsidies had given it rights; they would do nothing without consulting it, and I have since known that while they were playing at negotiation, the British government declared to the Emperor of Russia that even the stipulations of Lunéville were too favorable to France. All these difficulties could be condensed into a single phrase: " We want war ! " We had war, therefore, or, rather, this scourge continued to devastate Germany, and presently menaced and invaded France. I ought, moreover, to point out that what contributed to render our position extremely critical in case of a reverse, was that Prussia was now carrying on not merely a war of soldiers, but a war that had become national by the rising of the *landwehr* and the *landsturm*, and hence a war a thousand times more dangerous than the tactics of the best disciplined of armies. To all these perplexities was added the fear, soon justified, of seeing Austria develop from the lax and nonchalant mediatrix that she was, into a declared enemy.

Before going further, it seems proper that I should turn back to two or three circumstances which I have involuntarily omitted, and which relate to our sojourn in Dresden before what may be called the second campaign of 1813. The first of these circumstances was the appearence at Dresden of the Duc d'Otrante, whom His Majesty had sent for. He had been seen but seldom at the Tuileries since the Duc de Rovigo had superseded him as minister of police, and I remember that his presence at headquarters surprised many persons, for he was supposed to be in complete disgrace. Those who are always seeking to explain the causes of the least events thought that it was His Majesty's intention to oppose the astute measures of M. Fouché's police to the then all-powerful police of Baron de Stein, the avowed chief of the secret societies which were forming on all sides, and who was regarded, not without reason, as the director of popular opinion in Prussia and Germany, and especially in the numerous schools, where the students were only awaiting the moment to take arms. These conjectures concerning the presence of M. Fouché in Dresden had no foundation. In summoning him, the Emperor had a real motive which he nevertheless disguised under an apparent pretext. The thought of Mallet's enterprise being incessantly present to his mind, His Majesty had considered it imprudent to leave at Paris, in his own absence, a malcontent so influential as the Duc d'Otrante, and I have many times heard him express himself on this subject in a manner which left me no room for doubt. However, to give a color to this real motive, the Emperor appointed M. Fouché governor of the Illyrian provinces, to replace Count Bertrand, then called to the command of an army corps and shortly afterwards to succeed the adorable General Duroc in the functions of grand marshal of the palace. However it might be with M. Fouché, it is a very certain thing that few persons were so convinced of the superiority of his talents for the police as His Majesty himself;

several times, when anything extraordinary had occurred at Paris, and notably when he heard of the Mallet conspiracy, the Emperor, when reviewing in the evening what had most affected him during the day, ended by saying: "It would not have happened if Fouché had been minister of police." This may have been a prepossession; for the Emperor certainly never had a more loyal and devoted adherent than the Duc de Rovigo, although there was a good deal of jesting in Paris over his captivity of several hours.

Prince Eugène having returned to Italy at the beginning of the campaign to organize a new army there, we did not see him at Dresden; the King of Naples, who arrived in the night of August 13–14, presented himself almost alone, having nothing in the grand army but the small number of Neapolitan troops whom he had left behind him at the time of his departure for Naples.

I was in the chamber of the Emperor when the King of Naples entered it and saw him for the first time. I do not know to what to attribute it, but I thought I noticed that the Emperor gave his brother-in-law a less cordial reception than of old. Prince Murat said he had been unable to remain longer in Naples when he knew that the French army, to which he had never ceased to belong, was fighting, and that he asked nothing but to combat in its ranks. The Emperor took him with him to the parade and gave him the command of the imperial guard; it would not have been easy to confide it to a more intrepid leader. Later on, he had the general command of the cavalry.

Throughout the whole duration of the armistice, occupied rather than filled by the tardy and useless conferences of the Congress of Prague, it would be impossible to give a notion of all the various tasks to which the Emperor applied himself from morning to evening, and frequently during the night. You would see him incessantly lying over his maps, rehearsing in advance, as it were, the battles that he meditated. However, growing frequently impatient with the slowness of the negotiations, as to the result of which he seemed to be no longer under any illusion, he told me, a little before the end of July, to see if everything had been prepared for him which was necessary for an excursion we were about to make as far as Mayence. He had appointed a meeting with the Empress there, and she was to arrive on the 25th, that the Emperor might arrange his departure so as to arrive shortly after she did. I report this journey, however, merely as a fact; for it was not signalized by any remarkable circumstance, unless that it was during our excursion to Mayence that the Emperor learned the death of the Duc d'Abrantès, who had just succumbed at Dijon to the violent attacks of the terrible malady from which he suffered. Although the Emperor, knowing already that he was in a deplorable state of mental alienation, must have expected this loss, he was none the less deeply affected by it, and sincerely regretted his former aide-de-camp.

The Emperor remained only a few days with the Empress, whom he had met again with lively satisfaction. But the great interests of his policy recalled him to Dresden; on the way thither he visited several places along the road, and we were back in the Saxon capital August 4. Travellers who had seen this beautiful city only in times of peace would have found difficulty in recognizing it. Immense works had metamorphosed it into a war city; numerous batteries had been erected in the suburbs so as to command the opposite bank of the Elbe. Everything assumed a warlike attitude; and the occupations of the Emperor became multiplied and pressing, to such a point that he remained nearly three days in his cabinet without leaving it.

Meanwhile, amidst the preparations for war, all was being arranged for the celebration of the Emperor's birthday, which had been advanced to August 10, because, as I think I have already mentioned, the armistice would expire precisely on the anniversary of Saint Napoleon, and it could be affirmed that, with his bellicose disposition, the resumption of hostilities was not a birthday gift which the Emperor would be tempted to disdain.

As at Paris, there was a free performance at Dresden on the eve of the Emperor's fête. The actors of the Théâtre Français played two comedies on the 9th, at five o'clock in the evening; and this representation was the last, the company having received immediately afterwards the order to return to Paris. The next day, at nine o'clock in the morning, the King of Saxony, accompanied by all the princes of his family, came to the Marcolini palace to congratulate the Emperor; afterwards there was a grand levee as at the Tuileries; and a review in which the Emperor inspected a part of his guard, several regiments, and a number of Saxon troops, who had been invited to dinner by the French troops. On that day the city of Dresden might have been compared without too much exaggeration to a vast dining-room. In effect, while His Majesty was dining in state at the palace of the King of Saxony, where the whole family of this prince was assembled, the entire diplomatic corps were seated at the table of the Duc de Bassano; Baron Bignon, envoy of France at Warsaw, was entertaining all the Poles of distinction who were in Dresden; Count Daru was giving a grand dinner to the French authorities; General Friant to the French and Saxon generals; and Baron de Serra, minister of France at Dresden, to the heads of the Saxon colleges. Finally this day of dinners was crowned by a supper of nearly two hundred covers which General Henri Durosnel, governor of Dresden, gave that very evening at the close of a magnificent ball in the hotel of M. de Serra.

On our return from Mayence to Dresden, I had learned that the house of General Durosnel was the meeting-place of the best society, whether Saxon or

French. During the absence of His Majesty, the General, taking advantage of his leisure, gave some entertainments, among others one to the actors and actresses of the Comédie Française. Concerning this I even recall a comic anecdote which was told me at the time. Without failing either in decorum or politeness, Baptiste junior, so they said, contributed greatly to the pleasantness of the evening. He presented himself under the title of Lord Bristol, an English diplomat on his way to the Congress of Prague. His disguise was so accurate, his accent so natural, his phlegm so imperturbable, that several persons belonging to the Saxon court were completely deceived by it. That did not surprise me; I saw by it that the talent of Baptiste junior for mystifications had suffered no diminution since the days when he so greatly diverted me at the breakfasts of Colonel de Beauharnais. What things had already happened since that epoch!

Meanwhile the Emperor, seeing that nothing could longer retard the resumption of hostilities, had at once divided his two hundred thousand infantrymen into fourteen army corps, the command of which was given to Marshals Victor, Ney, Marmont, Augereau, Macdonald, Oudinot, Davoust, and Gouvion Saint-Cyr,[1] Prince Poniatowski, and Generals Reynier,

---

[1] Marshal Gouvion Saint-Cry was at this time the youngest in date of the marshals of the Empire, having received the marshal's baton on the field of battle during the campaign of Moscow, after the combat of August 18.

Rapp, Lauriston, Vandamme, and Bertrand. The forty thousand cavalrymen formed six grand divisions under the orders of Generals Nansouty, Latour-Maubourg, Sébastiani, Arrighi, Milhaud, and Kellermann; and, as I have already said, the King of Naples had command of the imperial guard. In addition, in this first campaign we saw guards of honor appear for the first time on our battle-fields, choice troops recruited from the richest and most notable families, and amounting to more than ten thousand men, separated into two divisions under the simple title of regiments, one of which was commanded by General Count de Pully, and the other, if I do not mistake, by General Ségur. These young men, once idle, addicted to repose and pleasures, became, in a short time, an excellent body of cavalry, and distinguished themselves on several occasions, notably at the battle of Dresden, of which I shall presently have to speak.

The reader has already seen what was the strength of the French army. The combined army of the allies amounted to four hundred thousand infantry soldiers, and its cavalry was scarcely less than a hundred thousand horses, without counting a reserve army corps of eighty thousand Russians ready to start from Poland under the orders of General Beningsen. Thus the foreign soldiers were more than two to one against us.

At this period of entering on campaign, Austria had just declared against us. This blow, although expected, struck the Emperor very hard; he often spoke plainly on the subject in presence of all those who had the honor to approach him. I have heard say that M. Metternich almost warned him of it in his last interviews with His Majesty at Dresden; but the Emperor had been long reluctant to believe that the Emperor of Austria would make common cause with the coalitionists of the North against his daughter and his grandson. At last all doubts were removed by the arrival of Count Louis de Narbonne, who returned from Prague to Dresden, bearing the Austrian declaration of war. Every one foresaw from this time that France would soon count among her enemies every country no longer occupied by her troops. The event justified the prevision but too well. Still all was not lost, and we had not yet been obliged to put ourselves on the defensive.

CHAPTER VIII

THE war began again without the negotiations having been precisely broken off, since the Duc de Vicenza was still with M. de Metternich; hence the Emperor, while mounting his horse, said to the numerous generals by whom he was surrounded, that he was marching to the conquest of peace. But what hope could one retain after the declaration of Austria, and above all when one knew that the allied sovereigns had increased their demands with every concession that the Emperor made? The Emperor left Dresden at five o'clock in the afternoon, by the road of Koenigstein. He spent the next day at Bautzen, where he examined the battle-field which was the scene of his latest victory. There the King of Naples, who had refused to receive royal honors, rejoined him at the head of the imperial guard, the aspect of which was as imposing as it had ever been.

We arrived on the 18th at Görlitz, where the Emperor found the Duc de Vicenza, who was returning from Bohemia. He confirmed the news His Majesty had already received at Dresden of the determination taken by the Emperor of Austria to make common cause with the Emperor of Russia, the King of Prussia, and Sweden against the husband of his daughter, of that princess he had given him as a pledge of peace. It was also from the Duc de Vicenza that the Emperor learned that General Blücher had just entered Silesia at the head of an army of one hundred thousand men, and that, without respect for the most sacred conventions, he had seized Breslau on the day before that fixed for the rupture of the armistice; that on the same day General Jomini, a Swiss by birth, but up to then in the service of France, chief of staff to Marshal Ney, and loaded with the benefits of the Emperor, had deserted his post and repaired to the head-quarters of the Emperor Alexander, who had welcomed him with every demonstration of lively satisfaction.

The Duc de Vicenza entered into some details concerning this desertion which seemed to afflict His Majesty more than all the other tidings. He said, among other things, that when General Jomini had arrived in presence of Alexander, he found that monarch surrounded by chiefs, among whom some one pointed out General Moreau; and it was then that the Emperor received the first intimation of Moreau's presence at the enemy's headquarters. The Duc de Vicenza added that the Emperor Alexander had presented General Jomini to Moreau, who gave him a cool reception, which Jomini acknowledged by a simple inclination of the head, after which he retired without saying a word, and remained sorrowful and silent all the evening in a corner of the salon opposite to that where Moreau was standing. This coolness had not escaped the notice of Alexander; hence the next morning at his levee, addressing Marshal Ney's ex-chief of staff, he said: "General Jomini, what was the reason of what happened yesterday? I should have thought it would be agreeable to you to meet General Moreau." "Anywhere else, Sire."—"How so?" "If I had been born a Frenchman, like the General, I should not be in Your Majesty's camp to-day." The Duc de Vicenza having thus terminated his report to the Emperor, His Majesty said with a bitter smile: "I am sure that miserable Jomini thought he had performed a fine action. Ah! Caulaincourt, it is the deserters who will ruin me!" Possibly Moreau, in himself greeting Jomini coldly, had thought that if he had still been serving in the French army, he would not have played false with arms in his hand; and, after all, it is not an unnatural thing to find two traitors blushing at one another, each cherishing illusions concerning his own treason, and never thinking that the sentiment he experiences is also that which he inspires.

However it may be, the news imparted by M. de Caulaincourt to the Emperor caused him to make some alterations in the plans he had formed for the campaign. His Majesty did in reality give up the idea of moving in person on Berlin as he had manifested his intention of doing.

The Emperor, recognizing the prime necessity of knowing the truth about the march of the Austrian grand army, commanded by the Prince of Schwarzenberg, penetrated into Bohemia; but learning, through the army scouts and spies, that eighty thousand Russians had been left from the opposite side with a considerable body of Austrian troops, he retraced his steps, after several engagements in which his presence decided the victory, and on the 24th we found ourselves again at Bautzen. From this residence His

Majesty despatched the King of Naples to Dresden to reassure the King of Saxony and the inhabitants of that city, who knew that the enemy was at its gates. The Emperor assured them that it would not be entered by the hostile forces, since he had returned to defend its approaches, urging them, nevertheless, not to allow themselves to be intimidated by a sudden attack that might be attempted by some isolated detachments. Murat arrived just at the right time, for we afterwards learned that a universal consternation was prevailing in the city; but such was the prestige attaching to the Emperor's promises that all regained courage on learning his presence.

While the King of Naples was fulfilling this mission, Colonel Gourgaud was summoned in the morning to the Emperor's tent, where I was at the time. "To-morrow I shall be on the road to Pirna," His Majesty said to him; "but I will stop at Stolpen. Do you make haste to Dresden; go with all speed; be there to-night. When you arrive, see the King of Naples, Durosnel, the Duc de Bassano, and Marshal Gouvion; reassure them all. See the Saxon Minister de Gersdorf also; tell him that you cannot see the King because you are leaving at once, but that to-morrow I can put forty thousand men into Dresden, and that I am preparing to arrive there with all the army. At daybreak go to the quarters of the commandant of the engineer corps; examine the redoubts and the enceinte of the city; and when you have thoroughly seen them, come back to me at

Stolpen as fast as you can. Report to me the real condition of things, as well as the opinion of Marshal Saint-Cyr and the Duc de Bassano. Be off." The Colonel started instantly, without having broken his fast that day.

By eleven o'clock the next evening Colonel Gourgaud was back with the Emperor, after having executed all his commissions. Meanwhile, the allied army had come down into the plain of Dresden, and several attacks had already been made on the outposts. It appeared from the information given by the Colonel, that on the arrival of the King of Naples the city was in the greatest consternation, and had no hope but in the Emperor. Hordes of Cossacks were, in fact, already in sight of the faubourgs which they menaced, and their appearance had compelled the inhabitants of these faubourgs to seek shelter inside the city. "As I came away," said Colonel Gourgaud, " I saw a village in flames within half a league from the grand gardens, and Marshal Gouvion Saint-Cyr was preparing to evacuate that position." — " But after all," said the Emperor, sharply, " what is the opinion of the Duc de Bassano?" "Sire, the Duc de Bassano thinks they will not be able to hold out for twenty-four hours longer." — " And you?" "I, Sire? ... I think Dresden will be taken to-morrow, if Your Majesty is not there." — "Can I rely on what you tell me?" "Sire, I will answer for it with my head."

Thereupon His Majesty sent for General Haxo,

and said to him, his finger on the map: "Vandamme is advancing by way of Pirna beyond the Elbe. The eagerness of the enemy to penetrate as far as Dresden has been extreme. Vandamme is going to find them on his rear. It had been my intention to sustain his movement with the whole army; but the fate of Dresden disturbs me, and I will not sacrifice that city. I can be there in a few hours, and I am going to do it, although it costs me much to abandon a plan which, if well executed, might enable me to be done with the allies once for all. Luckily, Vandamme is still in sufficient force to supplement the general movement by partial attacks which will harass the enemy. Tell him, therefore, that he is to advance from Pirna upon Ghiesubel, to gain the defiles of Peterswalde, and then, intrenched in this impregnable position, to await the result of what is about to take place under the walls of Dresden. *It is to him that I reserve the task of picking up the sword of the vanquished.* But he will need to keep cool and pay no attention to the uproar made by the fugitives. Explain thoroughly to General Vandamme what I expect from him. He will never have a finer chance to win the marshal's baton."

General Haxo set off that very moment; the Emperor called Colonel Gourgaud in again and told him to mount a fresh horse and go back to Dresden faster than he came, in order to announce his arrival. "The old guard will precede me," said the Emperor. "I hope they will not be afraid when they see them."

The morning of the 26th, the Emperor was on the Dresden bridge on horseback, and commencing amidst shouts of joy from the young and the old guard the preparations for that terrible battle which lasted three days.

It was ten o'clock in the morning when the inhabitants of Dresden, reduced to despair and talking loudly of capitulating, saw His Majesty arrive. The scene changed in an instant. To the most complete discouragement succeeded the strongest confidence, above all when the haughty cuirassiers of Latour-Maubourg defiled upon the bridge, heads up and eyes fixed on the neighboring acclivities surmounted by the enemy. The Emperor alighted at once at the palace, where the King was preparing to seek an asylum in the new city. The arrival of the great man altered his arrangements. This interview was extremely touching.

I do not pretend to enter into the details of those memorable days when the Emperor covered himself with glory and exposed himself to greater risks than he had ever before incurred. Pages, equerries, aides-de-camp, fell dead around him, balls pierced the body of his horses, but nothing could touch him; the soldiers beheld him and renewed their ardor in renewing their confidence and admiration. I will merely say that on the first day the Emperor did not re-enter the château until midnight, and spent all the hours until day in dictating orders while striding up and down; that at daybreak he remounted his horse, the weather being frightful, with a heavy rain that lasted all day. In the evening the enemy was completely routed; then the Emperor turned back toward the palace in a fearful condition. He had been on horseback since six o'clock, and the rain had not ceased for an instant; hence he was so wet that one could say without exaggeration that his boots took water by the collar of his coat: they were entirely filled with it. His hat of very fine beaver was so deformed that it was flapping on his shoulders; his leather belt was completely soaked with water; in a word, a man who has just been pulled out of the river is not wetter than the Emperor was. The King of Saxony, who was waiting for him, saw him in this condition and embraced him like a beloved son who has just escaped from a great danger; this excellent prince had tears in his eyes as he pressed the savior of his capital to his heart. After a few reassuring and affectionate words, the Emperor entered his apartment, leaving everywhere behind him traces of the water which was dripping from all parts of his clothing. I had great difficulty in undressing him. Knowing that the Emperor liked a bath after a fatiguing day, I had prepared one; but experiencing an extraordinary fatigue, accompanied by a very characteristic chill, His Majesty preferred to go to his bed, which I warmed with all speed. Hardly had the Emperor lain down when he summoned Baron Fain, one of his secretaries, to have him read his back correspondence, which was very voluminous.

He did not take his bath till afterwards; he had been in it but a few minutes when he was seized with an extraordinary distress, soon followed by fits of vomiting, which obliged him to go back to bed. Then His Majesty said to me: " My dear Constant, a little repose is indispensable to me; see that no one wakes me up unless for matters of the very greatest importance; say so to Fain." I obeyed the orders of the Emperor, after which I remained in the salon leading to his bedroom, watching with the rigor of a sentinel that no one should awaken him or even go near his apartment. The Emperor rang for me at a rather early hour the next morning, and I went in immediately, being anxious to know how he had passed the night. I found the Emperor almost entirely recovered and very cheerful: he told me, however, that he had had a rather high fever; I ought to add that to my knowledge this was the only time the Emperor had a fever, for, during all the time I was with him, I never saw him ill enough to keep his bed for twenty-four hours. He rose at his usual time. When he came down, the Emperor experienced a very lively satisfaction, occasioned by the good appearance of the battalion on duty. These brave grenadiers, who had served as his escort the day before, had re-entered Dresden with him in the most pitiable condition; but in the morning we saw them drawn up in the court of the château in splendid style and with their weapons as polished as on a parade day on the Place du Carrousel. These brave fellows had spent the night in cleaning and drying themselves around the great fires they had kindled for that purpose, thus preferring to sleep and the repose they must have needed so much, the satisfaction of presenting themselves in good condition before the Emperor. A word of approbation repaid them for their fatigues, and one may say that no military leader has ever been so beloved by his soldiers as was His Majesty.

The last courier who had arrived from Paris at Dresden, and whose despatches were read to the Emperor as I have said, was the bearer of several letters for me, from my family and two or three of my friends; and all those who have followed His Majesty on his campaigns, in any capacity whatever, know how precious is the news he receives from his own people. They wrote me, I remember, about a famous suit then in progress before the Court of Assizes between Michel the banker and Reynier. This scandalous affair made so much noise in the capital that it almost divided with the army news the interest and attention of the public. They wrote me, also, about the journey which the Empress was about to make to Cherbourg, to be present at the rupture of the dikes and the invasion of the harbor by the sea. This journey, as may be imagined, had been advised by the Emperor, who sought every occasion to bring the Empress before the public and make her perform acts of sovereignty as regent of the Empire. She convoked and presided over the

council of ministers, and I have more than once
beheld the Emperor felicitating himself, after the
Austrian declaration of war, because *his Louise*, as
he called her, was entirely devoted to the interests
of France, and had nothing Austrian about her but
her birth. Hence he left to her the satisfaction of
publishing herself, and in her own name, all the
official news from the army; no bulletins were
drawn up any longer; the news was transmitted
to her all written out; and there is no doubt that
the object of this attention on the part of His
Majesty was to render the Empress-regent more
popular by making her the intermediary of govern-
mental communications to the public. Moreover, it
is strictly true that we, who were on the spot, though
we were immediately informed of the winning of a
battle or an unlucky reverse, were very often ignorant of the ensemble of the operations of the various
corps manœuvring over an immense line, except
through the means of the Parisian newspapers; it
may be fancied, then, how eager we were to read
them.

CHAPTER IX

Prodigies of valor of the King of Naples — Growing prudence of
several generals — The Emperor on the battle-field of Dresden
— Humanity toward the wounded and assistance to the poor
peasants — The Prince of Schwarzenberg believed to be dead —
His Majesty's remark — Fatalism and souvenir of the Parisian
ball — The Emperor undeceived — Inscription on the collar of a
dog sent to Prince de Neufchâtel — *I belong to General Moreau*
— Death of Moreau — Details of his last moments given by his
valet de chambre — The march on Berlin again decided on —
Fatal news and catastrophe of General Vandamme — Fine
remark of the Emperor — Painful resignation of the Emperor —
Definitive departure from Dresden — Marshal Saint-Cyr — The
château of Düben — The Emperor's projects known to the army
— Defection of the Bavarians and increasing discouragement —
Apathetic idleness of the Emperor — The Emperor yielding to
the generals — Departure for Leipsic — Universal joy of the staff
— Marshal Augereau alone shares the Emperor's opinion — The
hopes of the Emperor disappointed — Resolution of the allies to
fight only where the Emperor is not present — Proclamations of
the Prince-royal of Sweden to the Saxons — M. Moldrecht and
the Emperor's clemency — Leipsic the centre of the war — Three
enemies to one Frenchman — Ammunition exhausted — The
retreat ordered — The Emperor and Prince Poniatowski —
Indignation of the King of Saxony against his troops and consolations imparted by the Emperor — Imminent danger of His
Majesty — Final and affecting farewells of the two sovereigns.

DURING the second day of the battle of Dresden,
at the close of which His Majesty experienced
the access of fever, of which I have spoken in the

preceding chapter, the King of Naples, or rather Marshal Murat, had performed prodigies of valor. Much has been said of this truly extraordinary prince; but only those who have seen him can form an exact idea concerning him, and even then they would know him but imperfectly if they have not seen him on a field of battle. There he was like those great actors who produce a complete illusion amidst the enchantments of the stage, but who do not resemble heroes in private life. Whenever, in Paris, I was present at a representation of Luce de Lancival's *Mort d'Hector*, I never listened to the verses in which the author describes the effect produced on the Trojan army by the appearance of Achilles without thinking of Prince Murat, and it may be said, without exaggeration, that his presence produced the same effect as soon as he showed himself in front of the Austrian lines. Being naturally of an almost gigantic figure, which would have sufficed to render him remarkable, he further sought all possible means of attracting notice, as if he wished to dazzle those he sought to strike. His regular and strongly marked countenance, his beautiful blue eyes rolling in their orbits, enormous whiskers, and black hair falling in ringlets on the collar of a *kurtka* with tight sleeves astonished at first glance; add to this the richest and most elegant costume that any one ever thought of wearing, even on the stage: a Polish coat, embroidered in the most brilliant manner and clasped by a gilded belt from which depended the scabbard of a light sabre with a straight and pointed blade, without an edge and without a guard; wide trousers of amaranthine purple, embroidered in gold on the seams, and nankeen bottines; a big hat embroidered in gold and surmounted by four large ostrich feathers, from the midst of which rose a magnificent tuft of heron plumes. And lastly, the horse of the king, chosen from among the strongest and largest that could be found, covered with a long, sky-blue housing, magnificently embroidered, and kept in place by a saddle of Hungarian or Turkish shape, curiously wrought, and accompanied by a bridle and stirrups not exceeded in richness by the rest of the equipment. All these things combined to make the King of Naples a being by himself, an object of terror and of admiration. But what idealized him, so to say, was a bravery that was veritably chivalrous and frequently urged even to temerity, as if danger ought not to exist for him. Besides, this temerity was far from displeasing to the Emperor; without always approving the use to which it was put, His Majesty seldom failed to praise it, above all, when he thought it needful to oppose it to the increasing prudence of some of his ancient companions in arms.

On the 28th, the Emperor visited the field of battle, which presented the most frightful spectacle; he gave orders that the sufferings of the wounded should be alleviated as much as possible, and those of the inhabitants, the peasants whose houses and fields had been ravaged, burned, and pillaged; and afterwards ascended the heights whence he could watch the march of the retreating enemy. Nearly all the attendants had followed him in this excursion. There was brought to him a peasant from Nothlitz, a small village where the Emperor Alexander and the King of Prussia had had their headquarters on the two preceding days. This peasant, interrogated by the Duc de Vicenza, said that he had seen a great personage brought to Nothlitz who had been wounded the day before in the midst of the allied staff; he was riding beside the Emperor of Russia at the moment when he was struck, and the Emperor seemed to take the keenest interest in his fate. He had been carried to the headquarters of Nothlitz on the crossed pikes of Cossacks; nothing had been found to cover him with but a mantle soaked with rain. On reaching Nothlitz, the Emperor Alexander's surgeon had amputated both of his legs and sent him on a couch to Dippoldiswalde, escorted by several detachments, Austrian, Prussian, and Russian.

On learning these details, the Emperor persuaded himself that this must be the Prince of Schwarzenberg. "He was a brave man," said he, "and I regret him." Then, after a silent pause, His Majesty resumed : "Then it is he who purges the fatality! That occurrence at the ball has always weighed on my heart as a sinister omen. . . . It is very evident now, that the omen was intended for him."

However, while the Emperor was indulging in this sort of conjectures and recalling his former presentiments, the prisoners brought before His Majesty were interrogated, and he learned that Prince Schwarzenberg had not been wounded, that he was in good health and had directed the retreat of the Austrian grand army. Who then was the important personage who had been struck by a French ball? Conjectures were beginning anew on this point when Prince de Neufchâtel received from an envoy of the King of Saxony a collar taken from the neck of a stray dog which had been found at Nothlitz; it was engraved with these words: *I belong to General Moreau.* Still this was merely an indication, but the suspicions it gave rise to were soon confirmed by abundant information.

Thus, Moreau received his death-blow the first time that he bore arms against his country, after having so often braved with impunity the fire of her enemies. History has passed an irrevocable sentence on him; nevertheless, in spite of the enmity that had long existed between them, I can affirm that the Emperor did not hear of his death without emotion, indignant though he was that so famous a French general should have taken arms against France and donned the Russian cockade.

This unexpected death produced a great effect in both camps. Our soldiers beheld in it a just punishment from Heaven, and a favorable presage for the Emperor. However that might be, here are some details which came afterwards to my knowledge, such as they were related by the valet de chambre of General Moreau.

The three sovereigns of Russia, Austria, and Prussia had watched the fighting on the 27th from the heights of Nothlitz, whence they had departed as soon as they saw that the day had gone against them. That same day, General Moreau had been wounded by a cannon-ball, near the intrenchments established before Dresden. Towards four o'clock in the afternoon he was taken to the country seat of a banker named Salir, at Nothlitz, where the Emperors of Russia and Austria had established their headquarters. Both legs of the General were amputated below the knee. After the amputation, he asked for something to eat and a cup of tea; three fried eggs and some tea were offered him, but he took nothing but the tea. Toward seven o'clock he was placed on a stretcher and borne to Passendorf by Russian soldiers. He spent the night in the country house of M. Tritschier, grand master of the forests. There he took nothing but another cup of tea, and complained greatly of his sufferings. The next day, August 28, he was transported, again by Russian soldiers, from Passendorf to Dippoldiswalde, where he had a little white bread and a glass of lemonade at the house of a baker named Watz. An hour later, he was taken still nearer the frontiers of Bohemia. Russian soldiers carried him in the body of a coach detached from the train. During this passage the cries wrung from him by the intensity of his pains were incessant.

Such are the details I received at the time concerning Moreau's catastrophe, and it is well known that the General did not long survive his wound. The same ball which broke his two legs carried off an arm from Prince Ipsilanti, then an aide-de-camp of the Emperor Alexander; so that if the harm that one inflicts could repair the harm that one suffers, one might say that the ball which took General Kirchner and Marshal Duroc away from us was that day sent back to the enemy, but alas! those are melancholy consolations which one extracts from reprisals.

It is plain from the preceding pages, and especially from what appeared to be the decisive winning of the battle of Dresden, that wherever our troops were sustained by the all-powerful presence of the Emperor, they always gained advantages. Unluckily, it was not the same at several remote points on the line of operations. However, seeing the allies routed by the army that he commanded in person; sure, moreover, that General Vandamme would have maintained the position he had indicated to him through General Haxo, His Majesty returned to his first idea of marching on Berlin. He was already making his preparations to do so when the fatal tidings came that Vandamme, the victim of his own temerity, had vanished from the field of battle, and that his ten thousand men, hemmed in on all sides and overwhelmed by the enemy, had been cut to pieces. Vandamme was supposed to be dead, and it was only by later tidings that we learned he had been taken prisoner with a part of his troops. We also learned that Vandamme, carried away by his natural intrepidity, and unable to resist his desire to attack an enemy whom he saw within his reach, had quitted his defiles for that purpose. He had conquered at first, but when, after his victory, he attempted to resume his position, he found it occupied by Prussians who had seized it. Then he fought with the courage of despair, but all in vain, and General Kleist, proud of this fine trophy, led him to Prague in triumph. It was in speaking of Vandamme's audacious attempt that the Emperor employed that fine expression which has been so justly admired: " For a flying enemy you must make a bridge of gold, or oppose to him a wall of steel."

The Emperor listened with his habitual calmness to the details of the losses he had just experienced. Nevertheless, his words more than once expressed the astonishment caused him by Vandamme's deplorable temerity; he could not get over the fact that so experienced a general should have allowed himself to be drawn from his position. But the harm was done, and in such cases the Emperor never lost time in empty recriminations. " Come," said he, addressing the Duc de Bassano, " you have just heard . . . That is war! away up in the morning, and away down in the evening."

After various orders given to the army and its

leaders, the Emperor left Dresden in the evening of September 3, to try and regain what had been lost by the audacious imprudence of General Vandamme. But this check, the first we had experienced since the resumption of hostilities, was like the signal for the long series of reverses which awaited us.   One might have said that victory, making a final effort in our favor at Dresden, was at last weary; the remainder of the campaign was but a series of disasters, aggravated by treasons of every description, and terminated by the horrible catastrophe of Leipsic.   Even before quitting Dresden, we had heard of the desertion to the enemy of a Westphalian regiment, with arms and baggage.

The Emperor left Marshal Saint-Cyr in Dresden with thirty thousand men, and orders to hold out to the last extremity; he desired to save this capital at all costs.   September passed in marches and countermarches around the city, without any events of decisive importance.   Alas! the Emperor was never again to see the garrison of Dresden.   Circumstances, becoming more difficult, made it imperative on His Majesty to oppose a prompt obstacle to the progress of the allies.   The King of Saxony, a rare model of fidelity among kings, wished to accompany the Emperor; he entered a carriage with the Queen and the Princess Augusta, under an escort from the grand headquarters.   Two days after his departure, the junction of the Saxon troops with the French army took place at Eilenburg, on the borders of the Mulde.

The Emperor exhorted these allies, whom he must have believed faithful, to maintain the independence of their country. He pointed out that Prussia was menacing Saxony and coveting its finest provinces; he reminded them of the proclamations of their sovereign, his worthy and faithful ally; finally, speaking in the name of military honor, he summoned them in conclusion to take him always for their guide, and to show themselves the worthy rivals of the soldiers of the grand army, with whom they were making common cause, and beside whom they were going to fight. The Emperor's words were translated and repeated to the Saxons by the Duc de Vicenza. This language on the lips of him whom they regarded as their sovereign's friend and the savior of their capital, seemed to produce a profound impression. We began the march, therefore, with confidence, not foreboding the approaching defection of these very men who had so often saluted the Emperor with enthusiastic shouts while swearing to fight to the death rather than desert him.

At this time, His Majesty's scheme was to fall on Blücher and the Prince-royal of Sweden, from whom the French army was separated only by a river. Hence we quitted Eilenburg, leaving in that residence the King of Saxony and his family, the Duc de Bassano, the grand park of artillery and all the equipages, while we turned towards Düben. Blücher and Bernadotte had retired, leaving Berlin exposed. Then the Emperor's plans became known; it was known that it was Berlin and not Leipsic toward which he was moving, and that Düben was merely a point of junction, whence the various corps there assembled could march together upon the capital of Prussia, of which the Emperor had twice possessed himself already.

Unhappily, the time was past when the mere indication of the Emperor's intentions was regarded as a signal of victory; the leaders of the army, until then submissive, were beginning to reflect and even permitting themselves to disapprove of projects the execution of which alarmed them. When the Emperor's intention of marching on Berlin became known in the army, it was the signal for an almost universal dissatisfaction. The generals who had escaped the disasters of Moscow and the dangers of the double campaign of Germany were fatigued, and perhaps in haste to enjoy their fortune and at last to taste repose in the bosom of their families. Some went so far as to accuse the Emperor of wishing to prolong the war. "Have not enough of us been killed?" said they, "must we all be left here?" Nor were these complaints made only in private; they were openly expressed, and sometimes so loudly that they reached the Emperor's ears; but in such cases His Majesty knew how not to hear.

It was during this suspicious attitude of a considerable number of the army chieftains that the defection of Bavaria became known. This added new force to the anxieties and discontent arising from the Emperor's resolve; an unheard-of thing occurred;

his staff went in a body to the Emperor, entreating him to abandon his plans on Berlin and march on Leipsic. I saw how deeply the soul of the Emperor suffered from the necessity of listening to such remonstrances.

In spite of the respectful forms in which they were concealed, His Majesty remained undecided for two entire days; how long those forty-eight hours were! Never was bivouac or deserted cabin more dismal than the dismal château of Düben. In this lamentable residence I saw the Emperor for the first time completely idle; the indecision to which he was a prey kept him so absorbed that no one could have recognized him. Who would have believed it? to that activity which urged, which one might say incessantly devoured him, had succeeded an apparent nonchalance of which no idea can be formed. I saw him, during nearly an entire day, lying on a sofa, with a table in front of him covered with maps and papers which he did not look at, with no other occupation for whole hours together but that of slowly tracing large letters on sheets of white paper. It was because his mind was then wavering between his own will and the supplications of his generals. After two days of the most painful anxiety, he yielded, and thenceforward all was lost. Would to God that he had not listened to their complaints, that he had once more obeyed the presentiment that sought to master him! How many times he sadly repeated, in thinking of the concession he then made: " I would have avoided many disasters had I always followed my first impulse. I failed only by yielding to those of others."

The order to depart was given. Then, as if the army were prouder of having overcome the Emperor's will than of fighting the enemy under the sway of his high previsions, there was a general outburst of almost immoderate joy. Every face was radiant. "We are going," they repeated on all sides, "we are going to see France again, to embrace our children, our parents, our friends." The Emperor, and with him General Augereau, were the only persons who did not share the universal gladness. The Duc de Castiglione had just arrived at headquarters, after having avenged in part, on the army of Bohemia, the defeat of Vandamme; like the Emperor, he was impressed with gloomy presentiments concerning the results of this retrograde movement; he knew that defections would increase by degrees on the route of our enemies, and all the more dangerous ones because they were our allies but yesterday and knew our positions. As to His Majesty, he yielded with the conviction of the evil that would result, and I heard him end a conversation of more than an hour with the Marshal by these words, which he pronounced like a sentence of misfortune: "*They have willed it!*"

The Emperor, when moving on Düben, was at the head of a force which might be estimated at one hundred and twenty-five thousand men. He had taken this direction, hoping to find Blücher still on the Mulde; but the Russian general had recrossed the river, a measure which tended to accredit a rumor that had been in circulation for some time: they said that in a council of the sovereign allies, held previously in Prague, and at which Moreau and the Prince-royal of Sweden were present, it had been agreed that wherever it could be avoided, no battle should be engaged when the Emperor was present, and that operations should be directed solely against the corps commanded by his lieutenants. Doubtless it was impossible to render a more striking homage to the superiority of the Emperor's genius; but at the same time it was to enchain him in his glory and paralyze his ordinarily omnipotent influence.

However that might be, the evil genius of France having prevailed over the good genius of the Emperor, we took the road to Leipsic, and arrived there early in the morning, October 15. At this moment the King of Naples was fighting with the Prince of Schwarzenberg, and His Majesty, having heard the cannon, merely passed through the city and went to visit the plain where the battle seemed to be in active progress. On his return he received the royal family of Saxony, which had come to rejoin him.

During his short stay at Leipsic, the Emperor performed an act of clemency which will doubtless be considered very meritorious when the gravity of the circumstances we were placed in is remem bered. A merchant of that city, named Moldrecht, was accused and convicted of having distributed amongst the inhabitants, and even in the army, several thousand copies of a proclamation in which the Prince-royal of Sweden invited the Saxons to desert the Emperor's cause. When brought before a council of war, M. Moldrecht was unable to justify himself; and how could he have done so when several packages of the fatal proclamation had been found at his house? He was condemned to death. His weeping family came to throw themselves at the feet of the King of Saxony; but the facts were so evident and of so inexcusable a kind that the faithful King dared not show indulgence for a crime aimed still more at his ally than himself. But one resource was left to this unhappy family, that of appealing to the Emperor; but it was not easy to obtain access to him. M. Leborgne d'Ideville, interpreting secretary, proved willing to deposit a note on the Emperor's bureau. Having read it, His Majesty ordered a reprieve, which was equivalent to a full pardon. Events followed their course, and M. Moldrecht was saved.

Leipsic, at this period, was the centre of a circle in which fighting was going on at different points, and almost without interruption. The combats continued on the 16th, 17th, and 18th of October. His Majesty, ill-repaid for his clemency toward M. Moldrecht, reaped the bitter fruits of the proclamation scattered by means of this merchant. On that day the Saxon army deserted our cause and went over to Bernadotte. One hundred thousand men were now all that the Emperor had left, with three hundred thousand arrayed against him, so that if we had been one against two ever since the assumption of hostilities, we were now only one to three. The 18th, as is known, was the fatal day. In the evening, the Emperor was sitting on a red morocco camp-stool amidst the bivouac fires, dictating to Prince de Neufchâtel his orders for the night, when two artillery commanders presented themselves to His Majesty and told him that they were nearly out of ammunition. Within five days more than two hundred thousand discharges of cannon had been fired; the reserves were exhausted, and it would be hardly possible to keep up the firing for two hours. The nearest magazines were Magdeburg and Erfurt, whence it was impossible to obtain supplies soon enough; hence, the only step remaining was a retreat.

The retreat was ordered, therefore, and began the following day, the 19th, after a battle in which three hundred thousand men engaged in a deadly struggle over a space so contracted that its circumference did not exceed from seven to eight leagues. Before quitting Dresden, the Emperor charged Prince Poniatowski, who had just gained the baton of Marshal of France, with the defence of one of the faubourgs. "You will defend the southern faubourg," His Majesty had said to him. "Sire," the

Prince responded, "I have very few men."—"Eh well! defend yourself with what you have." "Ah! Sire, we will hold out. We are all ready to perish for Your Majesty." Moved by these words, the Emperor held out his arms, and the Prince threw himself into them with tears in his eyes. It was a parting scene, for this was their last interview; the nephew of the last King of Poland, as will presently be seen, found a death as glorious as it was deplorable in the waters of the Elster.

At nine o'clock in the morning, the Emperor went to take leave of the royal family of Saxony. The interview was short, but most affectionate and sorrowful on either side. The King manifested the utmost indignation at the conduct of his troops. "I never could have believed it," said he; "I thought better of my Saxons; they are nothing but cowards." His grief was such that the Emperor, notwithstanding the immense injury done him by the desertion of the Saxons during the battle, sought to console this excellent prince.

As His Majesty was pressing him to quit Leipsic, and not remain exposed to the dangers of a capitulation, which had become inevitable, the venerable prince replied in the negative. "No," said he, "you have done enough, and it is pushing generosity too far to remain here a few minutes longer for the sake of consoling us." Even while the King of Saxony was speaking, the detonation of a heavy fusillade was heard; then the Queen and the Princess Augusta united their entreaties to those of the monarch. In the excess of their alarm, they seemed already to see the Emperor taken and slaughtered by the Prussians. Some officers came up and announced that the Prince-royal of Sweden had forced the entrance of one of the faubourgs; that General Benningsen, General Blücher, and the Prince of Schwarzenberg were entering the city on all sides, and that our soldiers were reduced to defending themselves from house to house. The peril to which the Emperor was exposed was imminent; he had not a moment more to lose; at last he consented to withdraw and the King of Saxony having accompanied him to the foot of the palace staircase, they embraced each other there for the last time.

VOL. IV. — K

CHAPTER X

A proposed conflagration rejected by the Emperor — The King of
Saxony absolved from his fidelity — Exit from Leipsic impossible to the Emperor — His Majesty recrossing the city — The
mill bridge of Lindenau — Living souvenirs — Orders given
directly by the Emperor — His Majesty sleeping to the sound
of the combat — The King of Naples and Marshal Augereau at
the imperial bivouac — The bridge blown up — The Emperor's
orders badly executed, and his indignation — Absurdity of
several lying rumors — Unheard-of misfortunes — Marshal Macdonald swimming his horse across the Elster — Death of Prince
Poniatowski — Profound affliction of the Emperor and universal
regrets — The body of the Prince rescued by a fisherman —
Two days at Erfurt — The King of Naples makes his adieux
to the Emperor — The King of Saxony treated as a prisoner,
and the Emperor's indignation — Brilliant battle of Hanau —
Arrival at Saint-Cloud — Questions asked me by the Emperor
and truthful replies — Hopes of peace — Abduction of M. de
Saint-Aignan.

N OTHING was more difficult than to get out
of Leipsic, the city being surrounded on all
sides with hostile forces. It had been suggested to
the Emperor to burn the faubourg where the principal columns of the allied armies were presenting
themselves, in order to make his retreat more safe,
but he had indignantly rejected the proposition,
being unwilling to leave one of his cities in flames
as his final adieu to the faithful King of Saxony.
After having released him from his fidelity and exhorted him to consider nothing but his own inter-

ests, the Emperor, on leaving him, had turned in the direction of the Ranstadt gate; but he found it so encumbered that it was impossible to open a passage. Hence he was obliged to retrace his steps, to cross the city, to go out through the north gate, and to regain the only point whence he could carry out his intention of moving toward Erfurt by way of the western boulevards. The enemies were not yet completely masters of the city, and it was the general sentiment that it could still have been defended for a long time if the Emperor had not dreaded to expose it to the horrors of a taking by assault. The Duc de Raguse was still putting a good face on things in the Halle faubourg against the reiterated attacks of General Blücher, and Marshal Ney, on his side, still beholding the united efforts of General Woronzoff, the Prussian corps under General Bulow's command, and the Swedish army, recoil before his intrepidity.

Even valor like this must, nevertheless, succumb to numbers, and above all to treason; for, during the hottest of the fighting at the gates of Leipsic, a Baden battalion, which until then had fought valiantly in the French ranks, suddenly abandoned the Saint Peter gate which they had been ordered to defend, and thus gave the enemy entrance to the city. From that time, according to what I have heard related by several officers who were present in this affray, the streets of Leipsic presented the most horrifying spectacle. Constrained to withdraw, our men did not do so without disputing the ground. But an irreparable misfortune was soon to make the Emperor despair.

These are the facts which signalize that deplorable day, such as my memory even now recalls them. I do not know why it is, but not one of the great events of which I have been a witness presents itself so clearly to my mind as a scene which took place, so to say, under the walls of Leipsic. After having triumphed over incredible obstacles, we had at last succeeded in crossing the Elster on the mill bridge of Lindenau. I seem still to see the Emperor, himself placing officers on the road whom he charged with indicating the point of reunion of the corps to the isolated men who should present themselves. On that day, after an immense calamity, caused by numbers, his solicitude was extended to all as it was after a decisive triumph. But he was so overcome by fatigue that a few moments of repose were indispensably necessary, and he slept profoundly amidst the roar of cannon until a terrible explosion was heard. Soon after, I saw the King of Naples and Marshal Augereau enter the bivouac of His Majesty. They brought him melancholy tidings. The great bridge of the Elster had just blown up, and it was the last point of communication with the rear-guard, still twenty thousand strong, and left on the other side of the river under the command of Marshal Macdonald. "That is how they carry out my orders!" exclaimed the Emperor, seizing his head violently between his hands. Then he remained pensive for a moment, as if absorbed in his reflections.

His Majesty had in fact given orders to mine all the bridges across the Elster and to blow them up, but not until the whole French army had been put in surety by the stream. I have since heard different tales concerning this event; I have listened to many contradictory reports. It is not my business to seek to shed light upon a historical point so controverted as this one; I ought to limit myself to relating what was entirely within my cognizance, and it is that which I have done. At the same time, I may be permitted to submit here a simple observation to the reader which has presented itself to my mind whenever I have read or heard it said that the Emperor himself gave orders to have the bridge blown up, so as to shelter his own person from the enemy's pursuit. I beg pardon for the expression, but this supposition seems to me an absurdity which passes all belief; for it is very evident that if, in these disastrous circumstances, the Emperor had been thinking of his personal safety, we should not have found him voluntarily prolonging his stay in the palace of the King of Saxony, where he was exposed to a far more imminent danger than he could incur after leaving Leipsic. Assuredly, moreover, the Emperor did not enjoy the consternation that seized him when he learned that twenty thousand of his men were separated from him, and possibly forever.

How many misfortunes inevitably resulted from the destruction of the last bridge on the route from Leipsic to Lindenau! and what traits of heroism, the majority of which will remain forever unknown, signalized this disaster! Marshal Macdonald, seeing himself separated from the army, plunged with his horse into the Elster and was so fortunate as to attain the other bank; but General Dumortier disappeared and perished in the stream while attempting to follow his intrepid chief, and so did a large number of officers and soldiers; they had all sworn not to surrender to the enemy, and there were but few who submitted to the cruel necessity of becoming prisoners. The death of Prince Poniatowski was keenly regretted by the Emperor, and it may be said that all who were at headquarters were profoundly afflicted by the loss of the Polish hero. Details of this misfortune were eagerly sought for, irreparable though it was. It was known that His Majesty had charged him to cover the retreat of the army, and no one was ignorant that the Emperor's confidence could not have been better placed. Some related that, seeing himself pressed by the enemy against a river without a bridge, they had heard him say to those surrounding him: "Gentlemen, here we must succumb with honor." They added that, putting his heroic resolve at once into action, he had swum his horse across the Pleisse, in spite of the wounds received in a stubborn combat which he had maintained since morning. Finally, we learned that, finding no refuge but the waters of the Elster against inevitable captivity, the brave prince had plunged into them without considering the impracticable escarpment of the opposite bank, and in a few minutes both horse and rider were engulfed. Such was the end, at once deplorable and glorious, of one of the most brilliant and chivalric officers who have shown themselves worthy to figure among the élite of French generals.

Meanwhile the dearth of ammunition obliged the Emperor to retire promptly, although in the greatest order, upon Erfurt, a city richly provisioned with food, forage, armaments, equipments, in fine, with every kind of munitions. His Majesty arrived there the 23d, having had engagements every day, in order to secure his retreat, with forces four or five times more numerous than those remaining at his disposal. The Emperor remained in Erfurt only two days, and left it on the 25th, after receiving the adieux of his brother-in-law, the King of Naples, whom he was never to see again. I witnessed a part of this last interview, and thought I observed a nameless constraint in the attitude of the King of Naples, but His Majesty did not appear to notice it. It is true that the King did not announce his hasty departure, and that His Majesty was ignorant that this prince had secretly received an Austrian general.[1] However (and I ought to call attention to the

---

[1] This was Count de Mier, charged to guarantee Murat in the possession of his states if he would abandon the Emperor. He abandoned him; what did he preserve? — *Note by the editor*

fact because I have had frequent occasion to remark it), so many blows, precipitated so to say, one upon another, had been striking the Emperor for some time, that he seemed almost insensible to them; one would have thought him wholly intrenched in his ideas of fatality. But although unaffected by his own misfortunes, His Majesty gave full rein to his indignation when he learned that the allies considered the King of Saxony as their prisoner and had declared him a traitor precisely because he was the only one who had not betrayed him. Assuredly, if fortune had once more become favorable, the King of Saxony would have found himself the master of one of the largest kingdoms in Europe; but fortune was now always against us, even our triumphs being followed only by a useless glory.

Thus, for example, the French army was soon to cover itself with glory at Hanau, when it was obliged to pass through and overthrow the numerous army of Austrians and Bavarians assembled at that point under the command of General Wrede. Six thousand prisoners were the result of this triumph, which at the same time opened to us the approaches of Mayence, which we hoped to reach without encountering new obstacles. November 2, after a march of fourteen days from Leipsic, we saw once more the borders of the Rhine, and could breathe with some security.

After having devoted five days to the reorganization of the army, given his orders and assigned to each marshal and chief of corps the post he was to occupy during his absence, the Emperor left Mayence the 7th and on the 9th slept at Saint-Cloud, where he returned preceded by several trophies; for between Erfurt and Frankfort we had taken twenty flags from the Bavarians. These flags, brought to the minister of war by M. Lecouteulx, aide-de-camp of Prince de Neufchâtel, had preceded by two days His Majesty's arrival in Paris; and they had been already presented to the Empress, to whom the Emperor had offered them in the following terms: "Madame and dearest wife, I send you twenty flags taken by my armies in the battles of Wachau, Leipsic, and Hanau; it is a homage which I love to pay you. I desire you to see in it a mark of my great satisfaction with your conduct during the regency which I confided to you."

Under the Consulate and during the first six years of the Empire, whenever the Emperor returned to Paris after a campaign, it was because the campaign was terminated; the news of a peace concluded after victory had always preceded him. For the second time, it was otherwise when he came back from Mayence. On this occasion, as on that of the return from Smorghoni, the Emperor left the war still in progress, and returned, no longer to offer France the results of his victories, but to ask for more men and money in order to repair the failures and losses experienced by our armies. And yet, in spite of this difference in the result of our wars, the welcome given by the nation to His Majesty was still the same, at least in appearance. The addresses from the different cities of the interior were neither less numerous nor more chary of expressions of devotion; those who conceived fears for the future displayed even more loyalty than the others, lest their gloomy forebodings should be divined. For my part, it never once occurred to me that the Emperor might definitively succumb in the struggle he was maintaining; for my ideas did not go so far, and it is only in reflecting on it since that I have been able to appreciate the dangers which already menaced him at the period to which we have arrived. I was like those men who, having passed the night on the brink of a precipice, learn the peril to which they have been exposed only when the day reveals it. Nevertheless, I ought to say that everybody was tired of war, and that those of my friends whom I saw on returning from Mayence, all talked to me of the necessity of peace.

Even within the palace, I heard many persons attached to the Emperor use similar language when out of his presence; but they gave His Majesty quite a different version. When he deigned to question me, which was not infrequently, on what I had heard, I told him the exact truth; and when, in these confidential relations of the Emperor's toilet, the word *peace* issued from my mouth, he would exclaim several times: "Peace! peace! . . . and who desires it more than I do? . . . It is they who do not want it. The more I grant, the more they demand."

An extraordinary occurrence, which took place on the very day that His Majesty arrived at Saint-Cloud, gave some reason to believe, when it became known, that the allies had conceived the design of opening new negotiations. It was learned that M. de Saint-Aignan, His Majesty's minister at the ducal courts of Saxony, had been forcibly abducted and taken to Frankfort, where M. de Metternich, Prince Schwarzenberg, and the ministers of Russia and Prussia were then assembled. There most pacific overtures were made to him in the name of the sovereign allies; after which M. de Saint-Aignan was at liberty to repair at once to the Emperor in order to acquaint him with the details of the abduction and the resulting propositions. The offers of the allies, concerning which I knew nothing and, consequently, can say nothing, must, nevertheless, have seemed worthy of the Emperor's examination; for there was presently a general rumor throughout the palace that a new congress was to assemble at Manheim, that the Duc de Vicenza had been designated by His Majesty as his minister plenipotentiary, and that, in order to shed more lustre on his mission, he had just been intrusted with the portfolio of foreign affairs. I remember that this news was very favorably received; because, although it was doubtless the result of prejudice, every one knew that the general public were not pleased at seeing the Duc de Bassano in the position to which the Duc de Vicenza was called as his successor. The Duc de Bassano was supposed to anticipate what he believed to be the real wishes of the Emperor, and to be averse to peace. We shall see later on, by a response His Majesty made to me at Fontainebleau, how gratuitous and devoid of all foundation these rumors were.

It seemed at this time all the more probable that the allies really had the intention of treating for peace, since, by forcibly procuring a French negotiator, they had gone to unheard-of lengths in order to attribute the first proceedings to the Emperor. And what gave great weight to the belief in the pacific dispositions of Europe was, that there was question not merely of a continental peace, as at Tilsit and Schönbrunn, but of a general peace in which England could intervene as a contracting party; so that it was hoped that we should gain in security for the results what we might, perhaps, lose by the severity of the conditions. But, unhappily, the hope to which we yielded with anticipated joy was of short duration. We soon learned that the propositions communicated to M. de Saint-Aignan, after his abduction, were only a lure, an old diplomatic ruse to which the foreigners had resorted in order to lull the Emperor with false expectations. A month, in fact, had not elapsed, there had not been time to complete the exchange of preliminary correspondence, which takes place in such cases, when the Emperor learned of the famous declaration of Frankfort, in which, far from entering into negotiations with His Majesty, they affected to separate his cause from that of France. What intrigues! And how one blesses his own mediocrity with all his heart when comparing himself to men condemned to live in this labyrinth of high-toned cheating and honorary hypocrisy! The miserable certainty was acquired that the foreigners wanted a war of extermination, and it renewed consternation where hope was already reigning. But the genius of His Majesty was not abated, and thenceforth all his efforts were directed to the necessity of once more making head against the enemy, not now to conquer his provinces, but to guarantee from invasion the sacred soil of the fatherland.

IN speaking of the year 1813, mention should not be omitted of the incredible number of affiliations to the secret societies recently formed in Italy and Germany which took place that year. The Emperor, from the time when he was only First Consul, was not merely not opposed to the reopening of the Masonic lodges, but it is permissible to think that he covertly favored it. He was very sure that nothing would result from these reunions which could be dangerous to his person, or contrary to his government, since Freemasonry counted among its adepts, and even had for its chiefs, the greatest personages of the State. Moreover, it would have been utterly impossible that in these societies, into which some false brethren insinuated themselves, a dangerous secret, had there been such, could have escaped the vigilance of the police. The Emperor spoke of them sometimes, but as mere childishness, good to amuse simpletons; and I can affirm that he laughed heartily when he was told that the archchancellor, in his capacity as chief of the Grand-Orient, did not preside over a Masonic banquet with less gravity than he brought to the presidency of the Senate and the Council of State. Nevertheless the unconcern of the Emperor did not extend to the societies so well known in Italy under the name of *Carbonari*, and in Germany under various denominations. It must, in fact, be admitted that after the attempts of two young Germans affiliated to illuminism, it was very permissible in His Majesty not to see without inquietude the propagation of these *bonds of virtue* in which young fanatics were transformed into assassins.

I have known nothing special concerning the Carbonari, since we were not brought into close relations with Italy. As to the secret societies of Germany, I remember that during our stay in Dresden I heard a Saxon magistrate, with whom I frequently had the honor of being in company, talk about them in a manner that interested me greatly, even while it alarmed me for the future. He was a man of about sixty, who spoke French well, and in whom German phlegm and the gravity of age were wonderfully blended. In his youth he had lived in France, and had even made a part of his studies at the college of Sorèze. I attribute the liking he displayed for me to the pleasure he experienced in hearing a country spoken of whose memory he seemed always to have cherished. I remember perfectly, even now, the profound veneration with which this excellent man spoke to me of one of his former professors of Sorèze, whom he called Dom Ferlus; my memory must have been very ungrateful had I forgotten a name which I heard him repeat so often.

My excellent Saxon was called M. Gentz, but he was not related to the diplomat of the same name attached to the Austrian chancery. He was of the reformed religion and very exact in the performance of his religious duties; and I can affirm that I have never known a man more simple in his tastes or more penetrated by his duties as man and magistrate. I would not venture to say what he really thought about the Emperor, for he seldom mentioned him; and if he had had anything unpleasant to say about him, it may readily be fancied that he would have chosen some other confidant. One day when we went together to examine the works His Majesty was erecting all along the left bank of the Elbe, I do not know how the conversation happened to turn on the secret societies of Germany, a subject which I knew absolutely nothing about. As I asked questions for my own information, M. Gentz said to me: "It must not be believed that the secret societies, which are multiplying in such an extraordinary way in Germany, have been protected by the sovereigns. The Prussian government views their increase with alarm, although, at present, it is seeking to turn them to account in order to give a national appearance to the war it is waging on you since the defection of General Yorck. Some of the unions now tolerated have been the object of lively persecutions, even in Prussia. For instance, it is not long since the Prussian government took severe measures for the suppression of the society called *Tugendverein* (union of virtue). It succeeded in breaking it up; but at the very moment of its dissolution three others were formed from it which were to be directed by the members of the Tugendverein, though taking the precaution of disguising themselves under different names. Doctor Jahn put himself at the head of the *black knights*, who have since given birth to a body of partisans known as the *black legion*, commanded by Colonel Lutzoff. The memory of the late Queen, which is still vivid in Prussia, exercises a great influence over the new direction impressed on its institutions; she might be called their occult divinity. During her lifetime she gave Baron Nostitz a silver chain which, in his hands, became the decoration, or rather the rallying-sign, of a new society to which he gave the name of the *Louisa Union*. Finally, M. Lang is the declared chief of an order of *Concordists*, which he has instituted in imitation of the societies of the same name established some time since in the universities.

"My duties as a magistrate," continued M. Gentz, "have more than once put me in a position to obtain exact information concerning these new institutions, and you may regard what I say on this subject as perfectly authentic. The three chiefs of whom I have just spoken appear to direct three societies; but it is very certain that the three make only one, since these gentlemen are pledged to follow the track of the Tugendverein in every point. They have divided Germany between them merely to render their influence more immediate by their presence. M. Jahn has reserved Prussia more particularly to himself, M. Lang the north, and Baron Nostitz the south of Germany. This latter personage, knowing what influence a woman may exert upon young adepts, has associated with him a very beautiful actress of Prague, named Madame Brede, and she has already made a very important conquest for the Louisa Union, and one which may become still more so in the future if the French experience reverses. The former Elector of Hesse, affiliated through the agency of Madame Brede, accepted, almost immediately after his reception, the grand mastership of the Louisa Union, and on the very day of his installation he placed in the hands of Baron Nostitz the funds necessary for the formation and equipment of a free company of seven hundred men intended to enter the service of Prussia. It is true that once provided with this sum, the Baron did not trouble himself about the formation of this company, a fact which has greatly dissatisfied the old Elector; but by means of address and intrigues, Madame Brede has succeeded in reconciling them. It has, in fact, been demonstrated that Baron Nostitz did not appropriate to his own use the funds with which he was intrusted, but merely gave them another destination than the arming of a free company. Nostitz is, beyond all contradiction, the most zealous, ardent, and able of the three leaders; I do not know him personally, but I know that he is one of the men who are most capable of exerting a great mastery over those who listen to them. It was thus that he captivated Stein, the Prussian minister, to such a point that the latter kept two of his secretaries at the disposal of Baron Nostitz, to draw up under his direction the pamphlets with which Germany is inundated; but I cannot too often repeat to you," added M. Gentz, "that the hatred vowed against the French by these different societies is merely an accidental thing, born of circumstances only; for their original object was the overthrow of governments as they exist in Germany; and their fundamental principle is the establishment of a system of absolute equality. This is so true, that it has been hotly debated among the adepts of the Tugendverein whether or not to proclaim the sovereignty of the people throughout Germany; they say openly that war ought not to be made in the name of governments, which, according to them, are only instruments. I do not know what will finally result from all these machinations; but it is certain that by dint of assuming importance, the secret societies create one which is not assumed. To listen to them, you would believe that they alone determined the King of Prussia to declare openly against France, and they make a boast of not stopping there. After all, that will probably happen to them which almost always happens in such cases; if they are considered useful, they will be promised wonders in order to turn them to advantage, and they will be dropped when they are no longer needed, for it is utterly impossible that reasonable governments should lose sight of the real aim of their institution."

Such is the sum, which I believe exact, not of all that M. Gentz told me about the secret societies of Germany, but of all that I remember, and I recollect that when I was allowed to give an account of it to the Emperor, His Majesty deigned to pay great attention, and even made me repeat certain details, a fact which contributed not a little toward impressing them on my memory. As to the Carbonari, there is every reason to believe them to be affiliated by secret ramifications to the German societies; but, as I have said already, I have not been in a position to obtain certain information concerning them. Nevertheless, I will attempt to reproduce here what I have been told about the reception of a Carbonaro.

The recital of this history, which is, perhaps, merely an invention, impressed me greatly; moreover, I give it here with all reserve, not knowing even whether some one else has not made use of it, seeing that I was not the only listener to this narration. I had it from a Frenchman who lived in the northern part of Italy, at the very period from which dates my conversation with M. Gentz.

"A French officer, formerly attached to General Moreau, a man of an ardent yet sombre and melancholy temperament, had left the service after the trial instituted at Paris against his general. He had not been involved in the conspiracy, but being unchangeably attached to republican principles, simple in his manners and possessing enough to live on though in a very modest way, this officer quitted France at the time the Empire was founded, and took no pains whatever to disguise his aversion for the head of an absolute government; in fine, although very peaceable in his conduct, he was one of those who are styled malcontents. After travelling for some years in Greece, Germany, and Italy, he settled in a small town of the Venetian Tyrol. There he lived in a very retired manner, having few communications with his neighbors, occupied with the study of the natural sciences, and paying no further attention, it might be said, to public affairs. He was in this position, which appeared mysterious to some persons, when the affiliations to the *rentes*, or lodges of the Carbonari, were making such astonishing progress in the majority of the Italian provinces and notably on the borders of the Adriatic. Several notable inhabitants of the region, ardent Carbonari conceived the project of enrolling in their society, the French officer, with whom they were acquainted, as well as with his implacable resentment against the chief of the imperial government, whom he regarded as a great man, indeed, but also as the destroyer of his dear republic.

"In order to avoid ruffling the presumed susceptibility of the French officer, it was resolved to organize a hunting party which should direct itself toward the places he was accustomed to select for his solitary excursions. This plan was adopted and carried out, so that the desired meeting took place and appeared wholly fortuitous. The officer did not hesitate to take part in the conversation of the hunters, several of whom he knew, and after various circumlocutions the conversation was brought around to the Carbonari, those new adepts of a sacred liberty. That magic word *liberty* had not ceased to live in the depths of the officer's heart; hence it produced on him all the effect that could have been expected; it awakened the enthusiastic souvenirs of his youth and made him tremble with long unwonted joy. When therefore it was proposed that he should augment the number of brethren by whom he found himself surrounded, they experienced no difficulty. The officer was received; the sacramental signs, the words of recognition, were made known to him; his oath was accepted; he pledged himself to be always and at all times at the disposal of his brethren and to perish rather than betray their secret. Thenceforward he was affiliated and continued to live as he had done in the past, awaiting a summons at any moment.

" The adventurous character of the inhabitants of the Venetian Tyrol differs in many respects from that of the inhabitants of Italy, but it resembles it by a natural suspiciousness which is common to both; and among them the descent from suspicion to vengeance is a swift one. Hardly had the French officer been admitted to the number of the Carbonari, than some among them censured this affiliation and regarded it as dangerous. There were some who even went so far as to say that the mere fact of being a Frenchman should have sufficed to exclude him, and that, moreover, at a time when the police was employing clever men to take all disguises, it was necessary that the firmness and constancy of the newly elected man should be subjected to other trials than the simple formalities to which they had confined themselves. The sponsors of the officer, they who had, so to say, coveted him as a brother, made no objections, so sure were they of the excellence of their choice.

" Things were at this standpoint when the tidings of the disasters of the French army at Leipsic reached the provinces bordering on the Adriatic, and redoubled the zeal of the Carbonari. Nearly three months had elapsed since the reception of the French officer without his having received any notification from his brethren, and he was thinking that the labors of Carbonarism amounted to very little. Then, he one day received a mysterious letter, in which he was enjoined to repair, on the following night, armed with a sword, to a wood which was indicated, to be there precisely at midnight, and wait until some one should come to seek him. Exact to the rendezvous, the officer repaired thither at the hour prescribed, and remained until daylight without having seen any person appear ; whereupon he returned home, supposing that they had merely desired to make trial of his patience. This opinion was changed into conviction when, some days later, another letter having enjoined him to go in the same manner to the same place, he again spent the night in useless waiting.

"It was not the same with a third and similar appointment. The French officer kept it with the same punctuality, and without fatiguing his patience. He had been waiting several hours when, all of a sudden, instead of seeing his brethren arrive, he heard the clicking of swords that strike against each other. Carried away by a first impulse, he sprang in the direction whence the noise issued, and it seemed to recede as he advanced. He arrived, nevertheless, at a spot where a frightful crime had been committed ; he saw a man, bathed in his blood, whom two assassins had just struck down. Quick as lightning, he sprang, sword in hand, upon the two murderers ; but they had disappeared in the thick forest, and he was about to lavish his assistance on their victim when four gendarmes arrived upon the scene. The officer found himself alone, with a naked sword in his hand, close to the assassinated man. The latter, who was still breathing, made a last effort to speak, and expired in the act of designating his defender as his murderer. The gendarmes at once arrested him; two of them lifted the corpse, and the other two bound the officer's arms with cords and led him to a village about a league away, which they reached at daybreak. There he was conducted before the magistrate, interrogated and committed to prison.

"Imagine the situation of the officer, with no friends in the country, afraid to appeal to his own government to which his known opinions would have rendered him suspicious, accused of a horrible crime, seeing every proof against him, and, moreover, crushed beyond escape by the last words of the dying victim! Like all men of firm and resolute character, he looked his position in the face without flinching, saw that it was remediless, and resigned himself to his fate.

"Meanwhile a special commission had been appointed so as to preserve at least a show of justice. Led before the commission, he could only repeat what he had said to the magistrate who had questioned him at first; that is, to recount the facts as they had occurred, protest his innocence, and yet admit that all the appearances were against him. What could he answer when asked why, with what motive, he was alone at night and armed with a sword, in the depths of a wood? Here his oath as a Carbonaro impeded his words, and his hesitation was but an additional proof against him. And what could he reply to the deposition of the gendarmes who had taken him in the very act? Hence he was unanimously condemned to death, and led back to prison, where he was to remain until the day fixed for his execution.

"In the first place, a priest was sent to him; the officer received him with the greatest respect, but abstained from recourse to his ministry; next he was importuned by the visit of a confraternity of penitents. At last, the executioners came to lead him to the place of execution. As he was going thither, accompanied by several gendarmes, and between a long and double row of penitents, the funereal procession was interrupted by the unexpected appearance of a colonel of gendarmerie, whom chance had brought to the scene of action. This superior officer bore the name of Colonel Boizard, a name well known throughout upper Italy, and dreaded by all malefactors. The colonel ordered a suspension of proceedings that he might interrogate the condemned in person and learn the circumstances of the crime and the trial. When he was alone with the officer, he said to him: 'You see that everything is against you, and that nothing can rescue you from death; still, I can save you, but on one condition: I know that you are affiliated to the sect of the Carbonari; tell me who are your accomplices in these underhand machinations, and you may have your life at that price.' 'Never.'—'But consider . . .' 'Never, I tell you; have me taken to the place of execution.'

"Hence the road to the scaffold had to be resumed. The executioner was at his post. The officer mounted with a firm step the fatal ladder. Colonel Boizard sprang toward him and again begged him to save his life on the conditions he had named: 'No! no! never!' Then the scene changed, the colonel, the executioner, the gendarmes, the priest, the penitents, the spectators, all crowded around the officer: everybody wanted to embrace him; at last he was led in triumph to his dwelling. All that had happened was merely a reception; the assassins of the forest and their victim, as well as the judges and the pretended Colonel Boizard, had been playing their part, and the most suspicious of the Carbonari knew to what point their newly affiliated brother could push the heroism of constancy and the sacredness of an oath."

Such is very nearly the story to which I listened, as I have said, with the keenest interest, and I have thought I might be permitted to recall it here, yet without concealing from myself how much it must lose in being written down. Should it be accepted without reserve? That is what I dare not decide; but what I can certify is that the narrator said that it was true, and even declared that the details of it would be found in the archives of Milan, seeing that this extraordinary reception had been made at the time the object of a circumstantial report addressed to the Viceroy, whom fate had already condemned never to see the Emperor again.

CHAPTER XII

I WANDERED somewhat in the preceding chapter from my reminiscences of Paris, subsequently to our return from Germany after the battle of Leipsic and the Emperor's short sojourn at Mayence. Even to-day I cannot write the name of the latter city without recalling the spectacle of tumult and confusion it presented after the glorious break at Hanau, where the Bavarians were so roundly beaten the first time that they presented themselves as enemies in a serious affair to those in whose ranks they had previously combated. If I do not mistake, it was in that battle that the Bavarian General Wrede, and even his family, became the immediate victims of their treason. The General, whom the Emperor had loaded with favors, was mortally wounded; all the relatives he had in the Bavarian army were slain, and his son-in-law, Prince Oettingen, experienced the same fate. This was one of those events which seldom failed to make an impression on His Majesty's mind, because they chimed in with his fatalistic notions. It was likewise from Mayence that the Emperor issued a decree for the assembly of the Legislative Body on December 2; but, as we shall see, this opening was delayed, and would to God that it had been indefinitely adjourned; for then His Majesty would not have experienced the tribulations caused him later on by the symptoms of opposition which manifested themselves for the first time, and in a manner which was at least unseasonable.

One of the things which astonished me most, and which astonishes me still more when I think of it now, was the inconceivable activity of the Emperor; far from diminishing, it seemed daily to take a new extension, as if the very exercise of his forces had redoubled them. I could not give an idea of the manner in which His Majesty's time was occupied at the period of which I am writing. Besides, since he had once more seen the Empress and his son, the Emperor had regained his serenity: I no longer surprised in him, or at least but rarely, those external signs of depression which he had not always concealed in private life after our return to Moscow. He occupied himself still more ostensibly than usual in the numerous works he was having executed in Paris. This was a salutary diversion from his grand ideas of war and the afflicting news he was receiving from the army. Nearly every day troops equipped as by enchantment were reviewed by His Majesty and sent immediately to the Rhine, nearly the whole line of which was threatened; the danger, of which we scarcely dreamed, must then have seemed imminent to the inhabitants of the capital, who were not carried away as we were by the sort of charm exerted by the Emperor over all who had the honor of approaching his august person. It was at this period that for the first time we saw the Senate asked for a contingent of men not due until the following year, and moreover, each day brought disagreeable tidings. Thus, during the autumn, we witnessed the return of the prince arch-treasurer, who had been forced to leave Holland after the evacuation of that kingdom by our troops, while Marshal Gouvion Saint-Cyr was forced to sign a capitulation at Dresden for himself and the thirty thousand men whom he had retained in that city.

The capitulation of Marshal Saint-Cyr will assuredly not occupy an honorable place in the history of the cabinet of Vienna. It is not my business to criticise political combinations; but I cannot forget the indignation manifested by everybody in the palace when it was learned that this capitulation had been outrageously violated by those who had become the strongest. The capitulation provided that the Marshal should return to France with the troops under his command, bringing a part of his artillery; that these troops might be exchanged against an equal number of those of the allied powers; that the sick Frenchmen remaining in Dresden should be forwarded to France as fast as they recovered, and that, in fine, the Marshal should begin his march November 16. Nothing of the sort occurred. Fancy, then, the indignation of the Emperor, already so profoundly afflicted by the capitulation of Dresden, when he learned that, in defiance of all the stipulated agreements, his troops had been made prisoners by Prince Schwarzenberg. I remember that I was in His Majesty's cabinet one day when Prince de Neufchâtel was there, and that the Emperor said to him angrily: "You talk to me about peace! Eh! f——! how do you suppose that I can believe in the good faith of those people?— See what has happened to Dresden! No! I tell you, they don't want to treat; they are only trying to gain time. It is our business not to lose any." The Prince made no answer, or, at least, I did not hear his response, for I left the cabinet then, having executed the order that had called me there. Moreover, I can add, as a further proof of the confidence with which His Majesty deigned to honor me, that he never interrupted what he was saying on my entrance, no

matter how important it might be, and I dare affirm
that if my memory were better, these souvenirs would
be far more valuable than they are.

Since I have spoken of the bad tidings which assailed the Emperor almost uninterruptedly during
the latter months of 1813, there is one which I must
not omit to mention, because it affected His Majesty
so painfully: I refer to the death of Count Louis de
Narbonne. Of all the persons who had not begun
their career under the eye of the Emperor, M. de
Narbonne was probably the one whom he most liked;
and it must be owned that it would be impossible to
combine real merit with more attractive manners.
The Emperor considered him the most suitable person to conduct a negotiation successfully: "Narbonne is a born ambassador," he said of him one day.
It was known in the palace why the Emperor had
appointed him his aide-de-camp at the time when he
was forming the household of the Empress Marie-
Louise. It had been at first the Emperor's intention
to make him knight of honor to the new Empress;
but a cleverly contrived intrigue induced the latter
to refuse him, and it was as a sort of indemnity for
this that he received the appointment of aide-de-
camp of His Majesty. At that time there was not
one in France which was more highly esteemed.
Many foreign princes, and even sovereigns, vainly
solicited this high favor; among these I can adduce Prince Leopold of Saxe-Coburg, the husband of
the Princess Charlotte of England, who refused to be

King of Greece after having failed to become the Emperor's aide-de-camp.

I would not venture to say, after carefully consulting my memory, that nobody at court was jealous at seeing M. de Narbonne an aide-de-camp of the Emperor; but I forget the names. However that might be, he soon became a favorite, and the Emperor daily appreciated more highly his qualities and services. Concerning this I recollect hearing His Majesty say, and I think it was at Dresden, that he had never well understood the cabinet of Vienna until *Narbonne's sharp nose* — these are his own expressions — had *smelled out* its old diplomatists. After the pretence at negotiations of which I have spoken already, and which occupied the whole time of the armistice of 1813 at Dresden, M. de Narbonne had resided in Germany, where the Emperor had confided to him the government of Torgau. It was there he died, November 17, in consequence of a fall from his horse, in spite of the skilful attentions lavished on him by Baron Desgenettes. Since the death of Marshal Duroc and that of Prince Poniatowski, I do not recollect having seen the Emperor display more regret than on this occurrence.

Meanwhile, almost at the time when he lost M. de Narbonne, but before hearing of his death, the Emperor had provided a substitute near his person in the man whom he had loved most, not excepting General Desaix. He had just summoned General Bertrand to the high functions of grand marshal of the palace, and this choice was generally approved by all those who had the honor of knowing Count Bertrand. But what can I have to say here of a man whose name history will never separate from that of the Emperor? The same period had seen the death of the Duc d'Istrie, one of the four colonels-general of the guard, and of Marshal Duroc; the same nomination united the names of their successors; Marshal Suchet was appointed at the same time as General Bertrand, and replaced Marshal Bessières as colonel-general in the guard.

At this period His Majesty made several other changes in the personnel of the superior administration of the Empire. A decree of the Senate having conferred on the Emperor the right to select the president of the Corps Législatif, His Majesty appointed the Duc de Massa to that post, replacing him in his functions as chief justice by Count Molé, the youngest minister the Emperor ever had. The Duc de Bassano resumed the secretaryship of State, and the Duc de Vicenza received the portfolio of foreign relations.

I have said that during the autumn of 1813, His Majesty went several times to visit the public works. He generally went on foot and almost alone to see those of the Tuileries and the Louvre; afterwards he would mount a horse, accompanied by at most one or two of his officers, and M. Fontaine, to examine those which were more distant. One day, nearly at the end of November, having profited by His Majesty's absence to take a few turns in the faubourg Saint-Germain, I unexpectedly found myself near him at the moment when he reached the entrance of rue de Tournon on his return from the Luxembourg, and I cannot describe with what lively satisfaction I heard the shouts of *Long live the Emperor!* as he approached. I was thrust very near the Emperor's horse by the pressure of the crowd; I did not suppose, however, that His Majesty had recognized me. I had proof to the contrary on his return: the Emperor had seen me; and as I was assisting him to change his garments, he said to me cheerfully: "Well! *M. le drôle*, and what were you doing in the faubourg Saint-Germain? I see what it is! . . . that is very fine! . . . You go to spy upon me when I go out!" And many other speeches of the same sort, for on that day the Emperor was very gay; whence I inferred that he had been satisfied with his visit.

When, at this period, the Emperor experienced any anxieties, I thought I noticed that he liked to dispel them by showing himself in public, perhaps more frequently than during his other sojourns in Paris, yet always without affectation. He even went several times to the play; and, thanks to the kindly attentions of Count de Rémusat, I was very often present at those assemblies, which on such occasions always had a very festive appearance. Certainly, on the day of the first representation of the ballet of *Nina*, at the Opéra, it would have been difficult to suppose when Their Majesties entered their box that the Emperor already counted enemies among his subjects. It is true that the mothers and wives in mourning were not there; but what I can affirm is that I have never seen more enthusiasm. The Emperor enjoyed it this time from the bottom of his heart, more perhaps than after his victories. The idea of being loved by the French people made the most vivid impression on him. In the evening he spoke of it; shall I dare to say that he talked about it to me like a child who prides himself on the reward he has just received? Then, with all the simplicity of a private man, he often repeated: "My wife, my good Louise! she must have been well satisfied!" The fact is that there was such eagerness in Paris to see the Emperor at the play, that, as he always occupied the side box looking on the front of the stage, whenever it was supposed that he would be present the boxes on the other side of the theatre were taken with the utmost promptness; even the highest tier of boxes was preferred to the best ones on that side of the theatre whence it was most difficult to see him. No one who lived in Paris at that time can fail to recognize the exactness of these souvenirs.

Not long after the first representation of the ballet of *Nina*, the Emperor was present at another performance which I also witnessed. As on the previous occasion, he was accompanied by the Empress, and during the representation I could not escape the thought that possibly the Emperor experienced certain souvenirs capable of distracting his attention from the harmony of the music. It was at the Italian theatre, then located at the Odéon. Nazzolini's *Cleopatra* was given, and the performance was one of those that are styled *extraordinary*, because it was for the benefit of Madame Grassini. It was within a very short time that this singer, celebrated on so many accounts, had first shown herself in public upon a Parisian stage; in fact, I think that on this day she appeared for the third or fourth time at most, and to be exact, I must say that she did not produce on the Parisian public all the effect that was expected from her immense reputation. It was a long time since the Emperor had received her more privately. And yet, until then the tones of her voice and that of Crescentini had been reserved for the privileged ears of the spectators of Saint-Cloud or of the Tuileries theatre. On this occasion the Emperor was very generous to the beneficiary, but there was no interview, because, as was said by a poet at the time, the Cleopatra of Paris had not to do with another Antony.

Thus, as one sees, the Emperor stole a few evenings from the vast affairs which occupied him, less for the sake of enjoying the play than to show himself in public. All the useful establishments were the object of his cares; he did not even rely solely upon the information furnished by men who justly enjoyed his confidence, but he examined everything himself. Among the establishments specially protected by His Majesty was one which he particularly liked. I do not believe that the Emperor ever came to Paris in the intervals between one war and another without paying a visit to the establishment of the demoiselles of the Legion of Honor, under the direction of Madame Campan, at Ecouen in the first place, and afterwards at Saint-Denis. The Emperor went there in the month of November, and I recall an anecdote concerning these visits which I heard the Emperor relate and which greatly diverted him. I cannot be sure, however, whether it belongs to the visit of 1813 or to a previous one.

It must be known, to begin with, that, conformably with the regulations of the house of the demoiselles of the Legion of Honor, no man except the Emperor was admitted to the interior of the establishment; but as the Emperor always went there with some display, his suite was considered as part of himself and entered with him. In addition to his officers, two pages usually attended him. Now it happened in the evening, after returning from Saint-Denis, the Emperor said to me with a laugh on entering his chamber, where I was waiting to undress him: " Well, well ! here are my pages trying to resemble the ancient pages. The little rogues ! Do you know what they do ? When I go to Saint-Denis they wrangle with each other as to who shall go with me ! Ah! ah ! " As he spoke, the Emperor was laughing and rubbing his hands; then, after repeating " The little rogues ! " in the same tone a number of times, he added, as a consequence from one of those singular

reflections which occurred to him now and then :
"Constant, I would have been a very poor page ;
such an idea would never have come into my head.
However, they are good young fellows ; fine officers
have come from them already. Marriages will result from it some day." It was seldom, in fact,
that an apparently frivolous matter did not elicit a
serious conclusion on the part of the Emperor. To
me, also, barring some recollections of the past, there
now remain none but serious things, and often very
sad ones to relate ; for here we are at a point where
all assumes a grave appearance and is invested with
colors that are often very sombre.

CHAPTER XIII

FOR the last time the anniverary of His Majesty's coronation was celebrated in Paris. The gifts of the Emperor on this occasion were the innumerable addresses he received from all the cities of the Empire, and in which offered sacrifices and protestations of loyalty seemed to augment with the increasing difficulties of the situation. Alas! four months were enough to demonstrate the value of these protestations; and yet, how in this unanimous agreement could one fail to believe in a not less complete unanimity of unreserve?

That would have been impossible to the Emperor, who to the end of his reign thought himself beloved by France with all the affection he bestowed; the truth, a truth sufficiently proved by the events that followed, is that the Emperor became more popular with that class of inhabitants which is called the people when he began to be unfortunate. His Majesty acquired the proof of this in a visit he made to the faubourg Saint-Antoine, and it is very certain that if, under other circumstances, the Emperor could have induced himself to flatter the people, a means distasteful to him on account of his souvenirs of the Revolution, the entire population of the Parisian faubourgs would have taken arms in his defence. How could any one doubt it after having read the fact to which I here allude?

Toward the close of 1813 or in the beginning of 1814, the Emperor went to the faubourg Saint-Antoine; for at present I cannot give the exact date of this unexpected visit. At any rate, on this occasion he displayed a confidence that even amounted to good-natured familiarity, so much so as to embolden those who came nearest to address him. Now, this is the conversation that ensued between His Majesty and several of the inhabitants, faithfully reported and acknowledged to be exact by several spectators of this truly affecting scene.

An Inhabitant. — Is it true, as they say, that affairs are going so badly?

The Emperor. — I cannot say that they are going any too well.

The Inhabitant. — But how is it going to end, then?

The Emperor. — God knows.

The Inhabitant. — But how is it? Can the enemies enter France?

The Emperor. — They might, and even come as far as here, unless people help me: I haven't a million arms. I can't do everything myself.

Many voices. — We will help you! we will help you!

Still more voices. — Yes! yes! count on us.

The Emperor. — In that case, the enemy will be beaten, and we shall preserve all our glory.

Many voices. — But what ought we to do?

The Emperor. — Enlist and fight.

A new voice. — We would do it willingly, but we would like to make some conditions.

The Emperor. — Well, speak out. Let us see; what are they?

Many voices. — We don't want to cross the frontier.

The Emperor. — You shall not cross it.

Many voices. — We would like to enter the guard.

The Emperor. — Well, be off to the guard.

Hardly had His Majesty pronounced these last

words when the immense crowd surrounding him made the air ring with cries of *Long live the Emperor!* and increasing all along the route which he followed in making his way slowly to the Tuileries, it was environing him with an innumerable escort when he arrived at the gateway of the Carrousel. We heard these noisy acclamations from the palace, but they were so singularly interpreted by the commandants of the palace posts that, thinking there was an insurrection, they had the gates of the Tuileries fastened on the court side.

When I saw the Emperor, a few minutes after his return, he seemed to me more moved than satisfied; for he was highly displeased by anything that bore the appearance of disorder, and there was always something that annoyed him in a popular tumult, no matter what might be the excuse for it. However, this visit, which His Majesty might have repeated, caused a strong impression among the people and produced an immediate result, since in the course of the day more than two thousand individuals voluntarily enlisted and formed a new regiment of the guard.

On the anniversary of the coronation and of the battle of Austerlitz, there were, as usual, free performances in all the theatres of Paris; but the Emperor did not make his appearance at them, as he had often done. There were games also, distributions of comestibles, illuminations; and twelve young girls, dowried by the city of Paris, were married to former soldiers. I remember that of all that marked the formal occasions of the Empire, this kind of marriages was what pleased the Emperor best, and he often spoke of them with lively approbation; because, if I may venture to say so, His Majesty had a touch of what might be called the marriage mania.

We were then residing at the Tuileries, which the Emperor had not quitted since November 20, the day when he returned from Saint-Cloud, and which he did not quit until he set off for the army. His Majesty very often presided over the Council of State, the labors of which were always very active. I learned at this time, apropos of a decree, a circumstance which I thought singular; it had doubtless been a long time since the Montmorency commune had resumed the use of its former title ; but it was only at the end of November, 1813, that the Emperor legally withdrew from it the name of *Emile*, given it by the Republic in honor of J. J. Rousseau. It may be believed that if it had retained it for so long, it was only because the Emperor had not thought of it sooner.

Perhaps it will be thought inexcusable in me to have mentioned a fact apparently so puerile, at a time when so many great measures were adopted by His Majesty. In fact, each day necessitated new arrangements, for the enemies were making progress at all points; the Russians were occupying Holland under command of General Witzingerode, who had been so bitter against us during the Russian campaign. The speedy return to Amsterdam of the inheritor of the House of Orange was already spoken of; in Italy Prince Eugène was contending only by dint of skill against the much more numerous army of Marshal de Bellegarde, which had just crossed the Adige; that of Prince Schwarzenberg occupied the confines of Switzerland; the Prussians and the troops of the confederation were crossing the Rhine at several points; the Emperor had not a single ally left, the King of Denmark, the only one who had remained faithful to him, having given way at last before the torrents from the north by concluding an armistice with Russia; while in the south all the ability of Marshal Soult barely sufficed to retard the progress of the Duke of Wellington, who was advancing toward our frontiers at the head of an army more numerous than that we could oppose to it, and one which was not exposed to the same privations as the French army. I very well remember having heard generals blame the Emperor at this time for not having abandoned Spain and brought all his troops back to France. I adduce this souvenir, but it may well be believed that I would not permit myself to hazard an opinion on such a matter. However it might be, it was evident that we were surrounded by war on all sides, and in this state of things, our former frontiers being threatened, it would have been strange had there not been a general aspiration after peace.

The Emperor desired it also, and at present no one

professes a contrary opinion. All the works I have read which have been written by those who were in the best position to know the truth on all these subjects, are in agreement on this point. It is known that His Majesty had a letter written by the Duc de Bassano, in which he gave his adhesion to the bases proposed at Frankfort by the allies, for a new Congress. It is known that the city of Mannheim was designated for the assembly of this Congress, whither the Duc de Vicenza was afterwards to be sent. The latter, in a note of December 2, again repeated the adhesion of the Emperor to the general bases and summaries indicated for the Congress of Mannheim. Count Metternich replied on the 10th to this communication, that the sovereigns would acquaint their allies with the adhesion of the Emperor. All these negotiations dragged their slow length along solely though the fault of the allies, who ended by declaring at Frankfort that they would not lay down arms. By December 20 they were openly announcing their intention to invade France through Switzerland, the neutrality of which country had been formally recognized. I must admit that at the period at which I am speaking, my position kept me in complete ignorance of these things; but on learning them afterwards, they have awakened memories which have powerfully contributed to demonstrate their truth to me. Everybody, I hope, will admit that if the Emperor had desired war, it is not before me that he would have taken the trouble to speak of his wish for peace, as I often heard him do, and this does not belie what I have related concerning a response of His Majesty to Prince de Neufchâtel, since even in that he attributed the necessity for war to the bad faith of his enemies. Neither the immense renown of the Emperor nor his fame stand in need of my testimony, and I am under no illusion on that point; but I feel able, like any one else, to deposit my grain of verity.

I said before that at the time of his journey to Mayence, the Emperor had convoked the legislature for December 2. By another decree, this convocation was prorogued to December 19, and the annual ceremony was marked by the introduction of unaccustomed usages. In the first place, as I have said, to the Emperor alone belonged the right of appointing the president without the presentation of a triple list, as had formerly been the usage of the Senate; moreover, the Senate and the Council of State went in a body to the hall of the Legislative Body to be present at the opening session. I remember that this ceremony was looked forward to with more than common interest, so curious and eager was all Paris to hear the Emperor's speech, and to know what he would say about the situation of France. Alas! we were far from supposing that this annual solemnity would be the last!

The Senate and the Council of State having successively occupied the places indicated for them in the hall of sessions, the Empress came in and took her seat in a reserved gallery, surrounded by her ladies and the officers of her household; finally the Emperor made his appearance a quarter of an hour after the Empress, being introduced by the customary ceremonial. When the new president, the Duc de Massa, had taken the oath between the hands of the Emperor, His Majesty delivered the following discourse:

" Senators;

" Councillors of State;

" Deputies from the departments to the legislature;

" Brilliant victories have distinguished the French arms in this campaign. Unexampled defections have rendered these victories useless. Everything has turned against us. Even France would be in danger without the energy and union of the French.

" In these great circumstances, my first thought has been to call you near me. My heart requires the presence and the affection of my subjects.

" I have never been deluded by prosperity; adversity will find me superior to its assaults.

" I have several times given peace to nations when they had lost all. From a part of my conquests I have raised thrones for the kings who have abandoned me.

" I had conceived and executed great designs for the welfare of the world! . . . . Monarch and father, I am sensible of what peace adds to the security of thrones and families. Negotiations with the allied powers have been entered into. I have adhered to the preliminary bases presented by them. I had hoped, therefore, that before this session opened the Congress of Mannheim would have assembled; but new delays, which are not attributed to France, have deferred that moment which the world is eagerly awaiting.

"I have given orders that all the original documents in the portfolio of my department of foreign affairs shall be communicated to you. You will obtain cognizance of them through the agency of a committee. The speakers of my council will acquaint you with my wishes on this subject.

"On my part there is no obstacle to the restoration of peace. I know and share all the sentiments of the French people. I say of the French people, because there is not one of them who would desire peace at the expense of honor.

"It is with regret that I ask new sacrifices from this generous people, but they are required by its noblest and most cherished interests. I must reinforce my armies by numerous levies: nations only treat securely when they deploy all their forces. An increase in the receipts has become indispensable. What my minister of finance will propose to you is conformable to the financial system I have established. We shall meet all expenses without a loan which will exhaust the future, and without paper money, which is the greatest enemy of social order.

"I am satisfied with the sentiments displayed toward me under existing circumstances by my Italian peoples.

" Denmark[1] and Naples alone have remained faithful to my alliance.

" The republic of the United States of America is successfully continuing its war against England.

" I have recognized the neutrality of the nineteen Swiss Cantons.

" Senators ;

" Councillors of State ;

" Deputies from the departments to the legislature;

" You are the natural organs of this throne ; it is for you to give the example of an energy which shall recommend our generation to future generations. Let them not say of us : *They sacrificed the chief interests of the country, they recognized the laws which England has sought in vain during four centuries to impose on France.*

" My people cannot fear that the policy of their Emperor will ever betray the national glory. On my part, I am confident that the French people will be ever worthy of themselves and of me!"

This discourse was greeted with unanimous cries of *Long live the Emperor!* and when His Majesty returned to the Tuileries he seemed very well satisfied. However, he had a slight headache, which half an hour's repose dispelled. It did not recur that evening, and the Emperor questioned me as to what I had heard. I told him the truth; namely, that all the persons of my acquaintance agreed in saying

---

[1] Denmark, as I have said, had concluded its armistice with Russia, but the news did not reach Paris until some days later.

that everybody wished for peace. "Peace! peace!" said the Emperor. "Eh! who desires it more than I do! Go, my son, go." I withdrew, and His Majesty went to rejoin the Empress.

It was about this time, though I cannot be exact about the day, that His Majesty made a decision in an affair which I had brought to his notice; and from this decision there will be evident what I may call His Majesty's profound respect for the rights of a legitimate marriage, and his antipathy against divorced persons. But I must go back a little in order to relate this anecdote which has just recurred to my memory.

In the Russian campaign, General Dupont-Derval had been killed on the field of battle after fighting valiantly. After His Majesty's return to Paris, his widow had tried several times, but always in vain, to bring a petition to his notice describing her painful position. Some one having advised her to address herself to me, I was affected by her distress, and took the liberty of presenting her request to the Emperor. His Majesty seldom rejected my solicitations of this sort, because I was very discreet about undertaking them; hence I was so fortunate as to obtain a considerable pension in favor of Madame Dupont-Derval. I do not remember how the Emperor happened to find out that General Dupont-Derval was a divorced man and had had a daughter by his first marriage, who was still living with her mother. He learned, moreover, that the woman whom General Dupont-

Derval had taken for his second wife was the widow of a general officer, by whom she had two daughters. None of these circumstances, as may be supposed, had been set forth in the petition, but when they came to the Emperor's knowledge, he did not withdraw the pension, the certificate for which had not yet been sent, but he changed its destination. He gave it to the first wife of General Dupont-Derval, and made it reversible to her daughter, who was rich enough to dispense with it, while the other Madame Dupont-Derval was really in need. Meanwhile, as one is always in a hurry to impart good news, I had lost no time in informing my solicitress of the Emperor's favorable decision. She came back again when she learned what had been done, a thing of which I was myself entirely ignorant, and when I heard it, I supposed that she was the victim of a misunderstanding. Under that impression, I took the liberty of speaking to His Majesty again. Judge of my surprise when the Emperor himself deigned to give me an account of the whole affair. Then he added: "My poor child, you let yourself be taken in like a ninny. I promised the pension, and I have given it to the wife of General Derval, that is, to his real wife, the mother of his child." The Emperor was not at all annoyed with me. I knew that the claims would not end there, even though I did not continue to interest myself in them; but events taking their course up to the abdication of His Majesty, matters remained as they had been settled.

CHAPTER XIV

Efforts of the allies to separate France from the Emperor — Truth
of His Majesty's words proved by events — Copies of the declaration of Frankfort circulating in Paris — A document to
compare with the Emperor's speech — Bad faith of the foreigners recognized by M. de Bourrienne — M. de Bourrienne under
supervision — The Duc de Rovigo his defender — The object of
the enemies partially attained — Count Regnault de Saint-Jean
d'Angély at the legislature — Legislative commission — The
Emperor's letter to the Duc de Massa — Reunion of the two
commissions at the house of the prince archchancellor — Cau-
tious behavior of the Senate — Frequent visits of the Duc de
Rovigo to the Emperor — Labors of the two commissions —
Address of the Senate well received — Remarkable response of
His Majesty — A promise more difficult to make than to keep —
Just criticism on the conduct of the Corps Législatif — Report of
the commission — Rude interruption and reply — The Emperor
thoughtful and striding up and down — A decision taken and
blamed — Seizure of the report and the address — Violent clos-
ing of the assembly hall — The deputies at the Tuileries — The
Emperor's dissatisfaction sharply expressed — The inflammatory
address — The Emperor's calmness — Melancholy forebodings
and the end of the year 1813.

IT was not with arms alone that the enemies of
France were trying to overthrow the power of the
Emperor at the close of 1813. Notwithstanding our
defeats, the name of His Majesty still inspired a
salutary terror, and numerous though they were, the
foreigners seemed to despair of victory so long as
there existed a mutual concord between the French

people and the Emperor. The reader has just seen
in what terms he had expressed himself in presence
of the great constituted bodies of the state, and
events have proved whether His Majesty concealed
the truth about the condition of France from the
representatives of the nation. To this discourse which
history has preserved, let me herewith oppose another
document of the same period. It is the famous declaration of Frankfort, copies of which were circulated
in Paris by the Emperor's enemies; and I would not
wager that any person of his court came to perform
his service without having one in his pocket. If
there still remain any doubts as to who was in good
faith at that time, the reading of what follows ought
to dissipate them, for here there is no question
of political considerations, but solely of comparing
solemn promises with the actions that followed them.

"The French government has just decreed a new
levy of three hundred thousand conscripts; the
motives of the Senate decree contain a provocation
to the allied powers. They find themselves once
more called upon to promulgate to the world the
views which guide them in the present war, the
principles which are the basis of their conduct,
their wishes, and their determinations. The allied
powers are not making war on France, but on that
openly proclaimed preponderance which, for the un-
happiness of Europe and of France, the Emperor
Napoleon has too long exerted beyond the limits of
his Empire.

" Victory has conducted the allied armies across the Rhine. The first use made of victory by Their Imperial and Royal Majesties was to offer peace to His Majesty the Emperor of the French. An attitude reinforced by the accession of all the sovereigns and princes of Germany has had no influence upon the conditions of peace. Those conditions are based upon the independence of the other states of Europe. The views of the powers are just in their object, generous and liberal in their application, reassuring to all, honorable to each.

" The sovereign allies desire that France shall be great, strong, and happy, because its great and strong power is one of the fundamental bases of the social structure. They desire that France may be happy, that French commerce may revive, that the arts, those benefits of peace, may flourish anew, because a great people cannot be tranquil except when it is happy. The powers confirm to the French Empire an extent of territory never possessed by France under its kings, because a generous nation does not decline when it has experienced reverses in a stubborn and bloody struggle in which it has combated with its customary audacity.

" But the powers also wish to be happy and tranquil. They desire a condition of peace which, by a prudent distribution of forces and a just equilibrium, shall henceforward preserve their peoples from the calamities without number which for twenty years have oppressed Europe.

"The allied powers will not lay down arms without having attained this great and beneficent result, the noble object of their efforts. They will not lay down arms until the political status of Europe shall be confirmed anew, until immovable principles shall have resumed their rights over novel pretensions, until the sanctity of treaties shall at last have assured a real peace to Europe."

Nothing but good sense is required to see whether the allied powers were in good faith in this declaration, the evident intention of which was to alienate from the Emperor the attachment of the French people by pointing him out as an obstacle to peace, and separating his cause from that of France; and here I am fortunate in being able to support my opinion by that of M. de Bourrienne, who surely will not be accused of partiality in favor of His Majesty. Several passages of his Memoirs, those especially in which he condemns the Emperor, have often pained me, and I am unable to conceal it; but in this circumstance he does not hesitate to recognize the bad faith of the allies, and that, according to my feeble judgment, is of great importance.

M. de Bourrienne was then in Paris, under the special surveillance of the Duc de Rovigo. I heard this minister speak of him to the Emperor several times, and always favorably; but either the enemies of the former secretary of the First Consul must have been very powerful, or His Majesty's prejudices very strong, for M. de Bourrienne never returned to favor.   The Emperor, who, as I have said, sometimes deigned to converse familiarly with me, never mentioned M. de Bourrienne on such occasions, and I never saw him after he ceased to see the Emperor. I perceived him for the first time among the officers of the National Guard on the day when those gentlemen, as will be seen hereafter, were received at the palace, and I have never seen him since; but as we all liked him very much, on account of the excellent way in which he treated us, he was often the subject of our conversation, and I may say of our regrets. Besides, I was ignorant for a long time that at the epoch of which I am speaking, His Majesty had offered him a mission to Switzerland, because I only learned that circumstance by reading his Memoirs. I cannot dissemble that this reading affected me painfully, because I would greatly have desired that M. de Bourrienne should by that time have abjured his resentment against His Majesty, who, at bottom, truly loved him.

However that may be, if it is plainly evident now to every one that the aim of the Frankfort declaration was to cause a rupture between the Emperor and the French people, what events have since explained was not even then a secret to the genius of the Emperor, and, unhappily, it was not long before the enemies partially achieved their object.   Not only did people express themselves in an unseemly manner about His Majesty in private society, but dissensions broke out in the midst of the Legislative Body.

After the opening of the session, the Emperor having decreed that a commission composed of five senators and five members of the legislature should be appointed, these two bodies assembled for that purpose. The object of the commission, as may be seen from His Majesty's speech, was to take cognizance of the documents relating to the negotiations entered into between France and the allied powers. Count Regnault de Saint-Jean d'Angély communicated the decree to the legislature, and supported it with his usual persuasive eloquence; he reminded them of the victories of France and the glory of the Emperor; but the result of the voting was to elect five members to the commission who were thought to be more attached to the principles of liberty than to the glory of the Emperor. They were MM. Raynouard, Lainé, Gallois, Flaugergues, and Maine de Biran. The Emperor seemed dissatisfied with this choice from the first, although he did not think that the commission would prove hostile, as it presently did. I remember very well that in my presence His Majesty said to Prince de Neufchâtel, with a touch of ill-humor, but no anger, "They have elected five lawyers!"

However, the Emperor gave no public evidence of his dissatisfaction. No sooner had he officially received the list of commissioners than he addressed the following letter, dated December 23, to the president of the legislature:

"Monsieur the Duc de Massa, president of the

legislature, we address you the following sealed
letter to acquaint you that it is our intention that
you should present yourself at noon to-morrow, the
24th instant, at the residence of our cousin, the
prince archchancellor, with the commission appointed yesterday by the legislature, in execution
of our decree of the 20th instant, and composed
of MM. Raynouard, Lainé, Gallois, Flaugergues,
and Maine de Biran, and this for the purpose of
taking cognizance of the documents pertaining to
the negotiation, as well as of the declaration of
the coalized powers, which will be communicated
by Count Regnault, minister of State, and Count
d'Hauterive, councillor of State, attached to the
office of foreign relations, who will be the bearer
of the said documents and declaration.

"It is also our intention that our said cousin shall
be chairman of the commission.

"Whereupon, etc., etc."

The senators designated to form part of the commission were M. de Fontanes, Prince de Bénévent,
M. de Saint Marsan, M. de Barbé-Marbois, and M.
de Beurnonville. With the exception of one of these
gentlemen, whose disgrace and opposition were pub-
licly known, the others were supposed to be sincerely
attached to the Empire; and whatever the subse-
quent opinion and conduct of all of them may have
been, they had not at this time to incur on the part
of the Emperor the same reproaches as the commissioners from the Legislative Body. No act of opposi-

tion, no sign of discontent, emanated from the conservative Senate.

At this epoch the Duc de Rovigo came very frequently, or rather every day, to see the Emperor. His Majesty liked him much, and that alone would suffice to prove that he was not afraid of hearing the truth, for after he became minister, the Duc de Rovigo did not spare him, which I can affirm because I witnessed it several times. In Paris, however, there was a universal outcry against him. Still I can cite a fact not mentioned by the Duc de Rovigo in his Memoirs, and of which I guarantee the authenticity. It can be seen from this anecdote whether or not the minister of police sought to augment the number of persons who daily compromised themselves by prating against the Emperor.

Among the employees of the treasury there was a former receiver of finances, who for twenty years had lived in a modest way, contented with a rather slender salary. He was, however, an enthusiastic man and very intelligent. His passion for the Emperor bordered on delirium, and he never spoke of him but in almost idolatrous terms. This employee was accustomed to spend his evenings in a club which met in the rue Vivienne. The habitués of the place, on which the police naturally kept an eye, did not all share the opinions of the man of whom I am speaking. They began to criticise the acts of the government with a certain freedom; the opponents gave vent to their dissatisfaction, and His Majesty's faithful adorer became all the more prodigal of admiring exclamations as his antagonists waxed lavish of reproaches. The Duc de Rovigo was informed of these discussions, which were daily growing sharper and more animated. One fine day, on going home, our worthy employee found a stamped letter from the office of the general ministry of police. He could not believe his eyes. What could the chief of police want with him, a good, simple, modest man, living remote from all grandeurs and devoted to the government? He opened the letter: the minister summoned him to his cabinet the next morning. He went there, as may be believed, with all imaginable punctuality; and then a dialogue very nearly like the following took place between these gentlemen:

"It seems, sir," said the Duc de Rovigo, "that you love the Emperor very much?"

"Do I love him? I would give my blood, my life!"

"Do you admire him much?"

"Do I admire him? The Emperor has never been so great! Never was his glory . . ."

"Very good, sir, and those are sentiments which do you honor and which I share; but I advise you to keep them to yourself; for otherwise, though I should doubtless greatly regret it, you would put me under the necessity of having you arrested."

"Me! Monseigneur! Arrest me!"

"Eh! certainly . . . not a doubt about it."

"How so?"

"Don't you see that you provoke the expression of

opinions which but for your enthusiasm would remain concealed, and that you in a manner force a good many worthy people to compromise themselves who will return to us when they see things better? Come, sir, let us continue to love, serve, and admire the Emperor; but at such a time as this let us not proclaim our good sentiments so loudly, lest we render men culpable who have merely gone astray."

The employee of the treasury thereupon left the office of the minister, after thanking him for his advice and promising to hold his tongue. I would not venture to guarantee that he scrupulously kept his word; but I can affirm anew that what has just been read is absolutely true; and I am sure that if this passage of my Memoirs falls under the notice of the Duc de Rovigo, it will remind him of a fact he may have forgotten, but the accuracy of which he will not fail to recognize.

Meanwhile the commission, composed, as I have said, of five senators and five members of the legislature, applied itself assiduously to the examination imposed upon it. Each of these great bodies of the State presented His Majesty with a separate address. The Senate had listened to the report made to it by M. de Fontanes, and its address contained nothing which could shock the Emperor; on the contrary, it was expressed in the most measured terms. Peace was asked for, but a peace which His Majesty should attain by an effort worthy of himself and the French people. " May your hand, so many times victorious," said the address, "let fall its weapons after having assured the repose of the world." The following passage was also remarked: "No, the enemy will not rend this fair and noble France which during fourteen hundred years has maintained itself with glory amid such varying fortunes, and which, even in the interest of neighboring peoples, is always able to put a considerable weight in the balance of Europe. As pledges of this, we have your heroic constancy and the national honor." And this other: "Fortune is not long wanting to nations which are not wanting to themselves."

This thoroughly French language, which was at least made imperative by the circumstances, pleased the Emperor, as may be inferred from the response he made, December 29, to the deputation from the Senate, presided over by the prince archchancellor of the Empire:

"Senators," said His Majesty, "I am affected by the sentiments you express to me. You have seen, from the documents I have had communicated to you, what I am doing for peace. The sacrifices implied in the preliminary bases proposed to me by the enemies, I have accepted; I shall make them without regret: my life has but one aim, — the welfare of the French people.

"Meanwhile Béarn, Alsace, Franche-Comté, Brabant, are encroached upon. The cries of this part of my family pierce my soul. I call the French to the succor of the French! I call the French of Paris, of Brittany, Normandy, Champagne, Burgundy, and the other departments to the relief of their brethren! Shall we forsake them in misfortune? Peace and deliverance of our territory ought to be our rallying-cry. At the aspect of all this people in arms, the foreigner will fly or will sign the peace on the terms he has himself proposed. It is no longer a question of regaining the conquests we had made."

One must have been in a position to know the character of the Emperor in order to understand what these last words must have cost him; but from that knowledge would also result the certitude that it would have cost him less to keep his promise than to make it. It would even seem as if this were understood in Paris; for on the day when the *Moniteur* published His Majesty's reply to the Senate stocks went up more than two francs, a fact which the Emperor did not fail to remark with satisfaction, for it is known that the price of stocks was to him the true thermometer of public opinion.

As to the conduct of the legislature, I heard it appreciated by a man of real merit who had always been imbued with republican opinions. He said one day in my presence some words which impressed me: "The legislature did then what it ought always to have done except on that occasion." From the language of the speaker of this commission, it was too easy to see that he believed the lying promises of the Frankfort declaration. According to him, or, rather, according to the commission, of which he was, after all, merely the organ, it was not the intention of the foreigners to humiliate France; they simply wished to confine us within our own limits and repress the vehemence of an ambitious activity which for twenty years had been so fatal to all the peoples of Europe. "The propositions of the coalized powers," said the commission, "appear to us honorable to the nation, since they prove that the foreigner fears and respects us." And finally the orator, continuing to read, and having arrived at a passage in which he alluded to *the Empire of the lilies*, added in so many words that the Rhine, the Alps, the Pyrenees, and the two seas enclosed a vast territory, several provinces of which had not belonged to ancient France, and yet *the royal crown of France was brilliant with glory and majesty among all crowns.*

At these words, the Duc de Massa interrupted the orator by exclaiming: "What you are saying there is unconstitutional." To which the speaker briskly replied: "I see nothing unconstitutional here except your presence." Then he went on with the reading of his report. The Emperor was informed every evening of what had taken place at the legislative session, and I remember that on the evening when this report was read to him, he seemed somewhat anxious. Before going to bed he walked up and down his room for some time with marked emotion, like one who is trying to form a resolution. Finally he decided not to allow the address of the legislature to pass; it had been communicated to him conformably to usage. Time pressed; the next day would have been too late; the address would be circulated throughout all Paris, where the public mind was already much excited. An order was given therefore to the minister of police to seize the copy of the report and the address at the printer's, and to break up the forms already composed. In addition, orders were given to close the doors of the legislative hall, which was done, and thus the legislature found itself adjourned.

I heard a great many persons express keen regrets at this time that the Emperor should have adopted these measures, and especially that, having done so, he should not have stopped there. They said that since the legislature was dissolved by force, it would have been better, no matter what might have been the result, to convoke another chamber, but that the Emperor ought not to have received the members of the one which was dismissed. His Majesty thought otherwise, and gave the deputies a parting audience. They came to the Tuileries, and there his too just resentment found expression in these terms:

"I have suppressed your address; it was incendiary. Eleven-twelfths of the Legislative Body are composed of good citizens; I know them; I shall know how to esteem them; but another twelfth contains the factions, the men who are devoted to England. Your commission and its reporter, M. Lainé, are of this number; he corresponds with the Prince-regent through the intermediation of the advocate Desèze: I know it, I have the proof of it; the four others belong to the factious party. . . . If there are

any abuses, is this the moment to come and make remonstrances, when two hundred thousand Cossacks
are crossing our frontiers? Is this the moment to
come and dispute over individual liberties and sure-
ties when political liberty and national independence
are in danger? We must resist the enemy; we
must follow the example of Alsace, the Vosges, and
Franche-Comté, who wish to march against him and
are asking me for arms. . . . You are seeking, in your
address, to separate the sovereign from the nation.
. . . It is I who represent the people here, for it has
given me four millions of suffrages. If I chose to
believe you, I would cede to the enemy more than he
asks for. . . . You will have peace in three months,
or I shall perish. . . . Your address was unworthy
of me and of the Legislative Body."

Although the journals were forbidden to reproduce
the details of this scene, the rumor of it spread
through Paris with the rapidity of lightning. The
Emperor's words were reported and discussed; and
the dismissed deputies very soon re-echoed them in
the departments. I remember having seen the prince
archchancellor come and ask audience of His Majesty next day; he wished to speak in favor of M.
Desèze, whose protector he then was. In spite of
His Majesty's menacing words, he found him disinclined to take severe measures; for his anger had
cooled down, as was always the case with the Emperor when he had been unable to restrain a fit of
passion. Nevertheless, the fatal misunderstanding

provoked by the legislative commission between that body and the Emperor produced the most unpleasant results in every way. It is easy to conceive that it must have delighted the enemies, who were promptly informed of it by their numerous agents in France. Under these gloomy auspices the year 1813 ended. In the sequel we shall see the consequences, and finally the history, until now unknown, of the Emperor's chamber at Fontainebleau; that is to say, of the most painful period of my life.

CHAPTER XV

IN order to neutralize the bad effect that might be produced in the provinces by the reports of the members of the legislature and the correspondence of the alarmists, His Majesty appointed from among the members of the conservative Senate a certain number of commissioners whom he charged to visit the departments and reanimate public spirit. This was surely a salutary measure and one imperiously required by circumstances, for discouragement was beginning to be felt among the masses of the people, and in such cases the presence of superior authorities is known to restore confidence to such as are merely timid. Meanwhile the enemies were advancing at several points; already they had trodden the soil of old France. When news of this sort reached the Emperor, it afflicted him profoundly, but did not cast him down; his indignation would break out sometimes, however, but this was chiefly when he saw by the reports that there were French emigrants in the hostile ranks. These he stigmatized as traitors, infamous wretches, scoundrels unworthy of pity. I remember that when Huningue was taken, he thus branded M. de Montjoie, who was serving in the Bavarian army after having assumed a German name which I have forgotten. He added, however: " But that fellow was at least ashamed to keep his French name ! " In the main, it was easy to pacify the Emperor on nearly all points, but he was pitiless toward those who bore arms against their country; and how many times have not I heard him say that in his view there was no greater crime!

To avoid increasing the complication of interests daily becoming more entangled, the Emperor had already thought of sending Ferdinand VII. back to Spain; I am even certain that His Majesty had had some overtures made to him on the subject during his last sojourn in Paris, but it was the Spanish prince who was unwilling, and who was, on the contrary, incessantly requesting the Emperor's support. His chief desire was to become the ally of His Majesty, and everybody knows that in his letters to His Majesty he was always asking him for a wife. The Emperor had thought seriously of marrying him to the eldest daughter of King Joseph, which seemed to be a means of conciliating the rights of Prince Joseph and those of Ferdinand VII. King Joseph would have asked nothing better than such an arrangement, and from the manner in which he had trifled with his royalty from the commencement of his reign, it is permissible to think that His Majesty did not greatly cling to it. Prince Ferdinand had agreed to this alliance, which seemed to please him very much; but just at the close of 1813 he asked for time, and in the end, events numbered this affair among those which are never more than projects. Prince Ferdinand finally quitted Valençay, but not until after the time when the Emperor authorized him to do so; for his presence had long been simply an additional embarrassment. For the rest, the Emperor had not to complain of his conduct toward him until after the events of Fontainebleau.

However, in the existing condition of affairs, what concerned the Prince of Spain was merely an accidental matter, like that of the sojourn of the Pope at Fontainebleau; the grand object, the object which took precedence of all others, was to defend the soil of France, which the first days of January beheld invaded at several points. That was His Majesty's great thought, although it did not prevent him from entering as usual into all the details of his administration, and we shall presently see what measures he took for the re-establishment of the National Guard at Paris. On this topic I have had positive documents and little known details from a person whom I am not permitted to name, but whose position enabled him to see all the machinery of its formation. These tasks required His Majesty's presence in Paris for nearly a month longer, and he remained there until January 25; but what gloomy tidings reached him during those twenty-five days!

In the first place, the Emperor learned that the Russians, as unscrupulous as the Austrians about observing the usually sacred conditions of a capitulation, had just trampled under foot the stipulations of that of Dantzic. In the name of the Emperor Alexander, the Prince of Würtemberg, who commanded the siege, had recognized and guaranteed to General Rapp and the troops under him the right of returning to France; these stipulations were no better respected than those agreed upon some months before with Marshal Saint-Cyr by Prince Schwarzenberg; hence the garrison of Dantzic were made prisoners of war with the same bad faith as the garrison of Dresden had been. This news, which arrived almost simultaneously with that of the surrender of Torgau, afflicted His Majesty all the more because it concurred in proving to him that the hostile powers were unwilling to treat of peace except for form's sake, and with the resolution of always recoiling from a definitive conclusion.

At the same epoch the news from Lyons was by
no means reassuring; Marshal Augereau had been
put in command there, and he was accused of lacking
the energy to prevent or arrest the invasion of the
south of France. However, I will not linger over
this matter here, as I propose, in the next chapter,
to bring together such of my souvenirs as have the
greatest bearing on the beginning of the French
campaign, and certain circumstances which preceded
it. At present I shall limit myself to recalling, so
far as my memory will permit, what relates to the
last days which the Emperor spent in Paris.

On January 4, although His Majesty had no hope
of inducing the foreigners to conclude a peace of
which all parties stood in so much need, he gave
the Duc de Vicenza his instructions and sent him
to the headquarters of the allies; but he had to wait
a long time for his passports. At the same time
special orders were despatched to the prefects of the
departments whose territory had been invaded, to
guide their conduct under such difficult circumstances. Thinking, moreover, that it was necessary
to make an example in order to reanimate the courage of the timid, the Emperor instituted a commission of inquiry charged with examining the conduct
of Baron Capelle, prefect of the department of the
Leman, at the time when the enemies entered
Geneva; finally a decree mobilized one hundred and
twenty battalions of the National Guards of the
Empire, and regulated the levy in mass in the east-

ern departments of all who were able to bear arms. Excellent measures, doubtless, but vain precautions! Destiny was stronger than the genius of a great man.

On January 3, however, the decree appeared which placed thirty thousand men of the National Guard of Paris on the active list; on the same day, by a dismal and singular coincidence, the King of Naples signed a treaty of alliance with Great Britain. The Emperor reserved to himself the command in chief of the Parisian National Guard, and regulated the composition of the staff in the following manner: A major-general second in command; four assistant major-generals, four adjutant commanders, and eight assistant captains. The legions were formed by arrondissements, and each legion was divided into four battalions subdivided into five companies. Afterwards the Emperor made the following appointments to the superior grades:

Marshal de Moncey, Duc de Conegliano, major-general second in command. Assistant major-generals: General of division Comte Hallin; Comte Bertrand, grand marshal of the palace; Comte de Montesquiou, grand chamberlain; Comte de Montmorency, chamberlain of the Emperor. Adjutant commanders: Baron Laborde, adjutant commander of Paris; Comte Albert de Brancas, chamberlain of the Emperor; Comte Germain, chamberlain of the Emperor; M. Tourbon. Assistant captains: Comte Lariboissière; Chevalier Adolphe de Maussion; MM.

Jules de Montbreton, son of the equerry of the Princess Borghese; Collin junior; Lecordier junior; Lemoine junior; Cardon junior; Mallet junior. Chiefs of the twelve legions: First legion, Comte de Gontaut senior; second legion, Comte Regnault de Saint-Jean d'Angély; third legion, Baron Hottinguer, banker; fourth legion, Comte Jaubert, governor of the bank of France; fifth legion, M. Dauberjon de Murinais; sixth legion, M. Lepileur de Brevannes; eighth legion, M. Richard Lenoir; ninth legion, M. Devins de Gaville; tenth legion, Duc de Cadore; eleventh legion, Comte de Choiseul-Praslin, chamberlain of the Emperor; twelfth legion, M. Salleron.

From the preceding names may be estimated the incredible tact with which the Emperor collected from among the élite of all classes those whose position rendered them most respectable and influential. At the side of names which had acquired greatness under the eyes of the Emperor and by assisting him in his glorious tasks, were seen those whose celebrity was of more ancient date, and, finally, those of the chief industrial leaders of the capital. His Majesty took much pleasure in these amalgamations; he must, in fact, have considered them of great political moment, for the idea preoccupied him to such a point that I have often heard him say: "I wish to blend all classes, all epochs, all glories: I desire that no title shall be more glorious than that of Frenchman." Why did fate will that the Emperor should lack time to accomplish his immense projects, of which he spoke so often, for the glory and welfare of France?

The staff of the National Guard and the chiefs of the twelve legions appointed, the Emperor left the nomination of the other officers, as well as the formation of the legions, in the province of M. de Chabrol, prefect of the Seine. This worthy magistrate, whom the Emperor greatly liked, displayed the greatest zeal and activity on this occasion, and in a short time the National Guard presented an imposing appearance. They vied with each other in arms, equipments, and uniforms; and this almost general alacrity was in these last days one of the consolations that affected the Emperor most deeply. He saw in it a proof of the attachment of the Parisians to his person, and a ground of security for the tranquillity of the capital during his approaching absence. However that might be, the bureaux of the National Guard were soon formed and established in the house occupied by Marshal Moncey, rue du Faubourg Saint-Honoré, near Place Beauveau. A master of requests and two auditors of the Council of State were attached to them, and the master of requests, Chevalier Allent, superior officer of engineers, soon became the soul of the entire administration of the National Guard, no one being more capable than he of giving a strong impulsion to an organization which demanded extreme promptitude. The person from whom I received some of the information which I am combining with my personal recollections, has assured me that in the sequel, that is to say, after our departure for Châlons-sur-Marne, M. Allent became still more influential in the National Guard, of which he was the real chief.   In fact, when King Joseph had received the title of lieutenant-general of the Emperor, which was conferred on him by His Majesty for the time of his absence, M. Allent found himself attached on one side to King Joseph's staff, as officer of engineers, and on the other side to the major-general second in command, as master of requests; whence it followed that he was the intermediary and counsellor of all the relations which must necessarily be established between the lieutenant-general of the Emperor and Marshal Moncey. The greatest benefits resulted from this on account of the rapidity of the decisions. That good and brave Marshal! he wrote his signature in full: *Le Maréchal Duc de Conegliano,* and so slowly that M. Allent had almost time enough to write the correspondence while the Marshal was signing it.

The functions of the two auditors of the Council of State were null, or nearly so; but they were not nonentities such as, it has been claimed, were some of those who slipped into the council, since the first condition required was to prove an income of at least six thousand francs. They were M. Ducancel, the dean of the auditors, and M. Robert de Sainte-Croix. The leg of the latter had been broken by a shell, on the return from Moscow; and this brave young man, a captain of cavalry, had come back astride of a can-

non from the banks of the Beresina as far as Wilna.
Having little bodily strength, but gifted with a firm
soul, M. Robert de Sainte-Croix must have owed it
to his moral courage that he did not succumb. After
undergoing the amputation of his leg, he abandoned
the sword for the pen, and thus it happened that he
became an auditor of the Council of State.[1]

Eight days after the Parisian National Guard was
put into active service, the chiefs of the twelve
legions and the staff were admitted to take the oath
of fidelity between the hands of the Emperor. Everything was already organized in the legions; but the
lack of arms was becoming evident; many citizens
could obtain nothing but lances, and those who could
not procure muskets found their ardor to equip
themselves somewhat cooled by that fact. However,
this citizen guard was not slow in assembling to the
desired number of thirty thousand men; gradually
it occupied the different posts of the capital; and
while fathers of families and citizens devoted to
domestic labors were enrolling themselves without
hesitation, those who had already paid their debt to

---

[1] M. Robert de Sainte-Croix, whose father, formerly ambassador
of France at Constantinople, was then prefect of Valence, had
had two brothers killed in Spain ; one of them was the captain of
a vessel, and the other General Charles de Sainte-Croix. Their
mother, born Mademoiselle Talon, and consequently the aunt of
Madame du Cayla, former lady of honor to the wife of Louis
XVIII., presented her son to that monarch in 1814. The King
having inquired after his family : "Sire," replied M. Robert de
Sainte-Croix, " out of us three brothers, this is the only remaining
leg." — *Note by the editor.*

their country on fields of battle were also asking for
a chance to shed for it the remainder of their blood;
even the invalids at last entreated leave to resume
their service; several hundreds of those heroes forgot their sufferings, and, covered with noble scars,
went to brave the enemy anew. Alas! very few of
those who then left the Hôtel des Invalides were so
fortunate as to return there.

Meanwhile the moment for the Emperor's departure was drawing near. Before departing he bade a
touching farewell to the National Guard, as will be
seen in the succeeding chapter, and confided the
regency to the Empress, as he had done during the
campaign of Dresden. Alas! this time it was not
necessary for His Majesty to take a long journey in
order to put himself at the head of his armies.

CHAPTER XVI

The campaign of miracles — Solemn promise violated — Violation
of Swiss territory — The Emperor's energy increasing with the
danger — Carnot governor of Antwerp and satisfaction of the
Emperor — Defection of the King of Naples — The King of
Naples and the Prince-royal of Sweden — Anger of the Emperor — The eve of the departure — Officers of the National
Guard at the Tuileries — Remarkable words of the Emperor —
Touching scene — The King of Rome and the Empress under
the safeguard of the Parisians — Scene of enthusiasm and tenderness — Tears of the Empress — Departure for the army —
Singular meeting — The old country curé recognized by the
Emperor — Arrival before Brienne — Blücher in flight — The Emperor believing Blücher a prisoner — Abominations committed by
the foreigners — The Emperor Alexander not troubling himself to
prevent disorder — The field of La Rothière — Childish combats,
and a bloody battle — Retreat on Troyes — Imminent danger
of the Emperor and the drawn sword — Blücher's army.

W E shall soon see the campaign of miracles begin.
But before reporting the things I witnessed
during this campaign, on which I might almost say
I never quitted the Emperor, it is needful that I
should here combine certain memories which might
be called an obligatory introduction to them. It is
known that the Swiss cantons had solemnly declared to the Emperor that they would not allow
their territory to be violated, and that they would
do everything to impede the passage of the allied

armies who were making for the French frontiers by way of the Brisgau. The Emperor counted on the destruction of the bridge of Bâle to arrest their march. But this bridge was not destroyed; and Switzerland, instead of guarding the neutrality which it had promised, entered into the coalition against France. The foreign armies crossed the Rhine at Bâle, Schaffousen, and Mannheim. The capitulations made with the generals of the coalized troops for the French garrisons of Dantzic, Dresden, and other fortified places had been openly violated, as has been seen. Thus Marshal Gouvion Saint-Cyr and his army corps, contrary to the pledge of treaties, had been surrounded by superior forces, disarmed, and taken prisoners into Austria; and twenty thousand men remaining from the garrison of Dantzic, were also arrested by order of the Emperor Alexander, and conducted into the deserts of Russia. Geneva opened its gates to the enemy. During the month of January, Vesoul, Épinal, Nancy, Langres, Dijon, Châlons-sur-Saone, and Bar-sur-Aube were occupied by the allies.

As the danger grew more pressing, the energy of the Emperor and his indefatigable activity continually increased. He hastened the organization of the new levies, and to provide for the most urgent expenses he drew thirty millions from the secret treasure that he kept in the vaults of the Marsan pavilion. But the levies of conscripts were made with difficulty. During the single year of 1813, *one million forty thousand* soldiers had been summoned beneath the flags. France was no longer capable of such enormous sacrifices. Yet veterans were enlisting on all sides. General Carnot offered his services to the Emperor, who was deeply affected by this proceeding and intrusted him with the defence of Antwerp. Every one knows with what courage the General acquitted himself of this important mission. Mobilized columns and partisan corps were arming in the eastern departments, some rich proprietors were raising and organizing volunteer companies, and bodies of picked cavalry were forming in which the riders equipped themselves at their own cost.

Amidst these preparations, the Emperor received a piece of news which afflicted him profoundly; the King of Naples had just joined the enemies of France. I had already heard the Emperor break into indignant reproaches when the Prince-royal of Sweden, after having been marshal and prince of the Empire, entered into the coalition against his former country; and yet the King of Sweden had more than one reason to adduce in his own justification. He was alone in the North, hemmed in by hostile powers, and utterly unable to cope with them, even had the interests of his new country been inseparable from those of France. By refusing to enter the coalition, he would have drawn down upon Sweden the wrath of his redoubtable enemies, and with the throne he would fruitlessly have lost and sacrificed the nation which had adopted him.

It was not to the Emperor that he owed his throne. King Joachim, on the contrary, was nothing except through the Emperor. It was the Emperor who had given him one of his sisters to wife, who had given him a throne, and had treated him as well and better than a brother. Hence it was the duty of the King of Naples not to separate his cause from that of the Emperor. Moreover, it was his interest as well: if the Emperor fell, how could kings of his family and his fashion hope to remain erect? Kings Joseph and Jérôme and the brave and loyal Prince Eugène had comprehended this. The latter was courageously defending in Italy the cause of his adoptive father. If the King of Naples had joined him, they might have marched on Vienna together; and this audacious and yet very practicable manœuvre would infallibly have saved France.

Such are some of the reflections I heard the Emperor make when speaking of the defection of the King of Naples. But he did not reason so calmly at the first moment; his anger was extreme, and yet there was blended with it sorrow, and even touches of compassion. "Murat," he exclaimed, "Murat betray me! Murat sell himself to the English! The unhappy wretch! He fancies that if they succeed in overthrowing me, they will leave him the throne on which I placed him. Poor fool! The worst that can happen to him is that his treason should succeed; for he will have less pity to expect from his new allies than from me."

On the eve of his departure for the army, the Emperor received the officers of the Parisian National Guard. The reception was held in the great hall of the Tuileries. The ceremony was imposing and sad. The Emperor made his appearance before the assembly with the Empress, and holding by the hand the King of Rome, who then lacked two months of being three years old. Although the speech he made on this occasion is already known, yet I will repeat it here, being unwilling that these beautiful and solemn words of my former master should be lacking to my Memoirs:

"Gentlemen officers of the National Guard, I have pleasure in seeing you assembled round me. I depart to-night to place myself at the head of the army. In quitting the capital, I leave with confidence under your protection my wife and my son, on whom are placed so many hopes. I owe you this mark of confidence in return for all those you have never ceased to give me in the principal epochs of my life. I shall go with a mind free from anxiety when they are under your faithful guard. I leave to you what, next to France, is dearest to me in all the world, and I intrust it to your care.

"It may happen that, through the manœuvres I am going to make, the enemy may find an opportunity to approach your walls. If that occurs, remember that it can only be a matter of a few days, and that I will soon come to your assistance. I recommend you to be united amongst yourselves and to repel all insinuations which would tend to divide you. Efforts will not be lacking to shake your fidelity to your duties; but I rely on your rejecting these perfidious instigations."

At the close of these remarks, the Emperor's glance rested on the Empress and the King of Rome, whom his august mother was holding in her arms; and indicating to the assembly by look and gesture this child whose expressive countenance seemed to reflect the solemnity of the occasion, he added in a voice that betrayed emotion: "I confide him to you, gentlemen; I confide him to the love of my faithful city of Paris." At these words of His Majesty, a thousand cries, a thousand arms arose, swearing to guard and defend this precious trust. The Empress, bathed in tears and pale from the different emotions by which she was agitated, would have fallen, if the Emperor had not supported her in his arms. At this sight, the enthusiasm reached its climax; tears fell from every eye; and there was not one of the spectators who did not seem, on retiring, ready to shed his blood for the imperial family. It was on that day that I saw M. de Bourrienne for the first time at the palace again; if I do not mistake, he wore the uniform of a captain of the National Guard.

January 25, after having conferred the regency on Her Majesty the Empress, the Emperor set out for the army. We slept at Châlons-sur-Marne. His arrival stopped the progress of the hostile armies and the retreat of our troops. Two days later he attacked the allies in his turn at Saint-Dizier. His Majesty's entry into this city was signalized by the most affecting tokens of enthusiasm and devotion. At the moment when the Emperor alighted, a former colonel, M. Bouland, an old man upwards of seventy, threw himself at His Majesty's knees, expressing to him the sadness he had felt in seeing the foreign bayonets and his confidence that the Emperor would wipe them from the soil of France. His Majesty raised the worthy veteran, and told him cheerfully that he would spare no pains to fulfil so favorable a prediction. The allies had behaved inhumanly at Saint-Dizier; women and old men were dead or ill from the bad treatment they had received; hence the presence of His Majesty was a subject of great joy to the country.

The enemy having been repulsed at Saint-Dizier, the Emperor learned that the army of Silesia was concentrating on Brienne. He set off at once across the forest of Déo. The soldiers who followed him seemed as indefatigable as himself. A halt was made at the town of Eclaron, where His Majesty gave the inhabitants money for the restoration of their church, which had been devastated by the enemies. The surgeon of this town having come forward to thank the Emperor, His Majesty examined him attentively and said: "Have you served, sir?" "Yes, Sire, I was with the army of Egypt."— "Why have you not the cross?" "Sire, because I have never asked for it."—"Sir, you are all the more worthy of it. I hope that you will wear the one I will send you." And in a few minutes his certificate was signed by the Emperor and handed to the new chevalier, whom the Emperor recommended to take the greatest care of the sick and wounded of our army who should be within reach of his assistance.[1]

On entering Mézières, His Majesty was received by the municipal authorities, the clergy, and the National Guard. "Gentlemen," said the Emperor to the National Guards who were pressing around him, "to-day we are fighting for our hearthstones; we must be able to defend them and prevent the Cossacks from warming themselves there; they are bad guests who would leave no room for you. Let us show them that every Frenchman is born a soldier and a good soldier." On receiving the homage of the curé, His Majesty perceived that this ecclesiastic was looking at him with interest and attention. This caused the Emperor to pay more attention in return, and he recognized him as one of his former regents of the college of Brienne. "What! is this you, my dear master?" exclaimed His Majesty. "Then you never quitted this region?

---

[1] It is known that the Emperor was not lavish with crosses of honor. Here is another proof of it: he was very well satisfied with the services of M. Veyrat, inspector general of the police, and the latter desired the cross. I presented several petitions for him to His Majesty, who one day said to me: "*I am satisfied with Veyrat; he serves me well; I will give him as much money as he wants: BUT THE CROSS, NEVER!*"

So much the better; you will be all the more able to serve the country's cause. I do not need to ask you if you know the neighborhood." "Sire," said the curé, "I could find my way about it with my eyes shut." — "Come along with us then; you will act as our guide, and we will talk." The worthy curé had his peaceable mare saddled at once, and took his place in the centre of the imperial staff.

That same day we arrived before Brienne. The Emperor's march had been so secret and so prompt that the Prussians knew nothing about it until he fell upon them. A number of general officers were made prisoners, and Blücher himself, who was tranquilly coming down from the château, had only time enough to turn heel and fly as fast as he could, pursued by the balls of our advance guard. For an instant the Emperor thought the Prussian general had been taken, and he shouted: "We will hold on to that old fighter; the campaign will not last long." The Russians established in the town set fire to it. Fighting went on in the middle of the fire. Night fell without separating the combatants. In the space of twelve hours, the town was taken and retaken several times. The Emperor was furious that Blücher had escaped him.

On his way back to headquarters, which had been established at Mézières, His Majesty narrowly escaped being pierced by the lance of a Cossack; but before the Emperor had had time to see the movement of this wretch, the brave Colonel Gourgaud, who was marching behind His Majesty, laid the Cossack low with a pistol-shot.

The Emperor had only fifteen thousand men with him, and they had fought with equal success against eighty thousand foreigners. At the close of this combat, the Prussians retreated on Bar-sur-Aube, and His Majesty established himself at the château of Brienne, where he passed two nights. I remembered, during the sojourn, the one I had made there with the Emperor ten years before, when he was going to Milan to add the title of King of Italy to that of the Emperor of the French. "To-day," I said to myself, "not merely is Italy lost to him; but also it is at the centre of the French Empire, it is within a few leagues of his capital that the Emperor is defending himself against innumerable enemies!" The first time that I saw Brienne, the Emperor had been received as a sovereign by a noble family which fifteen years before had welcomed him as a protégé. He had renewed there the sweetest memories of his childhood and youth; and in comparing what he was in 1805 with what he had been at the Military School, he had spoken with pride of *having made his way.* At the close of January, 1814, people were beginning to foresee where his path would end. Not that I wish to announce myself as having foreseen the Emperor's downfall. No; I did not go so far as that. Accustomed to see him rely upon his star, those who surrounded him relied on it no less than he. But yet we could not disguise from ourselves that there had been a change. To keep up an illusion on that subject it would have been necessary to close our eyes, so as neither to see nor hear these masses of foreigners whom until now we had never seen except in their own homes, and who were now in ours.

At every step, in fact, we met horrible proof of the passage of the enemies. After taking possession of cities or villages, they had arrested the inhabitants, maltreated them with sabre thrusts or the butt-end of their muskets, despoiled them of their clothes, and impressed into their service those they deemed competent to guide them. If they were not conducted as they desired to be, they sabred or shot their unfortunate guides. Everywhere they took possession of food, drink, forage, and, in a word, of all that could be useful to their army, made enormous requisitions, and when they had exhausted the resources of their victims, they generally finished their work of destruction by pillage and fire. The Prussians, and above all the Cossacks, distinguished themselves by their brutal ferocity. Sometimes these hideous savages would enter houses by main force, divide up all that fell under their hands, load their horses with booty, and break what they could not carry away; sometimes, not finding the wherewith to satisfy their avidity, they would take down the doors, demolish the ceilings so as to get the beams and windows, and with all these wrecks and the furniture which was too heavy to be taken along, they would make a fire which, communicating itself to the roof of every house, would consume in an instant the shelter of the unhappy inhabitants and force them to take refuge in the woods.

Elsewhere the better-off inhabitants would give them what they asked for, especially brandy, of which they were very greedy, hoping by this docility to escape their ferocity. But these barbarians, heated by drink, would then proceed to the last excesses; they would seize the daughters, wives, and servants, beat them frightfully in order to constrain them to drink some of the brandy, and when they were completely overcome by it, take infamous advantage of their helplessness. Many women and young girls had courage and strength enough to defend themselves against these brigands, but then three or four of them would come against one; and often, to revenge themselves for the resistance offered by these unfortunates, after having dishonored they would mutilate them, kill them with their weapons, or throw them into the middle of their bivouac fires. Farm-houses were burnt, and families but now opulent and comfortable reduced in an instant to beggary and despair. Husbands and old men were sabred when trying to defend the honor of their wives and daughters; and when some poor mothers would approach the fire, seeking to warm the infant hanging at their breast, they were scorched or killed by the explosion of packets of cartridges designedly thrown into it by the Cossacks, and their screams of anguish or of grief were silenced by the laughter of these monsters.

I should never finish were it necessary to recount all the atrocities committed by the foreign hordes. At the time of the Restoration it was the fashion to say that the complaints and reports of those who had been exposed to these excesses were exaggerated by fear or hatred. I have even heard well-intentioned persons jest very agreeably over the pretty tricks of the Cossacks. But these witty people had always kept at a distance from the scene of war, and had had the luck to inhabit departments which had not suffered from either the first or the second invasion. I would not have advised them to address their pleasantries to the unfortunate inhabitants of Champagne, and the eastern departments generally. It has also been claimed that the sovereign allies and the general officers, both Russian and Prussian, had severely interdicted all violence on the part of their regular troops, and that the harm was done only by undisciplined and ungovernable bands of Cossacks. A hundred times I have had occasion, more especially at Troyes, to acquire proof to the contrary. That city has doubtless not forgotten how it was that the Princes of Würtemberg and Hohenlohe, and the Emperor Alexander himself, did justice on the incendiarism, the pillage, rape, and assassinations without number which were committed under their eyes, not simply by the Cossacks, but also by enrolled and disciplined soldiers. Not one step was taken by the sovereigns or their generals to put an end to so many atrocities; and yet, when they departed from the city, it would have needed but an order on their part to disperse at once the cloud of Cossacks who were devastating the region.

The field of La Rothière, as I have said elsewhere, had been the rendezvous of the pupils of the Military School of Brienne. There, in childhood, the Emperor had preluded, by schoolboy conflicts, his gigantic battles. That of La Rothière was desperate, and it cost the enemy a great deal of blood to obtain the advantage which he owed solely to his immense numerical superiority. In the night which followed this unequal combat, the Emperor ordered the retreat on Troyes.

In returning to the château after the battle, His Majesty again incurred an imminent danger: he was suddenly surrounded by a troop of uhlans, and drew his sword to defend himself. M. Jardin junior, his equerry, who was close behind the Emperor, received a ball in the arm. Several chasseurs of the escort were wounded; but they finally succeeded in extricating His Majesty. I can attest that the Emperor displayed the greatest coolness in all encounters of this kind. On that day, as I was unbuckling his sword-belt, he half drew the weapon from its scabbard, saying: " Do you know, Constant, that those rascals made me draw my sword? The rogues are daring. They need a good lesson to teach them to keep at a respectful distance."

It is not my intention to tell in detail the story of this French campaign, in which the Emperor displayed an energy and activity which excited the highest admiration in all who surrounded him. Unhappily, the successive advantages which he gained exhausted his troops and inflicted on the enemy none but losses which were easy to repair. It was, as has been so well said by M. de Bourrienne, the combat of an Alpine eagle with a cloud of crows. "The eagle kills hundreds of them; each blow of his beak is the death of an enemy; but the crows come back in ever-increasing numbers, and press upon the eagle until they end by stifling him." At Champ-Aubert, at Montmirail, at Nangis, at Montereau, at Arcis, and in twenty other mêlées, the Emperor had the advantage of genius and our army that of courage; but this was in vain. Scarcely had the masses of the enemy been dispersed than they formed anew in perfectly fresh ones before our soldiers, harassed by continual battles and forced marches. Especially the army commanded by Blücher seemed to be incessantly reborn; everywhere beaten, it reappeared with forces equal, if not superior, to those which had been destroyed or scattered. How resist forever so great a superiority of numbers?

CHAPTER XVII

NEVER had the Emperor shown himself so admirable as during this fatal campaign of France; in struggling against fortune he renewed the prodigies of the first Italian wars, when fortune smiled upon him; aggression had signalized the commencement of his career; the end of it was marked by the finest defence commemorated in the annals of war. It may be said that everywhere and always His

Majesty was at once both general and soldier. On every occasion he gave the example of personal courage, and that to such an extent as to alarm those who surrounded him, and whose existence was bound up with his. It is known, for example, that at Montereau, the Emperor himself pointed the pieces of artillery, exposed himself gaily to the fire of the enemy, and said to the soldiers who were disturbed by this and wanted him to retire: " Let me do it, my friends; the cannon-ball that is to kill me has not yet been cast."

At Arcis, the Emperor again fought like a soldier; more than once he drew his sword to free himself from the enemies by whom he was surrounded. A shell having fallen at a few paces from his horse, the surprised animal sprang aside, and very nearly threw the Emperor, who, lorgnette in hand, was then deeply engaged in examining the field of battle. His Majesty having settled himself more firmly in his saddle, drove his spurs into his horse, which he urged toward the shell and forced to smell it; at that very instant the piece exploded and by some unprecedented chance, neither the Emperor nor his horse was hurt.

In more than one similar circumstance, the Emperor, during this campaign, seemed to have abandoned his hold on life; and yet it was only at the last extremity that he renounced the hope of preserving his throne. But it was painful to him to treat with the enemy while the latter was occupying French territory. His Majesty would have liked to purge the soil of France from the presence of foreigners before entering into arrangements with them. Thence proceeded his hesitations, his refusals to assent to the peace offered him on several occasions.

February 8, the Emperor, at the close of a long discussion with two or three of his confidential advisers, went to bed very late and in extreme preoccupation. He waked me often during the night, complained of not being able to sleep, and made me take away and fetch back his candle several times. Toward five o'clock in the morning, I was called again; I was sinking with fatigue; His Majesty observed it and said kindly: "You are knocked up, my poor Constant; we are making a rough campaign, aren't we? but keep up your courage a while longer; you are soon going to rest." Encouraged by the kindliness of His Majesty's tone, I took the liberty of replying that no one could think of complaining of the fatigue and privations we experienced, since they were shared by His Majesty; but that nevertheless the desire and hope of all the world was for peace. "Well, yes," returned the Emperor with a sort of concentrated violence, "they shall have peace; they shall see what a dishonorable peace is like!" I kept silence; the disturbance and vexation of His Majesty afflicted me profoundly, and at that moment I could have desired the Emperor to have an army of men of iron like himself. He would never have made peace but on the frontier of France.

The accent of kindness and familiarity with which

the Emperor spoke to me on this occasion, reminds me of another incident which I forgot to record in its own place, and which I will not now omit, because I think it calculated to give a notion of His Majesty's manners with the persons in his service, and particularly with me. Roustan was a witness of the fact, and it was from him that I learned the beginning of it.

In one of the campaigns beyond the Rhine (I cannot say in which), I had been up for several nights together, and I was tired. The Emperor went out toward eleven o'clock in the evening, and was absent three or four hours. I sat down to wait for him in his armchair, near his writing-table, intending to rise and withdraw when I heard him coming in. But I was so worn out with fatigue that slumber surprised me unawares, and I fell into a profound sleep with my head on my arm, and my arm on His Majesty's table. The Emperor at last came in, accompanied by Marshal Berthier and followed by Roustan. I heard nothing. Prince de Neufchâtel started toward me, intending to awake me and have me restore his chair and table to His Majesty; but the Emperor detained him, saying: "Let the poor fellow alone; he has passed I don't know how many sleepless nights." And then, as there was no other chair in the apartment, His Majesty sat down on the side of his bed, made the Marshal take a seat there also, and talked with him a long time, while I slept on. But requiring one of the maps which were on the table, and upon which my elbow was resting, His Majesty, although he tried to draw it away with precaution, waked me up, and I rose at once in utter confusion, and excusing myself for the liberty I had involuntarily taken. " Monsieur Constant," said the Emperor with a smile full of benevolence, " it distresses me to have disturbed you ; kindly excuse me." Such was the Emperor's thoughtfulness for his attendants. I desire that this, with other things of the same sort which I have already related, may serve as a reply to those who have accused him of severity in his household. I resume my narrative of the events of 1814.

In the night of the 8th–9th, the Emperor seeming to have decided to make peace, the night was spent in preparing the despatches, and at eight o'clock in the morning of the 9th they were brought to him to sign ; but he had changed his mind. At seven o'clock he had received news of the Russian and Prussian armies. When the Duc de Bassano entered, with the despatches in his hand, the Emperor was lying on his maps and planting his pins. " Ah ! it is you," said he to his minister; " there is no more question of that. See here, I want to thrash Blücher ; he has taken the Montmirail road. I am going to start. I shall fight him to-morrow and the day after to-morrow. The face of affairs is about to change and we shall see. We won't precipitate anything ; there will always be time enough to conclude such a peace as they propose to us." An hour later we were on the Sézanne road.

Then there were several days in succession during which the heroic efforts of the Emperor and his brave soldiers were crowned with the most brilliant success. Hardly had they arrived at Champ-Aubert, when the army, finding itself in presence of the Russian army corps with which it had already combated at Brienne, fell upon it without waiting to repose, separated it from the Prussian army, and made prisoners of the general-in-chief and several general officers. His Majesty, whose behavior toward his vanquished foes was always honorable and generous, had them dine at his table and treated them with the greatest courtesy. The enemies were again beaten at Ferme des Fréneaux by Marshals Ney and Mortier, and by the Duc de Raguse at Vaux-Champs, where Blücher was again on the point of being made prisoner. At Nangis, the Emperor dispersed one hundred and fifty thousand men commanded by Prince Schwarzenberg, and despatched in pursuit of them Marshals Oudinot, Kellermann, Macdonald, and Generals Treilhard and Gérard.

The eve of the battle of Méry, the Emperor went through all the environs of that little city, and his observing eye rested upon an immense extent of marsh, in the midst of which is the village of Bagneux, and a little further away the town of Anglure, where flows the Aube. After the rapid excursion he made over the moving ground of these dangerous marshes, he dismounted and sat down upon a bundle of reeds; there, with his back resting against the hut of a night watchman, he unrolled his campaign map; after examining it for some moments, he remounted his horse and set off at a gallop.

At this moment a cloud of teal and snipe flying in front of His Majesty, he cried with a laugh: "Go on, go on, my beauties; give place to other game." To all who surrounded him, His Majesty said: "This time we have got them!"

The Emperor was galloping toward Anglure, to see whether the rising ground of Baudemont, which is near that town, were occupied by the artillery, when the noise of cannon on the Méry side, obliged him to retrace his steps. He turned therefore toward Méry, saying to the officers who followed him: "Gallop, gentlemen, our enemies are in a hurry; it won't do to keep them waiting." Half an hour later he was on the field of battle.

The flames of the conflagration of Méry drove back enormous clouds of smoke upon the Russian and Prussian columns, and disguised in part the manœuvres of the French army. At that moment everything announced the success of the plan the Emperor had conceived that morning in the marshes of Bagneux; all was going well: His Majesty saw the allies defeated and France saved, while at Anglure everything was in desolation. The population of several villages were dreading to see the enemy approach, with not a piece of cannon there to cut off their retreat, not a soldier to prevent them from crossing the river.

The position of the allies was so critical that the whole French army believed them to be lost; they plunged with all their artillery into the marshes, and, riddled by grape-shot from our cannons, they should have stayed there. All of a sudden they were seen to make another effort, range themselves in order of battle, and prepare to cross the Aube. The Emperor, who could pursue them no longer without exposing his army also to the danger of sinking in the morass, arrested the impetuosity of his soldiers, believing that the hill of Baudemont was covered with artillery which would crush the enemy. Not hearing a single discharge from that quarter, he went with all speed to Sézanne to hasten the troops forward, but those whom he expected to find there had been sent on to Fère-Champenoise.

During this interval, a property owner at Anglure, named Ausart, had mounted a horse and galloped to Sézanne to warn the Marshal, who was there, that the enemy, pursued by the Emperor, was about to cross the Aube. On arriving near the Duke, and seeing that the army corps he commanded was not taking the road to Anglure, he made haste to speak. But as he seemed to have received no orders from the Emperor, he was not listened to, he was treated as a spy, and it was only with difficulty that this brave man avoided being shot.

While this scene was taking place, His Majesty was already at Sézanne; being surrounded by several of the villagers, he asked for some one to guide him to

Fère-Champenoise: a bailiff presented himself. The Emperor set off at once, escorted by some superior officers who had accompanied him to Sézanne; he said to his guide: "Go in front of me, sir, and take the shortest road." On arriving within a short distance of the battle-field of Fère-Champenoise, His Majesty saw that each detonation of artillery made the poor bailiff lower his head. "You are afraid, sir," said the Emperor. "No, Sire." — "In that case, why do you lower your head like that?" "Because I am not accustomed, like Your Majesty, to hear all this uproar." — "We have to get used to everything; don't be afraid: keep straight on." But the guide, more dead than alive, drew in his horse and trembled in every limb. "Come, come, I see you are really afraid, get behind me." He obeyed, turned rein and galloped back to Sézanne, promising himself never again to act as the Emperor's guide on a similar occasion.

At the battle of Méry, the Emperor threw a little bridge across a river which flows near the town, under the enemy's fire. This bridge was constructed in an hour with ladders fastened together and supported by pieces of wood; but this was not sufficient; to make it practicable, it was necessary to lay planks across it, and none were to be found, for the persons who might have procured some dared not approach the shot-riddled ground the Emperor was occupying at that moment. Impatient and even angry at not being able to board over the bridge, His Majesty had the shutters of several large houses near the river taken down, and then laid and nailed fast under his own eyes. While this work was going on, an extreme thirst tormented him, and he was going to dip up water in his hand to quench it, when a young girl who had despised danger in order to approach the Emperor ran to a neighboring house and brought him a glass of wine and water, which he drank with avidity.

Astonished to see this young girl in so dangerous a place, the Emperor smilingly said to her: "You would make a brave soldier, Mademoiselle. Will you take the epaulettes? you shall be one of my aides-de-camp." The young girl blushed, courtesied to the Emperor, and was about to go away, when he held out his hand, which she kissed. "Come to Paris after this," added His Majesty, "and remind me of the service you have rendered me to-day; you will be contented with my gratitude." The young person thanked the Emperor and withdrew, very proud of the words he had addressed to her.

On the day the battle of Nangis was fought, an Austrian officer came in the evening to headquarters and had a long secret interview with His Majesty. Forty-eight hours later, after the battle of Méry, a new envoy from Prince Schwarzenberg appeared, with a response from the Emperor of Austria to the confidential letter which His Majesty had written to his father-in-law two days before. We had quitted Méry, which was on fire, and in the little hamlet of Châtres, where the headquarters were established, no shelter was found for His Majesty but in the shop of a wheelwright. It was there the Emperor spent the night, either waking or lying in his clothes on the bed, without sleeping. There also he received the Austrian envoy, Prince Lichtenstein. The Prince remained a long time in private with His Majesty. Nothing transpired of their conversation; but no one doubted that it was concerning peace. After his departure, the Emperor displayed an extraordinary gaiety which communicated itself to all around him. Our army had made thousands of prisoners from the enemy; Paris had just received the Russian and Prussian flags taken at Nangis and Montereau: the Emperor had seen flying before him the foreign sovereigns who were for some time in dread lest they should not regain the frontier. Such success had restored all His Majesty's confidence in his fortune. But this confidence was unhappily but a dangerous illusion.

Prince Lichtenstein had barely left headquarters when I saw M. de Saint-Aignan arrive, the brother-in-law of the Duc de Vicenza, and equerry of the Emperor. M. de Saint-Aignan, I think, was coming to his brother-in-law, who was at the Congress of Châtillon, or rather who had been there, for the sessions of this Congress had been suspended for some days. It seems that before leaving Paris, M. de Saint-Aignan had had an interview with the Duc de Rovigo and another minister, and that they had intrusted him with a verbal message to the Emperor.

The mission was difficult and delicate ; he was anxious to have these gentlemen put into writing the representations they charged him to convey to His Majesty, but they had refused, and, as a loyal servitor, M. de Saint-Aignan had devoted himself to his duty, and was ready to say the whole truth, no matter what danger there might be in doing so.

At the moment when he arrived at the shop of the Châtres wheelwright, the Emperor, as has just been seen, was giving full rein to his most brilliant hopes. This was an unlucky circumstance for M. de Saint-Aignan, who was not the bearer of agreeable tidings. He came, as was afterwards learned, to announce to His Majesty that he could not rely on the temper of the capital ; that people there were complaining of the duration of the war, and that they would like the Emperor to seize the first occasion to make peace.   It has even been said that the word *disaffection* had issued, during this secret conference, from the sincere and truthful mouth of M. de Saint-Aignan.   I do not know whether that is true ; for the door was shut close, and M. de Saint-Aignan spoke in a low tone. It is certain, however, that his reports and his frankness excited to the utmost pitch the anger of His Majesty, who, in dismissing him with a harshness which he certainly had not deserved, raised his voice high enough to be heard by the gods.   M. de Saint-Aignan having withdrawn, His Majesty summoned me to my duties, and I found him still pale and disturbed by anger.   Some hours after this scene, the

Emperor having demanded his horse, M. de Saint-Aignan, who had resumed his duties as equerry, came up to hold His Majesty's stirrup; but as soon as the Emperor perceived him, he frowned, motioned him away, and shouted: *Mesgrigny!* in a loud voice. He was calling Baron de Mesgrigny, his other equerry. In conformity with the Emperor's wishes, M. de Mesgrigny took the service of M. de Saint-Aignan, who went to the rear of the army to wait until the storm should pass. Within a few days his disgrace ended, and all who knew him were rejoiced; Baron de Saint-Aignan was loved by every one for his amiability and loyalty.

From Châtres the Emperor marched on Troyes. The enemies were occupying this city and seemed at first inclined to defend it; but they soon surrendered and left it after a capitulation. During the short time the allies had been in Troyes, the Royalists had publically displayed their hatred against the Emperor and their devotion to the foreign powers, who, said they, were coming merely to replace the Bourbons on their throne. They had even been so imprudent as to raise the white flag and wear the white cockade. The foreign troops had protected them, although they were exacting and severe to those of the inhabitants who held a directly contrary opinion.

Unluckily for the Royalists, they were in a very slender minority, and the favor with which they were regarded by the Prussians and Russians made the population, crushed by the latter, hate the protected

as much as the protectors. Already, before the
Emperor entered Troyes, royalist proclamations, addressed to the officers of his household or of the
army, had fallen into his hands. He had shown no
sign of anger; but he had pledged those who had
received or were receiving documents of this kind to
destroy them and say not a word to any one. On
arriving at Troyes, His Majesty issued a decree in-
flicting the penalty of death on Frenchmen in the
service of the enemies, and on those who had worn
the signs and decorations of the former dynasty. An
unfortunate *émigré*, brought before a council of war,
was convicted of having worn the cross of Saint Louis
and the white cockade during the sojourn of the
allies at Troyes, and of having given the foreign generals all the information that he could. The council
sentenced him to death, for the facts were positive
and the law not less so. A victim of his premature
devotion to a cause which was then far from appear-
ing national, above all in the departments occupied
by the foreign armies, the Chevalier Gonault was
in fact executed.

CHAPTER XVIII

Negotiations for an armistice — Blücher and one hundred thousand men — Prince Schwarzenberg resuming the offensive — A stratagem of war — The Emperor going to meet Blücher — Halt in the village of Herbisse — The good curé — Politeness of the Emperor — Marshal Lefebvre a theologian — The Abbé Maury marshal and Marshal Lefebvre cardinal — Campaign supper — Awakening of the curé and generosity of the Emperor — Fatality of the name of Moreau — Battle of Craonne — M. de Bussy former comrade and aide-de-camp of the Emperor — General eagerness to give information — The brave Wolff and the cross of honor — Ability of General Drouot — Defence of the Russians — M. de Rumigny at headquarters and news of the Congress — Secret conference unfavorable to peace — Lively scene between the Emperor and the Duc de Vicenza — "You are a Russian !" — Vehemence of the Emperor — A victory in prospect — Tears of the Duc de Vicenza — March on Laon — The French army surprised by the Russians — Dissatisfaction of the Emperor — Taking of Rheims by M. de Saint-Priest — Valor of General Corbineau — We enter Rheims while the Russians are leaving it — Resignation of the people of Rheims — Good discipline of the Russians — The young conscripts — Six thousand men and General Janssens — Affairs of the Empire — The only indefatigable man.

AFTER the brilliant advantages gained by the Emperor within so short a space of time, and with forces so extraordinarily inferior to the masses of the enemy, His Majesty, feeling the necessity of allowing his troops a few days' rest at Troyes, had entered into arrangements for an armistice with

Prince Schwarzenberg. Under the circumstances, the Emperor was informed that General Blücher, who had been wounded at Méry, was descending both banks of the Marne at the head of an army of fresh troops estimated at not less than a hundred thousand men, and marching toward Meaux. Prince Schwarzenberg, on his side, having been told of this movement of Blücher, cut the negotiations short and immediately resumed the offensive at Bar-sur-Seine. The Emperor, whose genius comprehended within a single glance all the marches, all the operations of the enemy, but who could not be everywhere at once, resolved to go and fight Blücher in person, and yet, by means of a stratagem, to make it believed that he was confronting Schwarzenberg. Two army corps, therefore, one commanded by Marshal Oudinot and the other by Marshal Macdonald, were sent to meet the Austrians. As soon as the troops were within range of the hostile camp, they made the air ring with those shouts of confidence and joy which usually announced the presence of the Emperor. Meantime, we were hurrying to meet Blücher with all possible speed.

We came to a halt at the little village of Herbisse, where we spent the night in the presbytery. The curé, on seeing the Emperor arrive at his house with his marshals, aides-de-camp, orderly officers, the service of honor and the other attendants, was for a moment almost dazed. His Majesty, as he dismounted, said to him: "Monsieur le curé, we have come to ask your hospitality for one night. Don't let this visit alarm you; we will make ourselves very small so as not to crowd you." The Emperor, conducted by the good curé, who was perspiring with mingled eagerness and embarrassment, established himself in the only apartment, which served our host as kitchen, dining-room, bed-chamber, study, and parlor. In an instant His Majesty was surrounded by his maps and papers and had set to work as comfortably as in his cabinet at the Tuileries. But the members of his suite needed a little more time to install themselves. It was not an easy matter for so many people to find room in a bake-house, which, with the chamber occupied by His Majesty, comprised all there was of the presbytery of Herbisse; but these gentlemen, although there was more than one dignitary and prince of the Empire among them, were accommodating and quite inclined to make the best of matters. It was a remarkable thing, and very indicative of French character, to see the good humor of these brave warriors, in spite of the daily combats they had to sustain, and of events which at every instant took a more alarming turn.

The younger officers formed a circle around the niece of the curé, who sang them some provincial hymns. The good curé, amidst his continual goings and comings, and the pains he was taking to play worthily his part as host, was attacked on his own ground, that is to say, on his breviary, by Marshal

Lefebvre, who had made some studies for the priest-hood in his youth, and who said he had *retained nothing from his first vocation but the coiffure, because it was the soonest combed.* The worthy Marshal inter-larded his Latin quotations with military expressions, of which he was by no means sparing, and he made all present roar with laughter, including the curé, who said to him: "Monseigneur, if you had con-tinued your studies for the priesthood, you would have become a cardinal at the least." "Why not?" observed one of the officers; "if the Abbé Maury had been a sergeant-major in '89, he might possibly be a marshal of France to-day." "Or else dead," added the Duc de Dantzic, but employing a much more energetic word; "and so much the better for him; he would not see the Cossacks within twenty leagues of Paris." — "Oh! bah! Monseigneur," re-turned the same officer, "we shall chase them back." "Yes," muttered the Marshal between his teeth, "we shall see if they come."

At this moment arrived the canteen mule, long impatiently expected. There was no table, but one was made by laying a door across some casks; seats were improvised with boards. The principal officers sat down, the others ate standing. The curé took his place at the military table, on which he had him-self set the best bottles from his cellar, and his good-natured simplicity continued to enliven the guests. The conversation happened to turn on the situation of Herbisse and the neighborhood. The curé could not recover from his astonishment on finding that his guests knew the region even in its least details. "Ah!" said he, looking at them one after another, "So you are all Champagne men?" To put an end to his surprise, these gentlemen drew plans from their pockets on which they showed him the names of the smallest localities. But then his amazement merely changed its object; he had never imagined that military science required such exact studies. "What labors!" he repeated, "what exertions! and all that to fire cannon-balls!" The supper ended, the next thing was how to sleep, and a shelter and some straw was found in neighboring barns. Nobody remained outside, and near the door of the chamber occupied by the Emperor, but the officers on duty, Roustan, and me. Each had his bundle of hay for a bed. Our worthy host, having relinquished his own to His Majesty, stayed with us and rested as we did from his fatigues of the day. He was yet in his first sleep when the headquarters left the presbytery, for the Emperor rose and departed before daybreak. The curé, on awaking, manifested much chagrin at not having been able to bid His Majesty adieu. He was handed a purse containing the sum which the Emperor, when he stopped at the houses of private persons not greatly favored by fortune, was accustomed to leave behind him as an indemnity for their expense and trouble, and we resumed our march after the Emperor, who was hastening to meet the Prussians.

The Emperor wished to arrive at Soissons before the allies; but although they had had to traverse difficult roads, they were in advance of our troops, and on entering Ferté, the Emperor saw them retire upon Soissons. He was delighted to see it. Soissons was defended by a good garrison, and might delay the enemy, while Marshals Marmont and Mortier and His Majesty in person, attacking Blücher on the rear and the two flanks, would shut them up in a trap. But again the enemy escaped the combinations of the Emperor just when he expected to seize him. Hardly had Blücher presented himself before Soissons when the gates were opened to him. General Moreau, commandant of the place, had already delivered the city to Bülow, and thus assured to the allies the passage of the Aisne. On receiving this discouraging news, the Emperor exclaimed: " That name of Moreau has always been fatal to me!"

Continuing nevertheless his pursuit of the Prussians, His Majesty occupied himself with preventing the passage of the Aisne. March 5, he sent General Nansouty forward, who, with his cavalry, tore up the bridge, repulsed the enemy, and made a Russian colonel prisoner. After passing the night at Béry-au-Bach, the Emperor was marching on Laon, when some one informed him that the enemy was coming to meet us. It was not the Prussians, but a Russian army corps commanded by Sacken. On advancing, we found the Russians established on the heights of Craonne, and covering the Laon road. Their position seemed unassailable. Nevertheless our vanguard, led by Marshal Ney, rushed forward and succeeded in occupying Craonne. It was enough for that day, and the night was spent on both sides in preparing for the morrow's battle. The Emperor passed that night in the village of Corbeny, but without going to bed. Inhabitants from the neighboring villages were arriving every hour with information concerning the position of the enemy and the lay of the ground. His Majesty interrogated them himself, praised or even rewarded them for their zeal, and availed himself of their services and their knowledge. Thus, for example, having recognized in the mayor of a commune in the environs of Craonne one of his former comrades in the regiment of La Fère, he made him one of his aides-de-camp, and utilized him as a guide over this ground which no one knew better than he. M. de Bussy (such was the name of this officer) had left France during the Terror, and since his return had never resumed service, but lived in retirement on his estates.

The Emperor met still another of his former companions-in-arms of the La Fère regiment that night: this was an Alsatian named Wolff, who had been an artillery sergeant, with the Emperor and M. de Bussy as his superiors. He came from Strasburg, and testified to the good dispositions of the inhabitants in all the departments he had passed through. The shock given to the allied armies by the first attacks of the Emperor had been felt as far as the frontiers, and on all the roads the peasants had risen in arms, cut off the retreat, and killed a great many of the enemy. Partisan corps had been formed in the Vosges, led by officers of tried courage and accustomed to this style of warfare. The garrisons of the cities and strongholds of the East were full of courage and determination, and it would not be by their good will if France did not become, according to the wish expressed by the Emperor, the grave of the foreign armies. The brave Wolff, after having given this information to His Majesty, repeated it in the presence of many other persons, of whom I was one. He only stayed a few hours to rest himself, and then departed; but the Emperor did not dismiss him until he had decorated him with the cross of honor in recompense of his devotion.

The battle of Craonne began, or, rather, began again, at daybreak on the 7th. The infantry was commanded by Prince de la Moskowa and the Duc de Bellune, who was wounded on that day. Generals Grouchy and Nansouty, the first commanding the army cavalry and the second the cavalry of the guard, also received serious wounds. The difficulty was to hold the heights, not to ascend them. Nevertheless the French artillery, directed by the modest and skilful General Drouot, forced that of the enemy to cede the ground, little by little; but it was a horribly bloody struggle. The two sides of this hill were too craggy to admit of the Russians' being attacked in flank, so that their retreat was slow and murderous.

They recoiled nevertheless, and abandoned the field of battle to our troops. Pursued as far as the Angel Guardian tavern, they wheeled and kept up the fight for some hours longer in that locality.

The Emperor, who in this battle, as in all others of the campaign, had fought bravely and incurred as many dangers as the most exposed soldier, transferred his imperial quarters to the hamlet of Bray. Hardly had he entered the chamber which served as his cabinet, when he called me, took his boots off while leaning on my shoulder, but without saying a word, threw his sword and hat on the table, and stretched himself on his bed with a profound sigh, or rather with one of those exclamations of which one cannot say whether they are caused by discouragement or merely by fatigue. His Majesty's countenance was sorrowful and anxious; nevertheless he slept the sleep of lassitude for several hours. I awakened him to announce the arrival of M. de Rumigny, who brought despatches from Châtillon. In the existing disposition of the Emperor's mind, he seemed ready to accept all reasonable conditions which should be offered him; hence I avow that I had hopes (and many another beside me) that at last we were on the point of obtaining the peace so ardently desired. The Emperor received M. de Rumigny without witnesses, and the tête-à-tête lasted a long while. Nothing transpired of what was said, and it seemed to me that nothing good was to be inferred from this mystery. Very early the next morning, M. de Rumigny set off again for Châtillon, where the Duc de Vicenza was awaiting him, and from some words spoken by His Majesty as he was mounting his horse to go out to the outposts, it was easy to see that he had not yet been able to resign himself to the idea of making a peace which he regarded as dishonor.

While the Duc de Vicenza was at Châtillon or Lusigny to treat of peace, the Emperor's orders required him to delay or to press the conclusion of the treaty according to his successes or his disadvantages. At every gleam of hope he demanded more than they were willing to grant, and in this he imitated the example given him by the sovereign allies, whose requirements, ever since the armistice of Dresden, had gone on increasing as they came nearer France. When at last all was broken off, the Duc de Vicenza rejoined His Majesty at Saint-Dizier. I was in a little salon so close to the sleeping chamber that I could not avoid overhearing their conversation. As the Duc de Vicenza was continually returning to the charge and combating the Emperor's aversion to a positive decision, His Majesty exclaimed with great vehemence: "You are a Russian, Caulaincourt!" "No, Sire," the Duke responded quickly, "no, I am a Frenchman! I think I prove it by urging Your Majesty to make peace."

The discussion was kept up with warmth, in terms which, unfortunately, I cannot recall. What I know well is that every time that the Duc de Vicenza insisted, and tried to make His Majesty appreciate the reasons which to him seemed to make peace indispensable, the Emperor would reply: "If I gain a battle, as I am sure to do, I shall be master and can exact better conditions. . . . The tomb of the Russians is marked out under the walls of Paris! My measures are all taken and victory cannot fail me."

After this interview, which lasted more than an hour, and in which the Duc de Vicenza could obtain nothing, I saw him leave the chamber of His Majesty. He rapidly crossed the salon in which I was. Nevertheless I had time enough to notice that his face was extremely animated, and that, yielding to his deep emotion, great tears were falling from his eyes. Doubtless he had been acutely wounded by what the Emperor had said of his fondness for the Russians. However that might be, I never saw the Duc de Vicenza again until at Fontainebleau.

Meanwhile the Emperor marched with the vanguard and wished to reach Laon by the evening of the 8th; but to gain that city it was necessary to pass over marshy grounds by means of a narrow embankment. The enemy held this road and opposed our passage. After several discharges of cannon had been exchanged, the Emperor put off until the next day the attack to force the passage, and came back, not to go to bed (for at this critical time he seldom went to bed), but to pass the night in the hamlet of Chavignon. In the middle of that night, General Flahaut came to announce to the Emperor that the commissioners of the allied powers had just broken off the conferences of Lusigny. The army was not informed of this, although the news would probably have surprised nobody. Before day, General Gourgaud set off at the head of a troop picked from among the bravest soldiers of the army, and following a cross-road to the left, in the middle of the marshes, fell unexpectedly upon the enemy, killed many of them under favor of the darkness, and drew the attention of the allied generals in his direction, while Marshal Ney, still at the head of the vanguard, took advantage of this audacious manœuvre to force the passage of the embankment. The whole army hastened to follow his movement, and in the evening of the 9th it was in sight of Laon and in battle array before the enemy, who occupied the city and the heights. The army corps of the Duc de Raguse had arrived by another road, and was also in line before the Russian and Prussian army. His Majesty passed the night in expediting his orders and preparing everything for the grand attack which was to take place at daybreak the next morning.

The appointed hour having arrived, I had hastily completed the Emperor's short toilet, and he had already put his foot in the stirrup, when some cavaliers belonging to the army corps of the Duc de Raguse were seen running up, on foot and breathless. His Majesty had them brought before him and demanded in an angry tone the cause of this disorder. They said that their bivouacs had been unexpectedly attacked by the enemy, that they and their comrades

had offered every possible resistance to overwhelming forces, although they had barely time enough to
seize their weapons; but that they had at last been
obliged to give way to numbers, and that it was
only by a miracle that they had escaped the massa-
cre. "Yes," replied the Emperor, contracting his
eyebrows, "by a miracle of agility: we shall see
about that presently. What has become of the
Marshal?" One of the soldiers said that he had
seen the Duc de Raguse fall dead; another that he
had been made prisoner. His Majesty sent his aides-
de-camp and orderly officers to reconnoitre, and the
report of the cavaliers turned out to be only too
true. The enemy had not waited to be attacked; it
had fallen on the army corps of the Duc de Raguse,
surrounded it, and taken part of its artillery. The
Marshal, however, had neither been wounded nor taken
prisoner; he was on the road to Rheims, trying to
arrest and bring back the remnant of his army corps.

The news of this disaster still further increased
the chagrin of His Majesty. However, the enemy
was beaten back as far as the gates of Laon; but the
retaking of this city had become impossible. After
several fruitless attempts, or, rather, after several
feigned attacks the object of which was to conceal
his retreat from the enemy, the Emperor came back
to Chavignon, where we passed the night. The
next day, the 11th, we quitted this village and fell
back on Soissons. His Majesty dismounted at the
bishop's house, and at once summoned Marshal

Mortier and the principal officers of the place, to consider with them the means of putting the city in a state of defence. For two days the Emperor shut himself up to work in his cabinet, never leaving it but to go and examine the ground, visit the fortifications, give his orders everywhere and superintend their execution! Amidst these preparations for defence, His Majesty learned that the city of Rheims had been taken by the Russian general Saint-Priest, in spite of the vigorous resistance of General Corbineau, whose fate was unknown, but who was believed to be dead or fallen into the hands of the Russians. His Majesty confided the defence of Soissons to the Marshal Duc de Trévise, and went himself toward Rheims by forced marches. We arrived that very evening at the gates of the city. The Russians were not expecting His Majesty there. Our soldiers began the battle without having taken any repose, and fought with the determination which the presence and example of the Emperor never failed to inspire. The combat lasted all the evening and was even prolonged far into the night ; but General Saint-Priest having been grievously wounded, the resistance of his troops began to weaken, and they abandoned the city about two o'clock in the morning. The Emperor and his army entered by one gate while the Russians were departing by another. The inhabitants crowded around His Majesty, who, before descending from his horse, inquired what damage the enemy was supposed to have inflicted. He was told that the city had suffered no damage except what must inevitably result from a sanguinary nocturnal fight, and that for the rest, the hostile general had maintained rigorous discipline among his troops during their stay and up to the moment of his retreat. Among the persons surrounding His Majesty at this time was the brave General Corbineau; he was in citizen's dress and had remained concealed and in disguise in a private house of the city. The next morning he again presented himself before His Majesty, who received him very well and complimented him on the courage he had displayed in circumstances so difficult. The Duc de Raguse had rejoined the Emperor under the walls of Rheims, and his army corps had assisted in the taking of the city. When he made his appearance before the Emperor, the latter had broken out into sharp and severe reproaches on the subject of the affair at Laon; but his anger was not of long duration. His Majesty soon resumed with the Marshal the friendly tone with which he habitually honored him. They had a long conference together, and the Duc de Raguse stayed to dinner with the Emperor.

His Majesty spent three days at Rheims, in order to give his troops time to rest and recruit themselves before continuing this rude campaign. They needed it; for old soldiers would have found it hard work to endure continual forced marches that always ended in a sanguinary battle; and yet the majority of the heroes who obeyed the orders of the Emperor with such indefatigable ardor were conscripts levied in all haste and sent to fight against troops inured to war and the best disciplined in Europe. Most of them had not even had time to learn how to drill, and took their first lesson in front of the enemy. Brave youth, which sacrificed itself without a murmur and to whom the Emperor never but once failed to do justice, in a matter which I have previously described, and in which M. Larrey played so fine a rôle! It is perfectly true, in fact, that the terrible campaign of 1814 was for the most part made with new recruits.

During the stay of three days which we made at Rheims, the Emperor beheld, with a lively joy that he did not try to conceal, the arrival of an army corps of six thousand men, brought to him by the faithful General Janssens. This reinforcement of experienced troops could not have come at a more timely moment. While our soldiers were regaining breath for the renewal of a desperate struggle, His Majesty was applying himself to the most varied tasks with his accustomed ardor. Even amidst the cares and dangers of war, the Emperor neglected not a single affair of the Empire; every day he worked for several hours with the Duc de Bassano, received couriers from Paris, dictated his responses, and fatigued his secretaries almost as much as he did his generals and soldiers. As for himself, he remained always indefatigable.

CHAPTER XIX

THINGS had reached a point where the great question of triumph or defeat could not long remain undecided. To use one of the Emperor's most habitual expressions, *the pear was ripe*, but who was going to pick it? At Rheims the Emperor seemed not to doubt that the result would be to his advantage; by one of those bold combinations which amaze the world and change the face of affairs in a single battle, His Majesty, since he had been unable to prevent the enemies from approaching the capital, resolved to attack them in the rear, force them to wheel round and confront the army he was about to command in person, and thus save Paris from their presence. It was to execute this audacious combination that the Emperor left Rheims. Yet, thinking of his wife and son, the Emperor, before attempting this great enterprise, sent an order with the utmost secrecy to his brother, Prince Joseph, lieutenant-general of the Empire, requiring him to put them in a place of safety in case the danger should become imminent. I knew nothing of this order on the day it was sent, the Emperor having kept it secret from everybody. But when I afterwards learned that it was from Rheims that this injunction had been addressed to Prince Joseph, I thought I could fix the date of it as March 15 without fear of a mistake. That evening, in fact, His Majesty had said a good deal to me at his couchee concerning the Empress and the King of Rome ; and as in general, when the Emperor had been dominated during the day by a specially strong affection he nearly always recurred to it in the evening, I was able to infer from this that on that very day he had been occupied with securing from the dangers of war the two objects of his most intimate tenderness.

From Rheims we turned towards Epernay, whose

garrison and inhabitants had just repulsed the enemy who had endeavored to seize the place the previous evening. While there the Emperor heard of the arrival at Troyes of the Emperor Alexander and the King of Prussia. To evince to the inhabitants of Epernay his satisfaction with their admirable conduct, His Majesty rewarded them in the person of their mayor, to whom he gave the cross of the Legion of Honor. This was M. Moët, whose reputation has become almost as European as the renown of the wines of Champagne.

Without growing lavish of crosses of honor, His Majesty distributed several, during this campaign, to those of the inhabitants who had put themselves forward to repel the enemy. Thus, for example, I remember that before quitting Rheims he gave one to a simple farmer of the village of Selles, whose name I forget. This brave man, having learned that a detachment of Prussians was approaching his commune, had placed himself at the head of the National Guards, whom he had inflamed by his words and example, and the result of his enterprise was forty-five prisoners, three of them officers, whom he brought into the city.

How many incidents like this there were, which it is impossible to recall! However it may be with the numerous fine actions destined to oblivion, the Emperor, on quitting Epernay, marched on Fère-Champenoise, I will no longer say *in all haste,* for that is an expression one should use for all the

movements of His Majesty, who fell with the swift-
ness of an eagle on the point where he deemed his
presence most essential.   However, the hostile army
which had crossed the Seine at Pont and at Nogent,
having learned of the reoccupation of Rheims by
the Emperor and comprehended the assault he
planned upon its rear, began its retreat on the 17th
and tore up in succession the bridges it had built
at Pont, Nogent, and Arcis-sur-Aube.   On the
18th was fought the battle of Fère-Champenoise,
delivered by His Majesty to clear the road which
separated him from Arcis-sur-Aube, where the
Emperor and the King of Prussia were.   Hearing
of this new success, they beat a precipitate retreat
on Troyes.   The known intention of His Majesty
at this time was to go back as far as Bar-sur-Aube;
we had already crossed the Aube at Plancy and
the Seine at Méry, but we had to fall back on
Plancy.   This was the 19th, the very day on which
the Comte d'Artois arrived at Nancy and when the
Congress of Châtillon was broken off, a matter I
was constrained to speak of in the foregoing chapter by the order in which my souvenirs presented
themselves.

March 20, as is well known, was a day of pre-
destination in the Emperor's life, and was to become
still more obviously so a year later.   On March 20,
1814, the King of Rome was completing his third
year, while the Emperor was exposing himself still
more than usual, if that were possible.   At the

battle of Arcis-sur-Aube, which took place that day, His Majesty saw that at last he was to have new enemies to contend with; the Austrians came into line, and an immense army under command of Prince Schwarzenberg stretched out in front of him, when he thought he was to have nothing on his hands but an affair of the advance guard. Hence, and the coincidence may not seem unimportant, the Austrian did not begin to fight seriously and to attack the Emperor in person until the day after the rupture of the Congress of Châtillon. Was this the result of accident, or had the Emperor of Austria desired to remain in the background and show respect for the person of his son-in-law so long as peace seemed possible? That is a question which is not my business to decide.

The battle of Arcis-sur-Aube was terrible; it did not finish with the day. The Emperor held the city, notwithstanding the combined efforts of an army of one hundred and thirty thousand fresh troops, attacking thirty thousand harassed by fatigue. The fighting went on during the night, when the burning faubourgs lighted up our defence and the works of the besiegers. To hold out longer became impossible, and yet there was but one remaining bridge across which the army could effect its retreat. The Emperor had another constructed, and the retreat commenced, but in good order, in spite of the numerous masses which were pressing us close. This unhappy affair was the most disastrous that His Majesty had yet experienced during the campaign, since the roads to the capital were now exposed; but the prodigies of genius and valor were unavailing against numbers. One thing capable of giving an idea of the presence of mind the Emperor was able to retain in the most critical situations, is that before evacuating Arcis he sent a considerable sum of money to the Sisters of Charity, to provide for the principal needs of the wounded.

In the evening of the 21st we arrived at Sommepuis, where the Emperor passed the night. There, for the first time, I heard him mention the name of the Bourbons. His Majesty was extremely agitated, and spoke of them in an interrupted manner, which prevented me from catching other words than these, which he repeated several times : "To recall them myself ! . . . To recall the Bourbons. . . . What would the enemy say? No, no, impossible ! . . . Never!" These words, which escaped the Emperor in one of those preoccupations to which he was subject when his soul was under heavy pressure, struck me with inexpressible astonishment; for it had never once occurred to me that there could be any other government in France than that of His Majesty. Besides, it can readily be imagined that in my position I had seldom heard any one speak of the Bourbons, unless it were the Empress Josephine, and that only in the early days of the Consulate, when I was still in her service.

The different divisions of the French army and the masses of the enemy were at this time so serried against each other, that the latter immediately occupied the points we were obliged to abandon; thus on the 22d the allies took possession of Epernay, and to punish that faithful city for the defence it had previously made, it was given over to pillage. Pillage! The Emperor called that *the crime of war;* many a time have I heard him emphatically express the horror with which it inspired him; hence he would never authorize it during the long series of his triumphs. Pillage! And yet every proclamation of our devastators impudently declared that they were making war on the Emperor alone, and people had the audacity to repeat it, and were stupid enough to believe it! On that point, I saw too thoroughly what I saw, ever to have believed in those ideal magnanimities so highly vaunted since.

The 23d we were at Saint-Dizier, where the Emperor had recurred to his first plan of attack on the rear of the enemy. The next day, as His Majesty was mounting his horse to march on Doulevent, an Austrian general officer was brought to him whose presence caused quite a sensation at headquarters, because it delayed for some minutes the departure of the Emperor. I soon learned that it was Baron Weissemberg, Austrian ambassador at London, who was returning from England. The Emperor invited him to follow him to Doulevent, where he gave him a verbal message for the Emperor of Austria, while

Colonel Galbois was commissioned to carry a letter to that monarch which the Emperor had had written to him by the Duc de Vicenza. But in consequence of a movement of the French army on Chaumont and the Langres road, the Emperor of Austria, having been separated from the Emperor Alexander, had been obliged to retreat as far as Dijon. I remember that, on arriving at Doulevent, His Majesty received a secret notification from his faithful post-master-general, M. de La Valette. This notice, whose contents I did not know, seemed to affect the Emperor keenly; but presently he seemed to resume his accustomed severity; for some time I had seen plainly that it was only an appearance. I have since learned that M. de La Valette had informed the Emperor that there was not an instant to lose if the capital were to be saved. Such a warning, coming from such a man, could not be other than the expression of the most exact truth; and it was that very conviction which increased the anxieties of the Emperor. Until then the news from Paris had been favorable; people were speaking there of the zeal and devotion of the National Guard, which never flagged. Patriotic pieces had been performed in various theatres, and notably at the Opéra the *Oriflamme*,[1] circumstances apparently very trifling.

---

[1] It is rather singular that the opera of the *Oriflamme* should have furnished Geoffroy with the subject of his last article. This famous critic died a few days afterward, if not for the repose of his own soul, at least for those of the actors. — *Note by the Editor.*

but which nevertheless produce an effect on enthusiastic minds which is not to be despised. In a word, all the news we had represented Paris as entirely devoted to His Majesty, and ready to defend itself against an attack. Assuredly, it was not lying news; the fine conduct of the National Guard under the orders of Marshal Moncey, the enthusiasm of the colleges, the bravery of the pupils of the Polytechnic School soon gave abundant proof of this; but events were stronger than men.

Meanwhile time was advancing; we were approaching the fatal dénouement; each day, each hour, beheld the immense masses hastening from all the extremities of Europe to straiten Paris, to crush it with their myriads of arms, and during those last days one might say that the fighting was continual. On the 26th again, the Emperor, summoned by the noise of rather heavy firing, had marched on Saint-Dizier. Attacked by much superior forces, his rearguard had been forced to evacuate that city; but General Milhaud and General Sébastiani repulsed the enemy across the Marne, at the ford of Valcourt; the presence of the Emperor produced its usual effect, we re-entered Saint-Dizier, and the enemy dispersed in the greatest disorder over the road of Vitry-le-Français and that of Bar-sur-Ornain. The Emperor moved on the latter city, thinking that it was Prince Schwarzenberg he had against him; as he was on the point of arriving, he learned that it was no longer the Austrian generalissimo whom he had fought, but only one of his lieutenants, Count Wit-zingerode. Schwarzenberg had tricked him; he had effected his junction with Blücher as early as the 23d, and these two generals-in-chief of the coalition were urging their multitudes of soldiers on the capital.

Disastrous as the tidings might be which were brought to headquarters, the Emperor wished to verify their accuracy in person. On returning from Saint-Dizier he rode toward Vitry, to make sure that the allies were marching on Paris. He saw them; all his doubts were dispelled. Would Paris hold out long enough to let him crush the enemy beneath its walls? Henceforward that was his sole, his only thought. At once he was at the head of his army, and we were marching toward Paris by the road of Troyes. At Doulencourt he received a courier from King Joseph, which announced the march of the allies on Paris. That very instant he sent General Dejean to his brother, to advise him of his near arrival. Let them defend themselves two days, two days only, and the allied armies would have caught sight of the walls of Paris only to find their grave there. In what anxiety the Emperor was then! He set out with his attendant squadrons; I accompanied him; and he left me for the first time at Troyes, in the morning of the 30th, as will be seen in the succeeding chapter.

CHAPTER XX

WHAT a time, great God! what a time. What an epoch and what events are those whose deplorable souvenirs I must now recall! Behold me arrived at that fatal day when the coalized armies of Europe trod the soil of Paris, of that capital undefiled for centuries by the presence of the foreigner. What a blow for the Emperor! And how cruelly his great soul expiated his triumphal entries into Vienna and Berlin! It was in vain, then, that he had displayed so incredible an activity during the admirable campaign of France where his genius had renewed its youth and the marvels of those of Italy!

It was after Marengo that I first saw him on the morrow of a battle; what a contrast with his dejected attitude when I saw him, March 31, at Fontainebleau!

Having accompanied His Majesty everywhere, I was with him at Troyes, in the morning of March 30.

The Emperor left there at ten o'clock, followed solely by the grand marshal and the Duc de Vicenza. It was known then at headquarters that the allied troops were advancing on Paris; but we were far from suspecting that at the very moment of His Majesty's precipitate departure, the battle before Paris was raging with its utmost force; at least I had heard nothing which could induce me to believe it. I was ordered to go to Essonnes, and as means of transportation were scarce and difficult, I did not arrive until very early in the morning of the 31st. I had been there but a short time when a courier brought me an order to go to Fontainebleau, which I did at once. It was then I learned that the Emperor had gone from Troyes to Montereau in two hours, having travelled ten leagues in that short space of time. I also learned that the Emperor and his small suite had been obliged to have recourse to a covered cart in order to reach the Paris road, between Essonnes and Villejuif. He had advanced as far as the Cour de France, with the intention of marching on Paris; but there, having had the new and cruel certainty of the capitulation of Paris, he had despatched the courier of whom I have just spoken.

I had not been long at Fontainebleau when the Emperor arrived; he looked paler and more fatigued than I had ever seen him, and though he knew so well how to conceal the impressions of his soul, he apparently made no effort to hide the discouragement displayed in his attitude and countenance. One saw how he was tortured by all the disastrous events which for several days had been piling up in frightful progression.

The Emperor said nothing to any one, and shut himself up at once in his cabinet with the Ducs de Vicenza and de Bassano, and Prince de Neufchâtel. These gentlemen remained for a long time with the Emperor, who afterwards received several general officers. His Majesty went to bed very late, and I still thought him very much overcome; from time to time I heard stifled sighs escape him, and with them the name of Marmont, which I could not understand, as I had not yet heard how the capitulation of Paris had been made, and knew that the Duc de Raguse was one of those marshals for whom the Emperor had always had the most affection. That very evening I saw at Fontainebleau Marshal Moncey, who the day before had so valiantly commanded the National Guard at the barrier of Clichy, and the Marshal Duc de Dantzic.

I could not easily describe the sad and gloomy silence which pervaded Fontainebleau on the two days that followed. Prostrated by so many blows, the Emperor seldom went into his cabinet where ordinarily he devoted so many hours to work. He was so absorbed by his conflicting thoughts that often he did not perceive that the persons he had summoned were near him; he looked at them, one might say, without seeing them, and sometimes remained half an hour without addressing them a word. Then, as if scarcely roused from this state of stupor, he would ask a question the answer to which he did not seem to hear; even the presence of the Duc de Bassano and the Duc de Vicenza, whom he called for most frequently, did not always interrupt this almost lethargic state of preoccupation. The hours for meals were the same as usual, and they were served in the customary way, but everything passed in a silence broken only by the inevitable noise made by the attendants. The same silence marked the toilet of the Emperor; not a word issued from his mouth, and if in the morning I would suggest to him one of the potions he was in the habit of taking, I not only got no answer, but no expression on his face, which I observed attentively, could make me suppose I had been heard. This state of affairs was horrible for all who were attached to His Majesty.

Was the Emperor really overcome by his bad fortune? Was his genius stupefied like his body? I will say with all frankness that, seeing him so different from what he was after the disasters of Moscow, and even a few days before when I quitted him at Troyes, I firmly believed this to be the case;

but it was nothing of the kind: his soul was the victim of a fixed idea,—the idea of resuming the offensive and marching upon Paris. In fact, though he remained stupefied even when closeted with his most loyal ministers and most skilful generals, he was reanimated on beholding his soldiers, doubtless because he thought that the first would counsel him to prudence, while the others would never respond but by shouts of *Long live the Emperor*, to the most temerarious orders he might give. Hence, on the 2d of April, he momentarily shook off his depression to review, in the court of the palace, his guard, which had rejoined him at Fontainebleau. He spoke to his soldiers in a firm voice, and said:

"Soldiers! the enemy has stolen three marches from us and made himself master of Paris; we must drive him out of it. Unworthy Frenchmen, *émigrés* whom we had pardoned, have put on the white cockade and joined the enemies. The dastards! They will receive the price of this new attempt. Let us swear to conquer or to die, and to make respected this tricolored cockade which for twenty years has seen us on the path of glory and of honor."

The enthusiasm of the troops was extreme at the voice of their chief; they all cried: "Paris! Paris!" But on recrossing the threshold of the palace, the Emperor's depression returned in full force, doubtless because of his well-founded fear of seeing his immense desire of marching on Paris restrained by his lieutenants. I must add that it is only since then, in reflecting upon these events, that I have permitted myself to interpret in this fashion the struggles that were going on within the Emperor's soul; for at the time, wholly devoted to my service, I would not have dared even to conceive the notion of outstepping the circle of my ordinary functions.

Meanwhile events were becoming still more opposed to the plans and wishes of the Emperor. The Duc de Vicenza, whom he had sent to Paris, where a provisional government had been established under the presidency of Prince de Bénévent, came back unsuccessful from his mission to the Emperor Alexander, and each day His Majesty learned with keen sorrow the adhesion of the marshals and a great number of generals to the new government. That of Prince de Neufchâtel was especially painful to him, and I may say that, strangers as we were to the arrangements of policy, it struck all of us with astonishment.

Here I am under the necessity of speaking of myself, which I have done as seldom as possible in the course of my Memoirs, as I think my readers will do me the justice to admit; but what I have to say is too intimately connected with the last days I spent near the Emperor, and has too close a bearing on my personal honor, for me to suppose that any one will reproach me with it. I was, as may be believed, very anxious about the fate of my family, from whom I had received no news for a long time, and, moreover, the painful malady by which I was afflicted had made frightful progress in consequence of the fatigues of the last campaigns. And yet the moral sufferings to which I beheld the Emperor a prey so absorbed all my thoughts that I took no precaution whatever against the physical anguish which tormented me, and I had not even dreamed of asking a safeguard for the country-seat I owned in the environs of Fontainebleau. It had been seized by some free companies who had established their lodgings there after having pillaged, broken, and destroyed everything, even to the little flock of merino sheep which I owed to the kindness of the Empress Josephine. The Emperor having been informed of this, but not by me, said one morning at his toilet: "Constant, I owe you an indemnity." "Sire?"—"Yes, my child, I know that you have been pillaged; I know that you suffered considerable losses in the Russian campaign; I have given orders that you should receive fifty thousand francs to set over against that." I thanked His Majesty, who was indemnifying me in excess of my losses.

This happened in the early days of our last sojourn at Fontainebleau. At the same epoch, as the transportation of the Emperor to the island of Elba was already spoken of, the grand marshal of the palace one day asked me whether I could follow His Majesty to that residence. God is my witness that I had no other desire, no other thought than to consecrate all my life to the service of the Emperor;

hence I needed not an instant of reflection to reply to the grand marshal that there could be no doubt about that, and I immediately began the needful preparations for a journey which was not of great length, but to which no human intelligence could then assign a term.

Meanwhile, in his privacy, the Emperor daily became more sad and anxious, and whenever I saw him alone, which often happened, I tried to be near him as much as possible. I noticed that he was greatly disturbed by reading the despatches he received from Paris; this agitation was so extreme that I perceived that he had torn his thighs with his nails until the blood came, without his having noticed it himself. I took the liberty then of apprising him of it as gently as I could, hoping thus to put an end to those violent preoccupations which broke my heart. Several times, also, the Emperor demanded his pistols from Roustan; happily I had taken the precaution, on seeing His Majesty so tormented, to advise him never to give them to him, no matter how insistent the Emperor might be. I thought it my duty to acquaint the Duc de Vicenza with all this, and he approved entirely of what I had done.

One morning, I no longer remember whether it was the 10th or the 11th of April, but it was certainly one of the two, the Emperor, who had not spoken to me in the morning, sent for me during the day. I had scarcely entered his room when he said to me, with the accent of the most obliging kindliness: "My dear Constant, here is an order for one hundred thousand francs, which you will go and get cashed at Peyrache's; if your wife comes here before our departure, give them to her; if she delays, bury them in a corner of your grounds; take an exact description of the place and send it to her by a trusty person. When a man has served me well, he ought not to be poor! Your wife will buy a farm or invest the money; she will live with your mother and sister, and you will no longer be afraid of leaving them in want." Still more affected by the provident kindness of the Emperor, who was deigning to descend into the details of my family interests, than satisfied with the richness of the present he had just made me, I could scarcely find words to express my gratitude; and such, moreover, was our carelessness about the future, so far were we from the mere notion that the great Empire could have an end, that it was only then that I thought of the distress in which I would have left my family if the Emperor had not so generously provided for them. I had in fact no fortune, and possessed nothing in the world but my devastated house and the fifty thousand francs intended to repair it.

Under these circumstances, not knowing when I should see my wife again, I set about following the advice His Majesty had kindly given me. I converted my one hundred thousand francs into gold, which I put into five sacks. I took with me the wardrobe waiter, named Denis, whose probity was equal to every trial, and we went by the forest road, so as not to be seen by any of the persons inhabiting my house. We cautiously entered a small enclosure which belonged to me, and the door of which was concealed by the woods, though they were still devoid of leafage; with the assistance of Denis I succeeded in burying my treasure after having taken an exact description of the place, and I returned to the palace, far enough certainly from foreseeing what chagrins and tribulations were to be caused me by those cursed hundred thousand francs, as will be seen in one of the succeeding chapters.

VOL. IV.—T

Our position at Fontainebleau — Impossibility of believing in the Emperor's dethronement — Effect produced by the journals on His Majesty — The Duc de Bassano — The Emperor more affected by renouncing the throne for his son than for himself — Abdication of the Emperor — The Emperor's couchee — Frightful awakening — The Emperor poisoned — Remnants of the campaign sachet — Resignation of His Majesty — Determined to die — Order to call M. de Caulaincourt and M. Yvan — His Majesty's affecting words to the Duc de Vicenza — The Emperor's question to M. Yvan, and sudden fright — The Emperor finally takes a potion — His drowsiness — Awakening and complete silence on the events of the night — M. Yvan goes to Paris — Roustan's departure — Marshal Macdonald's farewell to the Emperor — The sabre of Murad Bey — The Emperor more chatty than usual — Remarkable proof of the Emperor's dejection — A fair lady at Fontainebleau — Another visit to Fontainebleau — Adventure at Saint-Cloud — My excursion to Bourg-la-Reine — The mother and daughter — Voyage to the island of Elba and marriage — Sorrowful return to the affairs of Fontainebleau — Question asked me by the Emperor — Frank reply — The Emperor's remark on the Duc de Bassano.

HERE I have greater need than ever of the reader's indulgence as to the order in which I report the facts I witnessed during the Emperor's stay at Fontainebleau and others connected with it, but which did not come to my knowledge until later; I also ask pardon for the possible inaccuracy of my dates, for I remember as it were in mass all that occurred during the wretched twenty days between the occupation of Paris and His Majesty's departure for the island of Elba ; and I was so absorbed myself with the unhappy state in which I beheld so good a master, that all my faculties barely sufficed for the sensations of the moment. We all suffered from the sufferings of the Emperor ; not one of us thought of impressing on his memory the souvenir of so many afflictions ; we lived, so to say, conditionally.

In the early days of our sojourn at Fontainebleau, those by whom we were surrounded were far from believing that the Emperor would presently cease to reign over France. It seemed obvious to everybody that the Austrian Emperor would not consent to the dethronement of his son-in-law, his daughter, and his grandson ; but this was a strange mistake. I remarked during those first days that more petitions than usual were addressed to His Majesty ; but I do not know whether they received favorable responses, or even whether the Emperor replied to them at all. He often picked up the gazettes, but after glancing at them he would throw them down with evident ill-temper, then take them up again and again reject them, and those who remember what horrible insults were then permitted themselves by writers, several of whom had often lavished praises on him, can readily understand that such transitions were well calculated to excite His Majesty's disgust. The Emperor very often remained alone, and the person he saw most frequently was the Duc de Bassano, the

only one of his ministers who was then at Fontainebleau; for the Duc de Vicenza, who was continually
charged with missions, was there only casually, as it
were, especially while His Majesty still hoped to see
his own government succeeded by a regency in favor
of his son.   In seeking to recall the different expressions whose signs I was constantly observing on the
Emperor's countenance, I think I may confidently
affirm that he was far more violently affected when
finally obliged to renounce the throne for his son
than when he relinquished it for himself.   When
the marshals or the Duc de Vicenza spoke to His
Majesty of arrangements concerning his own person, it was easy to see that he only listened to them
with extreme repugnance.   One day when some one
was speaking of the island of Elba, with I forget
what yearly income, I heard His Majesty sharply
reply: " It is too much, far too much for me.   If I
am no longer anything more than a soldier, I do not
need more than a louis a day."

However, the moment arrived when, pressed on
every side, His Majesty resigned himself to signing
the act of abdication, pure and simple, which was
demanded of him.   This memorable act was thus
expressed:

" The allied powers having proclaimed that the
Emperor Napoleon was the sole obstacle to the re-
establishment of peace in Europe, the Emperor Napoleon, faithful to his oath, declares that he renounces,

for himself and his heirs, the throne of France and Italy, and that there is no personal sacrifice, even that of life, which he is not ready to make in the interest of France.

"Done at the palace of Fontainebleau, April 11, 1814.   NAPOLEON."

I do not need to say that at the time I had no knowledge of the act of abdication that has just been read. It was one of those high secrets which emanate from the cabinet and are not likely to enter into the confidences of the bed-chamber. I merely remember that it was talked of that very day, though rather vaguely, by all the household; moreover, I had plainly seen that something extraordinary was going on; all day long the Emperor seemed more melancholy than he had ever been; and yet, how far I was from anticipating the torments of the night that followed this fatal day!

And now I entreat the reader to lend his whole attention to the event I am about to relate; at this moment I become a historian, since I have to retrace the painful souvenir of a fact of capital importance in the grand history of the Emperor, a fact which has been the subject of innumerable controversies, a fact concerning which surmises only were possible, and of which I alone could know all the painful details, — the poisoning of the Emperor at Fontainebleau. I do not need, I hope, to asseverate my veracity; I feel the importance of such a revelation too deeply to permit myself either to retrench or to add the least circumstance to the truth; I will tell the things therefore as they occurred, as I saw them, as the painful recollection of them will be eternally impressed upon my memory.

April 11, I put the Emperor to bed as usual; I think that it was even a little earlier than was customary, for, if I do not mistake, it was not quite half-past ten o'clock. At his couchee I thought he seemed better than during the day, and nearly in the state in which I had seen him on previous evenings. I slept in a chamber of the *entresol*, just above that of the Emperor, with which it communicated by a small private staircase. For some time I had taken care to go to bed all dressed, so as to reach His Majesty the more promptly when he summoned me. I was sleeping soundly enough when, at midnight, I was awakened by M. Pelard, who was on duty. He said the Emperor was asking for me, and on opening my eyes I saw such an expression of alarm on his countenance that it threw me into consternation. However, I jumped out of bed, and as we were going down stairs M. Pelard said: "The Emperor has mixed something in a glass and drunk it." I entered His Majesty's chamber in a state of anguish of which it is impossible to form an idea. The Emperor had lain down again, but on approaching the bed, I saw on the floor in front of the chimney-piece the fragments of a sachet of skin and black taffeta, the same that I have mentioned once before. It was, in fact, that which he wore around his neck during the Spanish campaign, and which I had kept for him so carefully in the intervals between those that succeeded it. Ah! if I could have suspected what it contained! At this fatal moment the frightful truth was suddenly revealed to me!

Meanwhile I was at the head of the Emperor's bed. "Constant," said he to me in a voice that was sometimes feeble and sometimes violently shaken, "Constant, I am going to die! . . . I cannot endure the torments I experience, especially the humiliation of seeing myself surrounded presently by agents of the foreigner! They have dragged my eagles in the dirt! . . . They have misunderstood me! . . . My poor Constant, they will regret me when I shall be no more! Marmont gave me the last blow. The unhappy wretch! . . . I loved him! . . . Berthier's desertion has broken my heart! . . . My old friends, my former companions in arms! . . ." The Emperor said several other things to me, which I fear to report in an unfaithful manner, and it may easily be conceived that, a prey as I was to the most violent despair, I was not trying to imprint on my memory the words that escaped at intervals from the Emperor's lips; for he did not talk consecutively, and the complaints I have reported were uttered after moments of repose, or rather of prostration. My eyes were fixed upon the Emperor's face, and through my tears I could see that it was drawn by convulsive movements, the symptoms of a crisis which caused me the greatest alarm; fortunately this crisis brought on a slight vomiting which gave me some hope. The Emperor had not lost his *sang-froid* in this complication of physical and moral sufferings; he said to me after this first relief: "Constant, have Caulaincourt and Yvan summoned." I half opened the door, so as to communicate this order to M. Pelard without leaving the Emperor's chamber. On returning to his bedside, I begged and entreated him to take a soothing potion; all my efforts were in vain, he rejected all my persuasions, so firm was his will to die, even in the presence of death.

In spite of the obstinate refusals of the Emperor, I was still supplicating him when M. de Caulaincourt and M. Yvan entered his chamber. His Majesty beckoned the Duc de Vicenza to approach his bed, and said to him : "Caulaincourt, I recommend my wife and child to you; serve them as you have served me. I have not long to live! . . ." At this moment the Emperor was interrupted by another fit of vomiting, but still slighter than the first one. Meantime I was trying to tell the Duc de Vicenza that the Emperor had taken poison; he divined rather than understood me, for my voice was so stifled by sobs that I could not pronounce a word distinctly. M. Yvan having drawn near, the Emperor said to him : "Do you think the dose was strong enough?" These words were really enigmatical for M. Yvan, for he had never known the existence of the sachet, at least to my knowledge; hence he responded : " I do not know what Your Majesty means ; " a response to which the Emperor made no reply.

All three of us, the Duc de Vicenza, M. Yvan, and I, having united our entreaties to the Emperor, we were fortunate enough, but not without a great deal of trouble, to induce him to take a cup of tea ; and even then he refused it after I had made it with all haste, saying : " Let me alone, Constant, let me alone." But on our renewing our entreaties, he finally drank, and the vomitings ceased. Soon after taking this cup of tea the Emperor seemed quieter ; he became drowsy ; the gentlemen softly withdrew, and I remained alone in his chamber, where I waited for him to awake.

After a slumber of several hours, the Emperor awoke, very much as usual, although his face still bore traces of what he had suffered, and when I assisted him to rise, he did not say a single word which referred, even in the most indirect manner, to the fearful night we had just passed. He breakfasted as usual, only a little later than common ; his appearance was perfectly calm, and he even seemed more cheerful than he had done for a long time. Was this a result of his satisfaction at having escaped the death which a moment of discouragement had caused him to desire, or was it not rather because he had acquired the certainty of not dreading it more in his bed than on the field of battle?

However that may be, I attribute the fortunate recovery of the Emperor to the fact that the poison contained in the fatal sachet had lost its efficacy.

When everything had returned to its usual order, without any one in the palace but those I have named having had cause to suspect what had occurred, I learned that M. Yvan had quitted Fontainebleau. Distressed by the question addressed him by the Emperor in presence of the Duc de Vicenza, and fearing lest he might be suspected of having furnished His Majesty with the means of attempting his life, this skilful surgeon, so long attached to the person of the Emperor, seems to have lost his head in thinking of the responsibility that might weigh upon him. Hence, after hastily descending from the Emperor's room, as he found a horse all saddled and bridled in one of the courts of the palace, he leaped upon it and made all haste to Paris. It was in the morning of the same day that Roustan quitted Fontainebleau.

April 12, the Emperor also received the last adieux of Marshal Macdonald. When he was introduced, the Emperor was still suffering from the consequences of the night, and I think the Duc de Tarente must have noticed, but possibly without divining the cause, that His Majesty was not in his usual condition. When he came, he was accompanied by the Duc de Vicenza, and at that moment the Emperor was still very despondent, and appeared so absorbed in his reflections that at first he did not

see these gentlemen, although he was already up.
The Duc de Tarente brought to the Emperor His
Majesty's treaty with the allies, and I left his
chamber just as he was preparing to sign it. Some
minutes later, the Duc de Vicenza came to call me,
and the Emperor said : "Constant, go and find the
sabre that was given me by Murad Bey in Egypt.
Do you know which it is ?" "Yes, Sire." I went
out, and almost immediately returned with this
magnificent sabre, which the Emperor had worn at
the battle of Mount Tabor, as I have often heard
him say. I gave it to the Duc de Vicenza, from
whose hands the Emperor took it and presented it
to Marshal Macdonald ; and as I was retiring, I
heard the Emperor speak to him with deep affection
and call him his worthy friend.

If I remember rightly, these gentlemen were present at His Majesty's breakfast, where, as I have said
already, he seemed more composed and cheerful than
he had been for a long time ; we were even much
surprised to find the Emperor chatting familiarly
and in the most amiable manner with persons to
whom of late his words had been brief and occa
sionally even harsh. However, this cheerfulness
did not last long ; and, as a rule, the moods of the
Emperor varied almost momentarily during the
whole duration of our stay at Fontainebleau. In
the course of a single day I have seen him plunged
for hours into the most frightful sadness ; an instant
later he would be striding back and forth in his

apartment whistling or humming *La Monaco;* then he would suddenly relapse into a sort of stupor so profound that he saw nothing that was around him and forgot the orders he had given me. Another point on which I cannot lay too much stress, is the inconceivable effect produced on the Emperor by the mere sight of the letters sent him from Paris ; as soon as he perceived them his agitation became extreme, I might even say convulsive without dread of being taxed with exaggeration.

In support of what I have said of the strange preoccupation of the Emperor, I may cite a fact which occurs to my memory. During our stay at Fontainebleau, Countess W——, of whom I have already spoken, came there, and having called for me, she told me how greatly she desired to see the Emperor. Thinking that this would be a distraction for His Majesty, I spoke to him about it that very evening, and was ordered to have her come at about ten o'clock. Madame W——, as may be readily believed, was punctual at the rendezvous, and I entered the chamber of the Emperor to announce her arrival. He was lying on his bed, and meditating so profoundly that I had to tell him twice before he answered : "Beg her to wait." She waited therefore in the room adjoining that of His Majesty, and I also waited there to keep her company. Meanwhile the night wore on ; the hours seemed long to the fair traveller, and she was so distressed on finding that the Emperor did not send for her that I took pity on her. I re-entered the chamber to apprise him of her visit for the second time. He was not asleep; but he was so profoundly absorbed in his thoughts that he made no reply. At last day began to break, and the Countess, fearing to be seen by the members of her household, retired heart-broken at having been unable to bid adieu to the object of her affections. She had been gone for more than an hour when the Emperor remembered that she was waiting, and asked for her. I told His Majesty what had happened, not concealing the despair of the Countess[1] at the moment of her departure. The Emperor was deeply affected by it : " Poor woman," said he to me, " she felt humiliated ! Constant, I am truly sorry ; if you see her again, be sure and tell her so. But I have so many things there !" he added in a very energetic tone, striking his forehead with his hand.

This visit of a lady to Fontainebleau reminds me of another of nearly the same kind ; an account of it will oblige me to go back a little.

When the Emperor had been married for some time to the Archduchess Marie-Louise, although he found in her a young and beautiful woman and really loved her very much, yet he scarcely pretended

---

[1] I have since learned that Countess W—— went with her son to see the Emperor at the island of Elba. This child greatly resembled His Majesty ; hence this journey caused a rumor to the effect that the King of Rome had been taken to the Emperor. Madame W—— remained only a short time at Elba.

to a more scrupulous conjugal fidelity than in the days of the Empress Josephine. During one of our sojourns at Saint-Cloud, he entertained a caprice for one Demoiselle L——, whose mother was married for the second time to a chief of squadron. These ladies lived then at Bourg-la-Reine, where they had been discovered by M. de ——, one of the most zealous protectors of pretty women near the Emperor. He had spoken to him of this young person, who was then seventeen. She was a brunette of medium height but very well made, with pretty feet and hands, and so graceful in every way that her appearance was enchanting; moreover, to the most tantalizing coquetry she united every pleasing accomplishment; dancing with much grace, playing on various instruments, and full of wit; in a word, she had received that brilliant education which makes the most delightful mistresses and the worst wives. The Emperor told me one evening, at eight o'clock, to go for her to her mother's house, and return by eleven o'clock at latest. My visit occasioned no surprise, and I saw that these ladies had been notified, doubtless by their obliging patron; for they were awaiting me with an impatience they did not try to hide. The young person's finery was dazzling and so was her beauty, and the mother beamed with joy at the mere idea of the honor intended for her daughter. It was plain that they fancied the Emperor could not fail to be captivated by so many charms, and would be smitten by a grand passion;

but that was only a dream, for the Emperor was never amorous but at his ease. We arrived at Saint-Cloud at eleven o'clock, and entered the château through the orangery, fearing to be regarded as indiscreet. However, as I had a pass key to every door in the château, I conducted her unseen to the Emperor's chamber, where she remained for some three hours. At the end of that time I took her back to her home, using the same precautions for our exit from the palace.

This young person, whom the Emperor saw only three or four times at most, also came to Fontainebleau, accompanied by her mother; but having been unable to see His Majesty, they determined, like Countess W——, to make a voyage to the island of Elba, where, I have been told, the Emperor married Mademoiselle L—— to a colonel of artillery.

What has just been read has carried me back, almost involuntarily, toward happier times. We must return, however, to the melancholy sojourn at Fontainebleau; and from what I have said of the state of depression in which the Emperor was living, it is not surprising that he was disinclined to gallantry while under the infliction of such overwhelming blows. I seem to see again the traces of that sombre melancholy which was preying on him; and, amidst such anguish, the goodness of the man, which seemed to increase simultaneously with the tortures of the fallen sovereign. With what amenity he talked to me in those latter days. Frequently he would deign to ask what people said of the final events. With my ordinary and very simple candor, I repeated to him exactly what I had been told, and I remember one day saying what I had heard said to many other persons, that the continuance of the last wars, which had been so fatal to us, was generally attributed to the Duc de Bassano. "That is a great mistake," he returned. "Poor Maret! They accuse him very wrongfully! . . . He never did anything but execute my orders." Then, as was his habit whenever he had spoken to me for a moment about serious things, he added : "What shame ; what humiliation ! Was it necessary that I should have a crowd of foreign commissioners in my palace ? "

CHAPTER XXII

The grand marshal and General Drouot the only great personages
with the Emperor — The Emperor's fate known — The commissioners of the allies — Request and repugnance of the Emperor — The eve of departure and a day of despair — Fatality of
the hundred thousand francs given me by the Emperor — Unexpected and inexplicable question of the grand marshal — What
I should have done — Inconceivable forgetfulness of the Emperor
— The money dug up — Dread of having been robbed — Frightful
despair — The spot mistaken and the treasure found — Prompt
restitution — Horror of my situation — I quit the palace — M.
Hubert's mission to me — Offer of three hundred thousand
francs to accompany the Emperor — I lose my head and fear to
act through interested motives — Painful reflections — The
Emperor departs — Unexampled situation — Physical pains and
moral sufferings — Complete solitude of my life — Visit from
a friend — False interpretation of my conduct in a newspaper —
M. de Turenne wrongfully accused — Impossible for me to defend
myself through respect for His Majesty — Consolations drawn
from the post — Examples and proof of disinterestedness on my
part — Refusal of four thousand francs — M. Marchand placed
with the Emperor by me — Gratitude of M. Marchand.

AFTER April 12, it may be said that none of
the great personages who ordinarily surrounded the Emperor remained with him, excepting the grand marshal of the palace and Comte
Drouot. The fate reserved for His Majesty, and
accepted by him, was soon known throughout the
palace. On the 16th, arrived the commissioners of

the allies who had been charged to accompany His Majesty to the place of his embarkation for Elba. They were Count Schouvaloff, aide-de-camp of the Emperor Alexander, for Russia; Colonel Neil Campbell for England; General Kohler for Austria, and Count Waldburg-Truchefs for Prussia. Although it was by his own request that His Majesty was to be accompanied by these four commissioners, I thought their presence at Fontainebleau seemed to produce an extremely disagreeable impression on him. These gentlemen were received very differently by the Emperor, and from certain words I heard His Majesty say, I was convinced on this occasion, as I had been on others, that he esteemed the English much more highly than his other enemies. Hence Colonel Campbell was much better received than the other commissioners; while the ill-humor of the Emperor was vented chiefly on the envoy of the King of Prussia, who could not help it and put the best possible face on the matter.

With the exception of the very slight apparent change induced at Fontainebleau by the presence of these gentlemen, no remarkable incident, at least to my knowledge, occurred to disturb the sad and uniform life of the Emperor in the palace. All remained gloomy and silent among the inhabitants of this last imperial abode; and yet I thought the Emperor was personally more tranquil since he had definitively come to a conclusion than while his mind was still wavering in the most painful indecision. He sometimes spoke in my presence of the Empress and his son, but not so often as I should have expected. One thing, however, which profoundly impressed me was that not a word ever issued from his lips which could recall the fatal resolution he had taken in the night of April 11–12, and which, as has been seen, did not have such disastrous results as might have been expected. What a night! what a night! While I live it will be impossible for me to think of it without a shudder.

After the arrival of the commissioners of the allied powers, the Emperor seemed gradually to acclimatize himself, as one might say, to their presence, and the chief occupation of the entire household was to make ready for departure. One day, while I was dressing His Majesty, he said to me with a smile : "Eh well? my son, get your cart ready ; we will go and plant our cabbages." Alas! when I heard these familiar words I was very far from supposing that by an unexampled concatenation of circumstances I was to be forced to submit to an inexplicable fatality which willed that, in spite of my ardent desire, I should not accompany the Emperor to the land of exile.

The day before that fixed for the departure, the grand marshal of the palace sent for me. After giving me some orders relative to the journey, he said the Emperor wished to know how much money I had received from him. I gave the account at once to the grand marshal, who found that the same amounted to some three hundred thousand francs, including the gold contained in a cash-box which had been remitted to me by Baron Fain, seeing that he was not to make the voyage. The grand marshal told me that he would give an account of it to the Emperor. An hour later he summoned me again and said that His Majesty thought there should be one hundred thousand francs more. I replied that I had, in fact, one hundred thousand francs given me by the Emperor, who had told me to bury them in my garden; in short, I related all the details which have been read in a previous chapter, and begged him to ask if these were the hundred thousand francs referred to by His Majesty. Comte Bertrand promised to do so, and then it was that I committed the enormous fault of not addressing myself directly to the Emperor. In my position, nothing could have been easier, and I had often experienced that whenever it was possible, it was always better to go to him in person than to have recourse to any intermediary whatever. It would have been all the better for me to act in that way, since if the Emperor had asked me to return the hundred thousand francs he had given me, which after all was scarcely supposable, I was more than inclined to restore them without permitting myself the least reproachful thought. Judge of my astonishment when the grand marshal brought back word that the Emperor did not remember having given me the sum in question. At the first moment I turned red with indignation and anger. What! The Emperor could have allowed Comte Bertrand to believe that I, his faithful servant, had wished to appropriate to my own use a sum which he had given me with all the circumstances I have detailed! That was the only thought I was capable of. I went out in a state impossible to describe, assuring the grand marshal that within an hour at most I would restore to him His Majesty's fatal gift.

In passing hastily through the court of the palace I met M. de Turenne, to whom I related what had just befallen me. "That does not surprise me," said he, "and we shall see many more such." Devoured by a sort of moral fever, my mind upset, my heart broken, I looked for Denis, the wardrobe waiter of whom I have already spoken ; I found him, very fortunately, and we ran with all speed to my country place, and God is my witness that the loss of the hundred thousand francs had nothing to do with my profound distress ; I did not even think of it. As on the first occasion, we went by way of the forest in order not to be observed. We began to dig in the ground for the treasure we had placed there, and in my eagerness to regain this wretched gold and return it to the grand marshal, I began further away than I ought. No, I can never describe the despair that seized me when, seeing that we found nothing, I thought that some one must have seen and followed us, and, in short, that I had been robbed. This was a still more crushing blow than the first : I foresaw the result of it with horror ; what would be said, what would be thought of me? would I be believed on my word? Surely the grand marshal, already prejudiced by the inexplicable response of the Emperor, would take me for a man devoid of honor. I was overwhelmed by these fatal thoughts when Denis made me observe that we had not been digging in the right place, but were several feet away from it. I caught eagerly at this glimmer of hope; once more we began to dig more eagerly than ever, and I can say without exaggeration that my joy bordered on delirium when I perceived the first of the sacks. We took out the whole five in succession, and with the assistance of Denis I brought them back to the palace. I placed them without delay in the hands of the grand marshal, along with the keys of the Emperor's dressing-case and the cash-box remitted to me by Baron Fain. As I was leaving him I said: "Monseigneur, I beg you to be so good as to inform His Majesty that I shall not follow him." "I will tell him so."

After this cold and laconic reply, I left the palace at once and was soon at the house of M. Clément, rue Coq-Gris, a bailiff who had long had charge of the repairs on my little house during the long absences necessitated by the journeys and campaigns of the Emperor. There I gave free vent to my despair. I was stifling with rage when I thought that any one could have suspected my honesty, after I had served the Emperor fourteen years with a disinterestedness so scrupulous that many people called it folly; when I had never asked the Emperor for anything, either for myself or my relatives! My head swam when I tried to explain to myself how it was possible that the Emperor, who knew this well, could have given me out to a third person as a dishonorable man; the more I thought of it, the more extreme became my indignation, and the less possible was it for me to discover the shadow of a motive for the blow that struck me. I was in the greatest violence of my despair when M. Hubert, ordinary valet de chambre of the Emperor, came to tell me that His Majesty would give me whatever I pleased if I would follow him, and that three hundred thousand francs would be counted out to me at once. In this first moment, I ask all honest men what I could do, and what they would have done in my place? I replied that when I resolved to devote my entire life to the service of the Emperor, I had no vile interest in view; but that it broke my heart to think he could have allowed Comte Bertrand to think me an impostor and a dishonest man. Ah! how happy would I have been then if the Emperor had never dreamed of giving me those cursed hundred thousand francs! Such ideas put me in torment. Ah! if I could have taken twenty-four hours for reflection, just as my resentment was, how I would have sacrificed it! I would have thought of nothing but the Emperor; I would have followed him; a painful and inexplicable fatality would not have it so.

This happened on April 19, the unhappiest day of my life. What an evening, what a night I passed! What grief was mine when I learned next day that the Emperor had departed at noon, after bidding farewell to his guard! By morning all my resentment had cooled down, on thinking of the Emperor. Twenty times I had wished to return to the palace; twenty times after his departure, I wanted to post after him until I could rejoin him; but I was chained fast by the very offer he had made me through M. Hubert. "Perhaps," thought I, "he may believe that it is that which brings me; it will doubtless be said by those around him, and what opinion will they have of me?" In this cruel perplexity I dared not come to a decision; I suffered all that a man can suffer, and at times that which was only too true seemed unreal to me, so impossible did it appear that I could be where the Emperor was not. Everything in this frightful position served to increase my anguish; I was sufficiently acquainted with the Emperor to know that, even should I return to him, he would never forget that I had wished to leave him; I felt unable to endure such a reproach from his mouth; moreover, the physical sufferings caused by the malady with which I was attacked had become extremely acute, and I was obliged to keep my bed for a long time. I could once more have overcome these physical sufferings, cruel though they were, but the frightful complication of my position reduced me almost to stupidity; I saw nothing that surrounded me: I heard nothing that was said to me.

After what I have said, the reader will surely not expect me to tell him anything about the farewell of the Emperor to his old and faithful guard, about which, for that matter, enough has been published to let the truth be known concerning an event which took place in public. Here my Memoirs might end. but I think the reader will not refuse me a few moments' attention for facts which I have a right to explain, and for certain others bearing on the return from Elba. I will continue on the first point; the second will be the subject of a final chapter.

The Emperor, then, had departed, and I was shut up alone in my country house, thenceforward very dismal to me; I held myself aloof from communication with any one whatever, reading no news, and not seeking to learn any. After a while I received a visit from one of my Parisian friends, who told me that the journals were talking of my conduct without knowing what it had been, and that they blamed it greatly; he added that it was M. de Turenne who had sent the editors the note in which I was criticised with extreme severity. I must say that I did not believe this; I knew M. de Turenne too well to believe him capable of so dishonorable a proceeding, all the more so because I had told him the whole thing frankly, and I have quoted his reply. But wherever it came from, the harm was none the less done, and I was reduced to silence by the incredible complexity of my position. Certainly, nothing would have been easier than to reply, to repel the

calumny by an exact recital of the facts; but ought
I to justify myself in that way, and, so to say, by
accusing the Emperor, and that at a moment when
so violent an excitement prevailed among his enemies? When I saw so great a man the target of
calumny, I, a pitiful member of the obscure multitude, could well endure that some of these enven-
omed shafts should likewise fall on me. At present
the time has come to tell the truth, and I have told
it without reserve, not to excuse myself; for, on the
contrary, I accuse myself of not having made a total
abnegation of myself and what would have been
said about me, and followed the Emperor to the
island of Elba. Yet, let me permitted to say in
my own favor, that in this medley of physical and
moral sufferings which simultaneously assailed me,
one ought to be very sure of never having failed
himself, before he utterly condemns the irritability
so natural to a man of honor who is accused of a
fraudulent abstraction. So this, I said to myself,
is the reward of so many cares, so many fatigues,
of a boundless devotion and a delicacy which the
Emperor — I can say it openly — has often praised,
and to which he afterwards did justice, as will be
seen when I have to speak of certain circumstances
belonging to the epoch of March 20 in the following
year.

The resolution to quit the Emperor, which I took
in my despair, has been gratuitously and maliciously ascribed to interested motives, whereas the

simplest good sense should suffice to make it plain that if I had been capable of being guided by my interests everything would have inclined me to follow His Majesty. In fact, the chagrin which he caused me, and the violent manner in which I was affected by it, have been more injurious to me than any other determination could have been. What could I hope for in France, where I had no right to anything? Is it not evident, moreover, to any one who will consider my position, one so confidential near the Emperor, that if I had been guided by the love of money my place would have allowed me to reap abundant harvests, without any detriment to my reputation; but my disinterestedness was so well known that I can defy any one to say that in all the time my favor lasted I ever made use of it to render any but disinterested services. Many a time I have refused to support a request simply because the solicitation to do so was accompanied by an offer of money,—offers that were often very considerable. Let me cite a single example among many others of a similar kind: I received one day an offer of four hundred thousand francs from a lady of very noble name, if I would induce the Emperor to receive favorably a petition in which she claimed what was due to her for a piece of ground on which the harbor of Bayonne had been constructed. I had succeeded in requests more difficult than this; well, I refused to lend it my support, solely because of the offer made me; I would have liked to oblige this lady, but simply for the pleasure of obliging her, and it was always with that single end in view that I solicited favors from the Emperor which he nearly always granted. Nor can any one say that I asked His Majesty for licenses, for lottery bureaux, or anything of that kind, a scandalous trade in which is known to have been often made, and, without any doubt, if I had asked for anything of the kind, the Emperor would have given it.

The confidence which had always been shown me by the Emperor was such that even at Fontainebleau, as it had been decided that none of the ordinary valets de chambre of His Majesty were to accompany him to the island of Elba, the Emperor left to me the selection of a young man who could second me in my service. I thought of an apartment waiter whose probity was perfectly well known to me, and who was, besides, the son of Madame Marchand, the first cradle-rocker of the King of Rome. I mentioned him to the Emperor, who approved of him, and I went at once to communicate the news to M. Marchand, who accepted the place with gratitude and showed me by his thanks how happy he was to accompany us; I say us, for at that moment I was far enough from foreseeing the succession of fatal circumstances which I have faithfully reported; and it will be seen hereafter, by the manner in which M. Marchand spoke of me at the Tuileries, during the Hundred Days, that I had not placed confidence in an ingrate.

CHAPTER XXIII

I begin to comprehend the greatness of the Emperor — Disembarkation of His Majesty — The good master and the great man — Delicacy and uncertainty of my position — Souvenir of the Emperor's kindness — Obliging words — Approbation of my conduct — Needless malevolence and justice rendered by M. Marchand — The Emperor at the Tuileries — A sergeant of the National Guard — Taking down the portraits of the Bourbons — The people at the wicket of the Carrousel — General Excelmans and the tricolored flag — Cockades preserved — Arrival of the Emperor — His Majesty carried in the arms of officers — First visits — The archchancellor and Queen Hortense — Two grenadiers from the island of Elba — His Majesty and the officers on half pay — Review on the Carrousel — The Emperor demanded by the people — Marshal Bertrand presented to the people by His Majesty — Touching scene and general enthusiasm — Two later souvenirs — Princess Catherine of Würtemberg and Prince Jérôme — The first cross of the Legion of Honor worn by the First Consul and Captain Godeau.

A STRANGER to all after the departure of the Emperor for the island of Elba, penetrated with ineffaceable gratitude for the favors heaped upon me by His Majesty during the fourteen years I had spent in his service, I thought incessantly of that great man and took pleasure in recalling to memory even the least souvenirs of my career. Concluding that a life of retirement best befitted my former position, I passed my time tranquilly enough with my family in the country house which I had acquired. Nevertheless a painful idea would recur in spite of me ; I feared lest men who were jealous of my former favor might succeed in deceiving the Emperor as to my unalterable devotion to his person, and foster the false opinion of me which they had momentarily succeeded in creating. Although my conscience reassured me on this point, the idea was none the less painful ; but, as will presently be seen, I had the happiness of gaining a certainty that my fears in this respect were not well founded.

Although totally unacquainted with politics, I read with keen interest the journal I received in my retreat after the great change which was styled the Restoration ; and the simplest common sense was all I needed to see the glaring difference that existed between the fallen government and the new one. I saw the series of titled men everywhere replacing the lists of distinguished men who, under the Empire, had given so many proofs of merit and courage ; but in spite of the great number of malcontents, I was far from thinking that the fortune of the Emperor and the wishes of the army would bring him back to the throne which he had voluntarily abdicated in order not to be the cause of a civil war in France. Hence it would be impossible for me to describe my astonishment and the multiplicity of different sentiments by which I was agitated when I received the first news of the Emperor's landing on the coast of Provence. I read with enthusiasm the admirable proclamation in which he announced that his eagles would fly from steeple to steeple, and that he would be close behind them in his triumphant march from the Gulf of Juan to Paris.

This is the place for the avowal: it was only after quitting the Emperor that I had comprehended all the immensity of his grandeur. Attached to his service almost from the beginning of the Consulate, at an epoch when I was still very young, he had grown, if I may say so, without my perceiving it, and what I had especially seen in him, on account of the nature of my service, was an excellent master still more than a great man; but how different an effect had distance produced on me from what it ordinarily produces! I had difficulty in believing, and I am even yet frequently astonished at the bold frankness with which I had often dared to sustain before the Emperor the things which I thought true; for very often, instead of being annoyed by my vehemence, he would say, with a gentleness accompanied by a benevolent smile: "Come! come! M. Constant; don't fly into a passion." Adorable kindness in a man of so lofty a rank! . . . Eh well! it is doubtful if I even noticed it when in his chamber; but since then I have felt all its worth.

On learning that the Emperor was to be restored to us, my first impulse was to go at once to the palace, so as to be there on his arrival; but reflection and the counsels of my family made me conclude that it would be more suitable to await his orders, in case he wished to recall me to his service.   I had to applaud myself for acting on the latter idea, since I had the happiness of learning that His Majesty approved my conduct; I learned, in effect, in the most positive manner, that the Emperor had barely arrived at the Tuileries when he deigned to say to M. Eible, concierge of the palace at the time : "Well, what is Constant doing? How is he? Where is he?" "Sire, he is at his country place, which he has not quitted."—"Good, very good. . . . He is lucky; he is planting his cabbages."   I also learned that in the first days of his return, His Majesty, having had a list of the pensions on his privy purse drawn up, had the goodness to append a note to mine requiring it to be augmented.   Lastly, I experienced a lively satisfaction, of another sort doubtless, but not less keen, — that of not having made an ingrate.   It has been seen that I had been fortunate enough to place M. Marchand with the Emperor; now this is what was reported to me by a witness.   In the beginning of the Hundred Days, M. Marchand happened to be in one of the salons of the Tuileries where several persons were assembled, some of whom expressed themselves concerning me in a rather ill-natured way. My successor with the Emperor quickly interrupted them, saying that there was no truth in the imputations of which I had been made the object, and adding that so long as I was in favor I had constantly obliged every member of the household who had had recourse to me, and had never injured any one. As to that, I dare affirm that M. Marchand said nothing but the truth; but I was none the less affected by the uprightness of his conduct with regard to me, and especially in my absence.

Not having been at Paris, March 20, 1815, as has just been seen, I would have nothing to say about the circumstances of that memorable epoch, if I had not received from some of my friends a number of details concerning the night which followed the return of the Emperor to the palace become once more imperial. It may easily be believed that I was eager to know all that related to the great man who was then regarded as the savior of France.

I will begin by reporting exactly the account given me by a brave and excellent man of my acquaintance, then a sergeant of the Parisian National Guard, and who was on duty at the Tuileries, March 20. "At noon," he said to me, "three companies of the National Guards entered the court of the Tuileries to occupy the inner and outer posts of the palace. I was a member of one of these companies, belonging to the fourth legion. My comrades and myself were all impressed by the incredible sadness inspired by the sight of an abandoned palace. Everything was deserted, in fact; at most, one caught sight here and there of some men in the royal livery, occupied in taking down and carrying away some pictures representing different members of the Bourbon family. We were also assailed by the noisy shouts of a really frenzied multitude, climbing up the gates, trying to get over them, and pushing against them with such force that at some places they bent so as to make it seem likely that they would come down. This multitude presented a frightful appearance and seemed inclined to pillage the palace.

"We had not been in the inner court more than a quarter of an hour when an accident, not very serious in itself, threw into consternation both ourselves and the crowd thronging the whole length of the railings of the Carrousel; we saw sparks rising from the chimney of the King's chamber; it had been set afire by an enormous mass of papers which had just been burned there. This accident gave rise to the most sinister conjectures, and a rumor soon spread to the effect that the Tuileries had been ruined before the departure of Louis XVIII. A patrol of fifteen men of the National Guard was instantly formed, commanded by a sergeant; they went through the château in every direction, examined all the apartments, visited the cellars, and made sure that there was no sign of danger anywhere.

"Although reassured on this point, we were still not without anxieties. As we were repairing to our post we had heard numerous groups shouting: *Long live the King! Long live the Bourbons!* and we soon had proof of the exasperation and fury of a portion of the people against Napoleon; for a superior officer who had imprudently donned the tricolored cockade too soon only reached us with the greatest difficulty, having been pursued all the way from the rue Saint-Denis. We took him under our protection, and brought him inside; and certainly he had need of it. At this moment we received orders to send away the people, who were more than ever bent or climbing over the gates, and to do so we were forced to use our weapons.

"We had occupied the post of the Tuileries for an hour at most, when General Excelmans, who had been made commander-in-chief of the château guard, ordered the tricolored flag to be hoisted over the middle pavilion. The reappearance of the national colors moved us to lively satisfaction; and thereupon, to the cries of *Long live the King!* the people suddenly substituted that of *Long live the Emperor!* and we heard no other all the rest of the day. As for us, when we were told to put on the tricolored cockade, it was a very easy matter; for a great many of the National Guards had preserved their old one, which they had merely covered with a scrap of folded white percale. We were told to stack our arms in front of the arch of triumph, and nothing extraordinary happened until six o'clock in the evening. Then lanterns began to be lighted along the road it was supposed the Emperor would take. A considerable number of officers on half pay had assembled beside the Pavilion of Flora; and I learned from one of them, M. Saunier, who had been decorated, that it was from this side that the Emperor would re-enter the palace of the Tuileries; I went there in all haste, and, as I was hurrying to catch a glimpse of him, I had the good luck to meet a commanding officer who placed me on duty at the very door of Napoleon's apartment, and I owe to this circumstance the fact of having witnessed what I have yet to tell you.

"I had been waiting for a long time, and almost in solitude, when, at a quarter of nine, an extraordinary hubbub on the outside announced to me the arrival of the Emperor. A few moments later I saw him appear amidst cries of enthusiasm, borne on the arms of the officers who had accompanied him to the island of Elba. The Emperor urgently entreated them to let him walk; but his prayers were in vain; they carried him in this way to the door of his apartment, where they set him down quite close to me. I had not seen the Emperor since the day he bade farewell to the National Guard in the grand apartments of the palace; and notwithstanding the fact that I was greatly excited by what was going on, I could not avoid noticing that His Majesty had grown considerably stouter.

"The Emperor had scarcely entered his apartment when my service became interior. Marshal Bertrand, who had just replaced General Excelmans in command of the Tuileries, ordered me not to allow any person to enter without first notifying him, and giving him the names of all who presented themselves to see the Emperor. One of the first who came was Cambacérès, who seemed to me paler than usual. Soon after came the father of General Bertrand; and as this venerable old man was about to begin by paying homage to the Emperor, the latter said to him: 'No, sir; nature first.' And in saying it, by a movement as prompt as his remark, Napoleon threw him, as it were, into the arms of his son. Next came Queen Hortense, accompanied by her two children; then Comte Regnault de Saint-Jean d'Angély, and many other persons whose names have escaped me. I did not see again those whose presence I announced to Marshal Bertrand, because they all passed out through another door. I continued this service until eleven o'clock in the evening, when I was relieved of my sentry duty and invited to supper at an immense table, laid, it seemed to me, for at least three hundred persons. All who were in the palace took their place in turn. I saw the Duc de Vicenza there, and I sat opposite General Excelmans. As to the Emperor, he supped alone in his chamber with Marshal Bertrand, and their supper was not nearly so splendid as ours, for it was composed merely of roasted chicken and a dish of lentils; and yet I learned from an officer who had not quitted him since he left Fontainebleau, that His Majesty had eaten nothing since morning. The Emperor was extremely fatigued; I had occasion to notice this every time that the door of his chamber was opened. He was sitting on a chair opposite the fire, with his feet up, resting against the mantlepiece.

"As we all remained at the Tuileries, some one came at one o'clock in the morning to say that the Emperor had just gone to bed, and that in case any of the soldiers who had accompanied him should arrive in the night, he had given orders to have them take the service of the palace conjointly with the National Guard. The poor wretches were hardly in condition to obey such an order. At two o'clock in the morning we saw two of them arrive in a pitiable state; they were emaciated and the skin was all worn off their feet; all they could do was to throw themselves down on their sacks, where they fell, one might say, fast asleep; for they did not wake up even when we made it a duty to dress their feet in the very apartment where they had but just arrived. There was no sort of attention we were not in haste to lavish on them; and I own I have always regretted not having inquired the names of these two brave grenadiers who inspired in all of us an interest which I could not describe.

"Having gone to bed at one o'clock, the Emperor was up at five in the morning; and orders were immediately given to the half-pay officers to hold themselves in readiness for a review. At daybreak they were drawn up in three ranks. At this moment I was told to watch an officer who had been pointed out as suspicious, and who, it was said, had arrived from Saint-Denis: it was M. de Saint-

Chamans. After a quarter of an hour of surveillance which involved nothing painful, he was simply asked to withdraw. Meanwhile the Emperor had descended from the palace and passed into the ranks of the half-pay officers, speaking to all of them, shaking hands with many, and saying to them: ' My friends, I have need of your services; I rely on you as you may rely on me.' Magical words in the mouth of Napoleon, which drew tears of emotion from all these heroes whose services had been contemned for more than a year.

"From morning the crowd grew rapidly larger at all the approaches to the Tuileries, and a mass of people assembled under the windows of the château were asking to see Napoleon. Marshal Bertrand having apprised him of this, the Emperor showed himself at a window, where he was saluted by the cries which his presence had so often excited. Afterwards the Emperor himself presented Marshal Bertrand to them, keeping his arm around the Marshal's shoulder, and pressing him to his heart with demonstrations of the liveliest affection. During this scene, which affected all the spectators and was greeted with loud acclamations, some officers, standing behind the Emperor *and his friend*, held above their heads flags surmounted by eagles, with which they formed a sort of national arch. At eleven o'clock the Emperor mounted a horse and went to review the different regiments which were arriving from all quarters, and the heroes of the island of Elba who

had reached the Tuileries during the night. We
could not weary of contemplating the faces of these
good fellows, tanned by the sun of Italy, and who
had just marched nearly two hundred leagues in
twenty days."

Such are the curious details furnished me by a
friend; and I can guarantee the exactness of his
story as if I had myself witnessed all that he saw
during the memorable night of March 20–21, 1815.

Having continued to live in my retreat during the
Hundred Days, and long afterwards, I have nothing
to say concerning this grand epoch of the Emperor's
history which is not as well known to everybody as
to me. I have shed many tears over his sufferings
at the moment of his second abdication, and over
the tortures he was subjected to at Saint-Helena by
the miserable Hudson Lowe, whose infamy will traverse the centuries incrusted in the glory of the Emperor. I will content myself with merely adding to
what has gone before a certain document which has
been confided to me concerning the former Queen of
Westphalia, and finally a word about the distinction
I thought fit to give to the first cross of the Legion
of Honor which had been worn by the First Consul.

Princess Catherine of Würtemberg, married, as is
known, to Prince Jérôme, is very beautiful; but she
is also endowed with more solid qualities which time
does not diminish, but increases. To much natural
intelligence she joins great cultivation of mind, a
character truly worthy of a sister-in-law of the Em-

peror, and a love of her duties which almost amounts to fanaticism. Events have not permitted her to become a great queen, but they could not prevent her from remaining an accomplished woman. Her sentiments are noble and elevated, but, nevertheless, she is not haughty to any one ; hence all who surround her take pleasure in praising the charms of her kindliness in private life, and in saying that she possesses the most fortunate of natural gifts, — that of inspiring love in all. Prince Jérôme is not lacking in a certain grandeur of manners and that showy generosity an apprenticeship to which he made on the throne of Cassel ; but in general people find him very haughty. Although since the great changes occasioned in Europe by the downfall of the Emperor Prince Jérôme owes the fine existence he still enjoys in great part to the love of the Princess, the latter none the less displays a truly exemplary submission to all his wishes. Princess Catherine is chiefly occupied with her children, of whom she has three, two boys and a girl, all of whom are very handsome. The eldest was born in August, 1814. Her daughter, Princess Mathilde, owes her education to her mother's special cares ; she is pretty, yet less so than her brothers, all of whom have their mother's features.

After the not flattering portrait just drawn of Princess Catherine, it will doubtless be found surprising that, gifted as she is with so many solid qualities, she has never been able to conquer an inexplicable leaning to petty superstitions. Thus, for example, she dreads extremely to sit down at a table where there are thirteen guests. Here is a fact whose authenticity can be guaranteed, and which may flatter the weakness of persons tainted by the same superstition as the Princess of Würtemberg. One day, at Florence, being present at a family dinner, she noticed that there were but thirteen covers; suddenly she turned pale and obstinately refused to sit down. Princess Elisa Bacciochi mocked at her sister-in-law, shrugged her shoulders, and said to her with a smile: "There is no danger; we shall be fourteen, for I am pregnant." Princess Catherine yielded, but with extreme reluctance. Not long after she had to put on mourning for her sister-in-law; and the death of Princess Elisa contributed not a little, as may be believed, to make her more superstitious than ever about the number thirteen. Eh well! let the strong-minded brag as much as they please; but I can console the feeble, for I venture to affirm that if the Emperor had witnessed a similar event in his own family, an instinct stronger than reflection, stronger than his all-powerful reason, would have caused him some moments of painful uneasiness.

And now nothing remains but to give an account of the use to which I put the First Consul's first cross of honor. Let nobody be disturbed; I did not make a bad use of it: it is on the breast of a hero of our old army. In 1817, I made the acquaintance of M. Godeau, a former captain of the imperial guard. He had been grievously wounded at Leipsic by a cannon-ball which ploughed through his thigh. I saw in him so plain and frank an admiration for the Emperor, he urged me so many times to give him something, no matter what, which had belonged to His Majesty, that I made him a present of the cross of honor I speak of, he having long been decorated with that order. This cross is, I may say, an historic monument; first, because it is, as I have said, the first that the Emperor wore. It is of silver, of medium size, and not surmounted by the imperial crown. The Emperor wore it for a year; it decorated his breast for the last time the day of the battle of Austerlitz. After that day, in fact, His Majesty took an officer's cross in gold with the crown, and never again wore the cross of a simple legionary.